The ri[g_]
didn't come easily...

Slowly Cal broke the kiss, passing his thumb over Dev's glistening lips. He inhaled unsteadily. "What am I going to do with you?"

Dev's voice was scratchy, her own breathing sporadic. "What do you want to do?" After the drugging beauty of his kisses and caring as deeply as she did, she was ready to accept anything he had to give.

"Dammit, Dev, I know what you're thinking—that I use women. But for the first time . . . I'm afraid to go on. I want us to be special together, and we can't be until I can give as well as take."

Dev ached to hold him. "Make no mistake, Cal Travis, I want you to love me . . . when you're ready."

Caressing her cheek, he murmured, "You'll be the first to know."

Eileen Nauman is a woman of action and feeling, vital ingredients she incorporates into every Temptation she writes. She has firsthand knowledge of fencing and test piloting. In fact, most things that fly appeal to her—even an ungainly pigeon given to her to raise. Eileen reports that Homely Homer is doing just fine....

Books by Eileen Nauman

HARLEQUIN TEMPTATION
51–TOUCH THE HEAVENS
76–DARE TO LOVE

These books may be available at your local bookseller.

Don't miss any of our special offers. Write to us at the following address for information on our newest releases.

Harlequin Reader Service
901 Fuhrmann Blvd., P.O. Box 1397, Buffalo, NY   14240
Canadian address: P.O. Box 2800, Postal Station A,
5170 Yonge St., Willowdale, Ont.   M2N 6J3

The Right Touch

EILEEN NAUMAN

Harlequin Books

TORONTO • NEW YORK • LONDON
AMSTERDAM • PARIS • SYDNEY • HAMBURG
STOCKHOLM • ATHENS • TOKYO • MILAN

To Judith McNaught,
my sister of the pen and my friend

To Jo Ann Prater and Lt. Scott Prater,
U.S. Naval Reserve,
and their son, Brandon,
for urging me to write about
courageous and very brave carrier pilots....

and

To my brother, Brent, and his wife, Jeanne,
and their little sprite, Erin,
who makes the sun shine for all of us....

Published April 1986

ISBN 0-373-25201-3

Printed in Canada

1

"COME ON, CAL, you need to get off this carrier for a while," Captain Scott Guthrie said as he entered the cramped quarters. He held his friend's icy gray glare.

"Tell the squadron commander I'm sick," Cal muttered, lying on the bunk, hands clasped behind his head as he stared grimly up at the ceiling.

Scott leaned against the hatch, shoving his hands into the pockets of his summer uniform. "You're the guy who's supposed to be heading up this shindig, remember? Hey, it isn't every day we get an unexpected week in a port like Hong Kong."

Cal flinched, his eyes darkening to charcoal. He and his copilot, Chief Stanton, had been the reason for the stay in Hong Kong. Repairs to the carrier's catapult system were being completed. Cal shut his eyes, unable to deal with the loss shearing through him. His copilot had been like a brother to him. Now he was dead. And Cal was alive. A fluke of fate.

"I'm not up to a party, Scotty. Much less an embassy function," Cal growled, wrestling with the pain that radiated outward in his chest. He hadn't slept well since the accident. Four days . . . God, four nightmarish days. He had been put on waivers immediately after the helicopter had fished him out of the South China Sea. Doctors had checked him over. Reports in triplicate and quadruplicate had been filled out. A talk with his squadron commander. A talk with the chaplain. And then a talk with the psychologist. Cal was sick to death of being poked, prodded and probed. All he wanted was to be left alone to mourn the loss of his best friend.

Scott's oval face was shadowed with concern as he studied his fellow aviator. "Look," he began earnestly, "maybe this is what you need, Cal. Get off the ship. Get away from here for a while. We don't have to report back aboard for three days. Hell, let's punch the ticket, do our bit for the American consulate, play escort and then hightail it to the Wanchai District over on the island and tie one on for Chief."

Cal drew in a ragged breath, opening his eyes, staring blindly at the ceiling. "Maybe you're right." Get drunk. That was a good idea. Maybe it would dull the pain. He was on flight waivers; he didn't have to worry about having alcohol in his bloodstream because he wasn't allowed near one of the combat jets he flew. Ordinarily, he'd toss down a beer or two with his friends. But right now, a couple of double scotches seemed a reasonable alternative. He could forget for a blessed while. He could finally get more than one or two hours' sleep a night. Cal rubbed his bloodshot eyes and slowly sat up, moving to his feet.

"That's more like it," Scott said as Cal pulled on his long-sleeved khaki shirt.

"Where is this party being held?" Cal asked, putting on the shirt and then straightening the tie of the same color at his throat.

"Over on Kowloon. Shangri-La Hotel. Supposed to be a five-star place." Scott shrugged, a grin curving his lips. "Hell, good chow, good booze and more than likely some very foxy ladies. Us bachelors couldn't ask for anything more."

Cal snorted, running a comb through his short, walnut-colored hair. "Right now, all I feel like is a dark corner with my drink and that's it, not a woman."

"Just turn on your marine corps charm, smile and be the handsome devil you always are and you'll survive," Scott drawled.

Cal picked up his jacket and shrugged into it. Hong Kong in late October was in the low eighties with ninety percent humidity. They'd sweat to death in their uniforms. All part of punching the ticket to get to test pilot school, he reminded himself. Only tonight, he wanted no part of official duties. He didn't want small talk, coy games being played by a woman—he didn't want any company at all. Grief wasn't something he could share. It was too personal. Too explosive in its pain, ripping him apart inwardly every waking moment. If only he could sleep . . . God, he could escape the hurt.

"I heard from Sam," Scott went on, "that we'll be playing escort to a group of national and Olympic amateur fencers from America. They're over here for an international competition this week. The American embassy is throwing a party for all the competitors. Isn't that something? Never met a fencer. I knew the sport existed, but I didn't know it had women in its ranks. Always thought of it as a man's game. They've even got the Russian and Chinese teams here for the meet."

Cal opened his locker and pulled out his service cap, making sure the black patent leather bill was dust and fingerprint free before he settled it on his head. He shrugged noncommittally. That would mean CIA types posing as businessmen littering the party. Those in the marine corps would be watched like hawks because one slip, one hint of top secret military knowledge would be just what the Russians would love to overhear—or so the undercover men would assume. Well, at the first opportunity, Cal was going to get rid of his assigned female and take a ferry over to Hong Kong and drown his misery in the Wanchai District.

Scott opened the hatch and they both stepped out. "I know what you're thinking, Cal, and we haven't got a thing to worry about: we've got the complete U.S. fencing team with us. All they gotta do is draw their swords and protect us from these undercover guys, if need be." He laughed genially as they ambled down the passageway toward the upper-deck stairs. "Wonder if those female fencers are built like bulldogs? Maybe tanks?"

Cal shrugged his broad shoulders. "We'll find out" was all he muttered.

"LOOK! HERE THEY COME!" Sarah whispered conspiratorially to Devorah. "Come on, Dev, at least *look* like you want to meet these gorgeous marine corps pilots."

Dev wrinkled her freckled nose, casting a quick glance toward the lobby. She could see a contingent of fifteen pilots from the U.S. carrier entering the huge marble and chandeliered area. "I *hate* blind dates. I don't care *who* they are. Why can't we attend this party alone?"

Sarah touched her short crop of blond hair, her green eyes dancing. "We're an international event, Dev! Of course the U.S. embassy is going to have us chaperoned." She rubbed her hands together, tossing her unenthusiastic friend a brilliant smile. "And marines! Oh! I just love a man in uniform. This is turning out better than I'd ever dreamed."

Dev rolled her eyes. "Correction: you're an international sensation, I'm not. You're the top foil fencer in the U.S." The comment went right over Sarah's petite head, and Dev smiled benignly. Well, what could she expect? Sarah was only twenty and she was twenty-eight. A world of difference and different experiences, Dev thought, trying to look philosophically upon the evening. Sarah had eyes for any man who was handsome but remained loyal to her steady boyfriend David back home. Besides, for Sarah, life was a nonstop adventure.

Sarah pouted. "You never give yourself credit, Dev. If you weren't important, they wouldn't have asked you along."

Dev grinned, her blue eyes sparkling. "Right. The woman épée specialist."

"Don't knock it. You and Sue Barnes not only made it acceptable for women to fence one another with heavier weapons, but you've also got it legally accepted at the national level. That's nothing to sniff at. It's impressive."

"I just wish Sue was here right now," Dev groaned.

"Well, if you were having a baby right now, you'd be home, too."

"Can I say I'm having morning sickness and gracefully bow out of this party we have to attend?"

Sarah laughed. "You're so funny, Dev. Guess it goes along with your funny name."

"And funny, gangly body."

"Oh, stop it!"

Dev laughed with her. "Hey, that's how I got into épée in the first place: I was too tall for foil. Did you ever see a *good* woman foil fencer over five-foot-six?"

Sarah shook her head. "Small means swift."

"Right. And large means a bigger target who's slower moving." She looked down at herself. "I'm five-foot-nine and a hundred and thirty pounds. That's why I went into épée. All épéeists are tall and slender. Merely a matter of self-defense." She tapped her head. "And smarts." Foil was a light weapon compared to the épée blade. Because of the difference in styles, many men thought women couldn't adjust to the more demanding and physical game of épée. Dev had proved them wrong.

"You're crazy, Dev! You always make me laugh."

Dev's full mouth curved into a smile as she watched her smaller friend's delight. "Yeah, that's what the guys at the TV station say, too."

"Have Minicam, will travel," Sarah agreed. And then she frowned. "You sure your wrist is healed enough? I mean, when that big guy tried to punch you out because you were the one with the camera . . ."

Dev looked at her right wrist. Ordinarily, the California sun would have tanned her whole arm; around her wrist the skin was white. The ace bandage had come off two days ago. Dev had spent every moment she could spare from her exhausting job as a camera operator fencing to rebuild the strained muscles. "It should hold up. Coach told me to tape it, but I don't know. I don't feel like losing in front of an international television audience. I need all the flexibility I can get to win." She hadn't told Coach Jack Gordon there were times when she experienced such excruciating pain that she dropped whatever she was carrying in her right hand. No, if Jack had known that, he would never have allowed her to come to this international meet. She was there to show the rest of the world that women were just as good in épée and sabre as any man in the sport.

Sarah frowned. "Yes, but if one of those big Russian women decides to poke you right there with the steel tip of an épée, you could really get it injured."

"Hey, don't worry about it." Dev put her hand on Sarah's bare shoulder. The cocktail-length black chemise made Sarah look smashing. Dev, on the other hand, wore a stunning strapless Victor Kosta dress of red-and-white stripes, complementing her auburn hair and blue eyes. "I'm supposed to be big sister, not you," she teased, laughing.

"I know, I know. Devorah Hunter is our den mother on this trip." At that moment, Sarah was distracted. Her eyes grew large as she eyed the pilots. "Oh, don't they look gorgeous?" she breathed.

Dev gave them a practiced once-over. "No," she drawled, amusement in her tone. "They look like they're on the prowl."

"Marines! Real men! Look at them!"

With a shake of her head, Dev excused herself and slid among the rest of the women fencers, making her way to the rear, resting her back against the marble wall. Mrs. Weintraub, wife of one of the officials from the American embassy, began to make introductions. Dev's eyes sparkled with laughter as she watched the older woman pairing off pilots with fencers based on the criterion of height. Couldn't have a short marine with a tall fencer, could we? Dev almost laughed aloud and then thought better of it. Most of the women were much younger than her; either Olympic hopefuls for 1988 or international foil fencers in their early twenties. And all short.

Her gaze roved without interest over the pilots. Most of them were short, too, and Dev wondered why, never having had much to do with the military services. The closest she got was when her television station had her and reporter Fred Tucker drive up to Edwards Air Force Base in the Mojave Desert to take pictures of Shuttle landings and astronauts waving as they disembarked from the huge white craft. Dev smiled as she saw Sarah blushing. A decidedly handsome pilot barely a head taller than her gallantly took her arm and escorted her toward the bank of elevators. Sarah was in love, Dev decided humorously, drowning in all that dashing derring-do of the fighter pilot image.

"Uh, Miss—let's see, dear . . ." The wife of the embassy official gave Dev a forced smile as she walked over quickly to her. Dev straightened. She saw the woman nervously riffling through the neatly typed lists in her hands. "Oh, dear . . . what *is* your name?"

"Dev. Dev Hunter, Mrs. Weintraub," she supplied, trying to look properly interested. Good! Maybe her name wasn't on the list, which meant she could go back to her room in the hotel and soak her wrist. It was aching and she had no desire to dance or do anything but rest her arm for the forthcoming meet.

"Oh, dear . . . I just *know* they have your name somewhere here."

Dev looked up. Up into dark-gray eyes that ruthlessly assessed her. She swallowed, caught in the web of his appraisal of her. He was tall. Much taller than any of the other pilots. And his lean face was closed, measured and disapproving. Her heart beat a little more quickly, a reaction that non-plussed her. Whoever he was, he was whipcord lean with squared broad shoulders that were thrown back confidently. An image flitted through her alerted mind: the expression in those almost colorless gray eyes with their huge black pupils warned that he was ready to pounce and shred his next victim. He looked like an eagle. His mouth, although well shaped, was thinned by obvious irritation. But Dev might have been more on guard if the corners of his mouth hadn't been turned softly upward. At some point, he must have laughed a great deal. He wasn't laughing now. No, if looks could kill, she'd be dead and so would poor Mrs. Weintraub, who was flustered by the faux pas.

Dev was far more concerned about Mrs. Weintraub's embarrassment. She appeared to be going into cardiac arrest as she tore through the sheaf of papers in her trembling fingers. Dev reached out and touched her elegantly clad silk shoulder. "It's quite all right, Mrs. Weintraub."

"Well, I just know you are a fencer . . . I feel terrible."

Dev risked a glance up at the marine corps officer, who was standing there as if bored to death. What was the matter with the arrogant idiot? He was just making Mrs. Weintraub that much more uncomfortable. Her blue eyes darkened when they met his gray ones. "Egotistical" flashed to mind. And then "cold." Cold and cruelly insensitive. She disliked him intensely in those seconds. Well, she didn't want to be here, either, but she wasn't acting like an ass, at least.

Dev's mouth pursed. "Look, Mrs. Weintraub, it's all right. I honestly didn't want to go to the party. I'm really tired with jet lag and—"

"Oh, my dear! I can't possibly let you go back to your room just because of a silly typing omission!"

Sure you can,
tised that she had
another plan formed
the stonelike officer or
smiles.

"Well, I'm sure the capta

"Major," he corrected her c

Dev waved her hand. "Of c
traub, I'm *sure* Major Travis wou
called it an evening." Her eyes widene
gesture as she held his insolent gaze. "
she asked sweetly. God, she hated herse
sickeningly sweet, femme fatale methods. Th
her. But at this point, Dev was willing to stoop
to get out of having to go anywhere with this in
ficer!

"Whatever the lady wants," he drawled with a sligh

I'll bet, you arrogant—

"My gracious, we just can't have that!" Mrs. Weintra
grabbed the officer by the arm and practically dragged him
over. "Dev Hunter, I'd like you to meet your escort for the
evening, Major Cal Travis." She moved from between them
and pushed them together. The instant Dev's forearm came
in contact with his hard, masculine body, Dev moved away
as if burned.

"Now come, come! Just go up to the twenty-first floor and
join the celebration." Mrs. Weintraub grabbed Cal's arm and
led them toward the bank of elevators.

Once inside one, Dev immediately went to the opposite
corner. Her heart was pounding like a snared rabbit's, yet she
met his hard eyes. "I don't like this any more than you do."

"Good, at least you aren't the type to play games," he said,
looking her over as if she were a piece of furniture to be ap-
praised. Cal saw a red stain come to her cheeks and suddenly
felt contrite. Come on, Travis, who do you think you're talk-

Dev thought, trying to look properly chas-
even suggested such an alternative. Then
in her mind, and she looked up, giving
e of her warmest and most brilliant

n out
and
wn.

her
she
n't

n, uh—"
olly. "Major Cal Travis."
ourse! Major. Mrs. Wein-
dn't mind a bit if we just
d slightly in a pleading
Would you, Major?"
If for such brash,
s just wasn't like
to such a level
pudent of-

t bow.

...p. If she had
put in an appearance for the
it was going to be agony. "Make it a double scotch, will you?"

He tilted his head, a thaw in his gray eyes and, if she wasn't imagining it, a *slight* hint of a smile pulling at one corner of his compressed lips. "We agree on two things. Stay here. I'll be right back."

Dev raised her chin, her blue eyes flaring. "Yes, sir. Or should I salute you, too?"

Some indecipherable emotion flicked across his face. "Just stand at parade ease and that will do, Ms Hunter."

Arrogant bastard! She stood there, seething. Well, to hell with him! Dev turned smartly on her white heels, perusing the huge room that was softly lit by the chandeliers overhead. The music was soothing, but she barely heard it as she prowled the perimeter of the two hundred or so guests. The women were in their finest and most colorful plumage, while the men wore a mixture of business suits or uniforms from the various services. *An impressive party,* Dev decided. Aha— a balcony. Just what she wanted. Perhaps if she went out there and hid, Major Travis with his vinegar personality might not find her and would go home—where he belonged. And then she could go to her room and sleep!

The scintillating lights of Victoria Harbor were mesmerizing as Dev lounged against the wrought-iron balustrade. The sparkling reds, greens and blues from the island of Hong Kong itself danced off the rippling ebony surface so that she quickly became absorbed in the beauty of the night. A heavy cape of stars covered the shoulders of the night above her, and a soft, tangy salt breeze caressed Dev's face. With a groan, she wriggled out of the heels, her feet already aching. She was used to wearing jogging shoes on the job and fencing shoes on the copper strip when going bouts with fellow fencers. Heels were something to be put in the darkest corner of her apartment closet and forgotten. Why women wore these tortuous, stilted monstrosities was beyond Dev. Then a silly grin split her squarish face. If she believed that, what was she doing wearing them tonight? The inconsistency of human behavior was alive and well, she decided.

After that, so engrossed did she become in the sight of Hong Kong in the distance and a junk sailing by that Dev forgot all about the party and her sourpuss escort.

Cal walked quietly across the huge stone patio that was embraced by carefully spaced, potted tropical plants towering above them. He missed little as he approached Dev: she had kicked her heels off, revealing shapely feet. The red-and-white cocktail dress outlined the fact that Dev Hunter was indeed tall and in good physical shape. Cal's gaze roved appreciatively from her bare shoulders and arms down her long, delicately curved back to her slender hips. He was irritated with himself for having drowned in her pleading blue eyes earlier when Dev had tried to gracefully dodge him and the party altogether. Her hair was an unruly mass of auburn color shot with gold and had been piled into a careless top-knot that obviously had refused to stay centered for very long.

Cal halted a few feet behind her, watching as she rested her elbows on the balustrade, chin cupped in her hands, a dreamy look on her face. She wasn't beautiful in a modeling sense. And he found himself applauding the fact that she wore very little makeup. Most women would have resorted to foundation to cover the riot of freckles across her slightly bumped nose and high cheekbones that insisted on staying after childhood had gone. Her lips were softly parted, full and expressive. Cal scowled, ordering his body to stop responding to that particular part of her anatomy. Her eyebrows were lightly winged, enhanced by a pair of wide, curious blue eyes framed with thick lashes. "Child" certainly fit her, he thought sourly. Innocent, childlike in one way, yet childish if he took into account the crack she had made earlier about saluting him. Mouth thinning, Cal decided to get the confrontation over with.

"If you were trying to lose me, it didn't work," he said, coming up beside her.

Dev gasped, startled. She turned quickly with a gazelle-like grace that only a fencer with years of training would have acquired. Her eyes widened as she met his dark, disapproving gaze, and her lips parted. Seconds hung suspended between them, and Dev felt an incredible dizziness sweep through her as he stood above her in the darkness. He was all at once a warrior, a male so vital and virile that he literally tore the breath from her, and she lost her voice. His eyes were large and intelligent looking as he stared down at her. Dev had to give herself a mental shake as he placed the cool tumbler of scotch and ice cubes in her hand. His eyes . . . had she detected sadness in them? He seemed so . . . desolate?

Alone? Yes, she decided, he was terribly alone. Knowing that, she dropped her defensive shield and refused to be drawn into his ugly mood.

"Thank you for the drink, Major. And yes, to be truthful with you, I was trying to hide." She took a sip, stealing a glance up at him to see what kind of effect her honesty had on him. Cal stood inches away from her, incredibly handsome in uniform, the silver wings over his left breast pocket gleaming in the semidarkness. With a slightly self-deprecating smile, she added, "Neither of us wants to be here, so I thought if I disappeared, you could be spared my company and have an adequate excuse to take off."

Cal relaxed slightly, leaning against the wrought iron, taking a good, long drink of his own double scotch. "You ran off because you were angry."

"Touché."

"Is that fencing talk, Ms Hunter?"

"It is, Major Travis. It means you scored one point against me."

"I believe I've caught you lying to me about the reason why you left."

Dev's brows drew down, her eyes turning cobalt. "It was a white lie. White lies don't hurt anyone," she snapped. "By shading the truth, I wanted to let you and myself off the hook. There's nothing wrong with that. Instead, you seem to like the bald truth, regardless of who it hurts." She took another sip, a longer one.

And so did he. They glared at one another.

"I'm not in the mood for games tonight, Ms Hunter."

Dev almost choked on her drink and backed off a good two feet from him, her eyes flashing. "Well, excuse me for being alive. You think you're the only one that has a bad day now and then?" She reached down, positioning her heels and angrily stabbing her feet back into them. She looked ominously at him. "Don't bother coming after me, Major. I'm in no mood for a sourpuss like you, either! I've got jet lag. I'm tired. My wrist hurts, and I've got the biggest competition of my life coming up. I don't need your arrogance, insensitivity and snarling disposition on top of all that!"

Cal leaned back, pursing his lips as he watched Dev Hunter march off the patio and then disappear into the crowd. He turned and frowned. The beaded coolness of the tumbler between his long, spare fingers sedated his temper. Just as well. How long he stood there, gazing blindly out into the night, he didn't remember. He did know when his tumbler was empty. Already, Cal could feel the numbing effect of alcohol, and he straightened and walked back to the noisy, crowded bar.

He was jostled into someone else and turned to say, "Excuse me." Dev Hunter was behind him with a pained expression on her face. He had stepped directly on her right foot. His moodiness was momentarily pushed aside when he saw tears gather in her luminous eyes.

"I'm sorry," he said, quickly reaching out to steady her as she leaned down to grasp the injured foot.

"What are you doing back here?" Dev gritted out.

"Same thing you are. Getting another double. Can you walk?"

Dev sucked in her breath, hobbling away from the bar. "Of course! Just let me go. Haven't you done enough damage for one night?" She sat down at a small table that had just been vacated, pulling off her heels. "I hate these things!" she griped, throwing them under the table.

Cal hovered nearby. "Can I make it up to you by getting you a drink?"

She snapped up her head, her lips compressed. "That's the least you can do. Just get me a pop and leave me in peace. One piece." Her pulse raced as she saw that slightly askew grin tug at one corner of his mouth again.

"Okay, redheaded witch, you've got a deal. I'll get you that drink and then leave you alone."

Dev was petulant when he returned. Her big toe was throbbing and bruised but not devastated. She barely acknowledged Cal when he set the drink down in front of her.

"Anything else before I leave?" he asked.

"Nothing."

"You're welcome."

Dev's mouth tightened. Now she was behaving like a spoiled child. At least he had had the manners to apologize for stepping on her foot! She looked up to apologize, but all she saw was the broadness of his shoulders tapering into a lean waist and hips as he was swallowed up by the milling, festive crowd. Following him with her gaze, Dev watched as Cal Travis went back out onto the patio. Alone. He was alone. Again. Angrily, Dev picked up the glass of pop. Why should she feel guilty? *He* was the one who had started this whole mess.

In her present feisty state, Dev didn't invite anyone to sit down with her. She drowned herself in thoughts of the forthcoming fencing competition, watching some of the women who would be her competitors and mentally reviewing each of their particular weaknesses or strengths against her own abilities.

Chewing on her lower lip, Dev glanced up, straining to catch a glimpse of Major Travis. Yes, he was still out there, drink between his hands, staring off into the darkness. Her conscience pricked her. She wriggled her toe. It felt much better. Rising, Dev picked up her heels in one hand and her small white purse in the other and went out to the nearly deserted patio.

"Major Travis?"

Cal blinked slowly as if coming back from some far corner of his mind. He turned his head. "Yes?"

Dev put her hands behind her back, gripping the straps of her heels. "I, uh, just wanted to come out and say I was sorry for the way I behaved earlier. You apologized for stepping on my foot, and I didn't even have the decency to thank you for getting my drink."

Cal's gaze lingered first on her flushed face, then traveled down her slender neck to her small breasts and finally to her feet. A slight grin pulled at his mouth. He was feeling no pain now with two doubles in him.

"Didn't your mother ever teach you not to go barefoot in public?"

Dev matched his burgeoning grin. "My mother taught me to be my own person. Besides, some big marine came by and stepped on my toe."

"The brute."

Her eyes glimmered with humor, and Dev walked over to where he stood, looking out over the bay toward Hong Kong. "Are all marines like that? Brutish?" she teased, relieved to find him less threatening.

Cal turned his glass around in his hands, studying it. "I don't know. Are they?"

She shrugged, enjoying his teasing, noticing that the hardness in his face was no longer quite so evident. "I've never met one. Until now."

Cal snorted softly and bowed his head for a moment. "I'm a lousy example, believe me," he muttered.

Her heart gave a funny lurch as Dev saw his face lose its coldness for just a second. What she saw in its place stunned her. Something tragic had happened to Cal. Now she really felt guilty about being nasty to him. "I don't think so," she countered, her voice husky with feeling. "I just think you're terribly alone."

Cal tipped his head, studying Dev intently. He shook his head. "You look like a child, you know that? Those big blue eyes, soft mouth and that vulnerable aura about you."

Heat rushed to her face; Dev didn't know quite what to do. "Nah, I just behave like a spoiled brat when I get my toes stepped on, that's all."

He gave her a perceptive look, one that said, *You don't fool me*. "By the way, how is your toe? I suppose it's the one you have to fence on?"

"It's feeling no pain right now, believe me. After a double?" She laughed softly, leaning languidly against the railing, totally at ease.

Cal turned, hip resting on the wrought iron, hungrily absorbing Dev into his memory. "No pain.... You know," he said with a slight slur, "you're right on target, Ms Hunter. No pain." He turned and threw his head back and moved his shoulders as if freeing himself from some imaginary load. "No pain."

"You can call me Dev if you want to," she said, watching him.

He set down the tumbler. "Okay, Dev. How about another?"

"No, thank you."

"Sure?" he asked, halting a few feet from her.

"Positive."

His eyes darkened and held hers captive. "Will you be here when I get back, or are you going to run away from me again?"

Dev trembled, the low vibration of his voice moving through her as if he had reached out and caressed her. She took a ragged breath. "No, I'll be here."

"Your word as a fencer? You're supposed to be chivalrous and all that."

Her smile was winsome, her laughter silvery. "I'll be here, Major."

"Cal. You can call me Cal."

"Okay, Cal. I'll be here when you get back," she promised softly.

He plunged through the crowd, head held high, shoulders pressed back like the wings of a proud eagle. Dev saw the women look up as he passed. A silly smile lurked on her lips. *Careful, Dev, this is not a man you mess around with and come away from unhurt.* She shivered with the memory of Cal's intense, heated look. Her experience warned her that he played for keeps. No. He was a taker. What was his, was his. Excitement spread through Dev as she allowed herself to wonder what it would be like to be his. To belong to him. Because Major Cal Travis was an owner. Which had its darker side—one who took, who owned, could be selfish. A hunter. A stalker. Cal was dangerous, her instincts finally shouted. Dev returned her attention to the picturesque view of Hong Kong and mulled over the sudden change in their adversarial relationship.

Cal joined her as noiselessly as he had left her, which put Dev a little in awe of him. She met his unreadable gaze as he stood next to her, his elbow lightly resting near her own. The heat of his body, the intoxicating scent of him encircled her, and she felt giddy. Giddy and out of control, as if someone had waved a magic wand and the two of them were the only people in the world at that moment.

"You stayed," he said, sipping the scotch.

"I told you I would. Fencer's word," she teased.

He cocked his head, studying her face for a long moment. "I don't know anything about fencing."

"I don't know anything about marine jet pilots, either."

His mouth lifted. "We're usually called jet jockeys. Or fighter jocks."

"Is that anything like Big Man On Campus?"

He shrugged nonchalantly. "Ask any marine who's the best military man in the world, and he'll tell you it's a marine."

Dev couldn't help but smile. "And along with that goes adjectives such as 'arrogant,' 'self-centered' and 'egotistical'?"

"Touché, Dev Hunter." Cal lifted his tumbler in salute to her and took another drink. "But be careful that you don't confuse my confidence with egotism. There's a difference."

"Touché, Cal Travis. I believe the score is now two to one for you."

He nodded. "In fencing, how many points do you score to a game?"

She laughed. "They're called bouts, and whoever scores five points first is the winner of that match."

Cal was feeling pleasantly drunk. "Anybody ever tell you that you're a feisty redhead?"

Dev rested her chin on her hands, smiling distantly. "Well, at our age, Cal, I'm sure we've both been called a few things. Don't you think?"

He scowled. "Age? God, you make it sound like we're both over the hill."

"Well, in two more years, I'll be thirty," she said lightly.

"You're not twenty-five?"

"No. But thank you for the compliment, anyway. Want me to guess your age?"

He shook his head. "If I don't look eighty, I should," Cal admitted, his face becoming tense once again. He stared off into the night. "Maybe a hundred. Hell, I don't know."

Dev licked her lower lip. Cal Travis was complex and changeable. Already, she had seen his cold, ruthless side, a bit of his teasing demeanor, and now that desolate expression was on his face again. Taking a deep breath, she decided to take a chance. "Cal?"

"Hmm?"

"Why are you so sad? I was watching you a while ago, and you seemed so unhappy."

He grimaced. "God, don't tell me I'm that transparent."

"No. I don't think you are. Maybe just to me. Fencers are trained to watch even the most minute of movements, facial expressions, that sort of thing."

Cal hesitated. "Listen, my redheaded witch, you don't want to open up Pandora's box," he warned.

"Why not?"

"Because it would be dangerous."

"In what way?"

The look he gave her revealed nothing. "Either you like to live dangerously, lady, or you're being naive."

"At twenty-eight, I'm hardly naive, Cal. You want to tell me why you're polishing off that third drink like your life depended on it? You won't be able to walk out of here if you do."

He held up the tumbler. "I guess fencers do like to live dangerously." His voice hardened. "And don't worry about me. I'll be able to make it over to Wanchai when I want to."

Dev was nettled by his attitude. "Maybe it would help if you could talk about it."

"Maybe I think you should mind your own business. I don't like women who think they can mother me."

"Why, you—God! You're really exasperating! One minute you can be nice and the next minute a real bastard."

Cal turned and blinked at her. Her eyes were narrowed midnight fire, her hair an unruly mass around her head by now, her hands resting imperiously on her slender hips. He smiled, feeling dizzy for a moment. "I was right: you are a witch."

"Yes, and if I had a broom, believe me, I'd knock you over the head with it! Where do you get off taking my concern for a human being as mothering?"

He shrugged, enjoying her spirit. "Aren't all women mothers?"

She set her lips, glaring at him. "I know some men that are real mothers."

"Like me, for instance?"

Dev burst out laughing, unable to maintain her fury when he was baiting her. "You're impossible."

"Yeah, that's what I've been told. 'Travis, you're a ring-tailed bastard whose mistress is an airplane and whose mother is the marine corps.'" He turned, giving her a glazed look. "Doesn't leave much room in my life for a wife, does it?"

"Who said anything about a wife?" she asked, watching him closely. His eyes were heavy lidded, and he was almost completely relaxed. Dev wondered when the alcohol was going to fell him.

"You."

"Me? I didn't, either!"

"See, there you go again. Exploding. You're more sensitive than a laser-fired rocket, you know that?"

"That's *your* fault."

His smile was devastating. "You'd make good wifely material, Dev Hunter."

"You're drunk, Travis. Stone cold drunk. And if you don't sit down, you're going to fall down."

Cal dismissed her with a wave of his hand, feeling no pain. At last, he was free of the anguish. He felt good. Dev made him happy just by being herself. "Sure, you'd make someone a great wife. Nice body, good sense of humor—"

"You want to look at my teeth before you buy, Travis?" she snapped back, becoming truly concerned as he leaned precariously on the rail. Dev reached out, taking the tumbler from his fingers before he dropped it. She heard someone approaching and looked up. Her heart sank—two marine pilots.

"Hey, Cal, you ready to go over to Wanchai? I think we've punched the ticket long enough. What do you say, buddy?"

Cal tipped his head toward Dev. "Nah, you go on, Scotty. Got my hands full here."

"You sure?"

Dev gave Cal Travis a deadly look and turned to the pilot named Scotty. "Correction: he hasn't got his hands full of anything. He's so drunk that he's ready to keel over. Why don't you take him back to the boat and—"

"Ship, Dev. It's called a ship, not a boat," Cal corrected her, grinning lopsidedly.

She glared at him. "Thanks for the naval lesson, Major Travis. Now if you gentlemen will excuse me, I don't want to keep you from Wanchai or whatever it's called!"

Cal looked dismayed, watching her stalk off in anger, her auburn hair a burnished red and gold beneath the light of the chandeliers as she went inside to the party that was still going full steam. "I'll be damned," he muttered. And then a grin creased his features. She didn't have her shoes on! He watched as she whipped between two groups of people. One of the heels she was carrying in her hand flew out of her grasp, dropping unnoticed to the floor.

Scotty shot a glance over to him. "Whew, she's a redhead, all right."

With a concentrated effort, Cal launched himself to his feet from his leaning position at the rail. "Yeah. Feisty. But nice. I was a little rough on her. Listen, you go on, there's one thing I've got to do before I leave," he told them, eyeing the white heel that lay on the floor.

"Going to apologize, Travis?" Scotty drawled.

"She'd probably nail me with a right hook if I tried to. No, she dropped one of her heels. I'll take it up to her and then grab a taxi over to Wanchai. You guys going to be at the Golden Dragon?"

"Is there any other place?"

"No. I'll see you in a little while."

Scotty grinned. "Yeah, well, try and stay on your feet, Travis. And don't get nailed."

2

IN THE MIDDLE of her beautifully appointed room, Dev wriggled out of her dress. She tossed the Victor Kosta on one of the double beds and stalked over to the mahogany dresser, jerking open a drawer. Who in the hell did Cal Travis think he was? What an arrogant ass! She yanked on a pair of her favorite threadbare jeans that were almost white from so much wear and a bright-red T-shirt emblazoned in white and silver with a fencer wielding an épée. She spotted one of her heels. Where was the other? Muttering under her breath, Dev searched every square inch of her room. Where could it be?

"Damn it." She sat back on her heels. In exasperation, she loosened her auburn hair, and it tumbled down around her shoulders in wavy abandon, framing her face. Throwing her hands on her hips, she glared around the area. "It's all your fault, Major Travis! My only pair of heels. I'll bet I lost it when I left the party." A knock on the door startled her. Immediately, her brows knit in a frown.

"Who is it?" she yelled. She wasn't in any mood for Sarah or any of her other fencing friends to visit her right now. All she wanted was to soak her aching wrist in Epsom salts, work on her fencing gear and then go to bed.

Another knock.

Dev leaped to her feet, angry at whoever it was because he or she didn't even have the decency to respond to her call. Barefoot, she marched down the long hall, unchained the door and removed the dead bolt. With a yank, the door was open.

"What do *you* want?" she demanded, glaring up at the marine. Dev tried to still her leaping pulse. Cal Travis looked remarkably relaxed.

"Is that the way you always answer your door?" he asked silkily. Damn, she looked gorgeous, Cal thought, his gaze hungrily taking in her unruly hair, slender body emphasized by nice rounded breasts and those delicious, beautifully curved thighs. He was coming to appreciate fencers and fencing, he thought, laughing to himself.

"When it's an arrogant marine corps pilot like you, you bet I do!" Dev flared back. "Now if you don't mind, I've lost one of my heels, and I've got to go back upstairs to find it."

Cal drew the white leather heel from behind his back, dangling it like a carrot before her. "I found it."

Dev pouted, feeling some of her anger abate. Well, he wasn't a total bastard, after all. She reached out for it, her long fingers wrapping around the strap.

He didn't let go.

Dev's mouth narrowed dangerously. His eyes were a warm, inviting gray. He was silently laughing at her.

"Let me have my shoe, Major."

"Only if you invite me in for a cup of coffee first," he said huskily.

Dev felt a thrill along her fingers as his hand remained lightly against her own. "If you think you're coming in for a roll in the hay, forget it. Go to your Wanchai or whatever it is."

Cal's mouth slowly drew into a mocking grin. "Are all fencers as blunt and paranoid as you?"

Her eyes glittered. Dev felt embarrassed and stupid standing out in the hall with her heel gripped firmly between them. A warning bell went off inside her: he reminded her of a big cat playing with a cornered mouse. And she was his dinner. "Only when they're under attack," she parried nervously beneath his heavy-lidded appraisal. God, the man could melt butter with those eyes of his!

"But I'm not attacking you. I brought you your heel, and I wanted to apologize for the way I behaved earlier."

"Apologize?" Her lips parted, and she ruthlessly searched his enigmatic expression for some telltale sign that he was lying through his playboy teeth.

Cal released the shoe, lounged against the doorjamb and stuck his hands deep into his pockets, watching her. She was sensuous in that outfit. Tall and built like a racing greyhound. And not an inch of fat or flab on her. "Yes, ma'am. I wasn't much of a gentleman earlier. I embarrassed the hell out of you in front of my friends." His voice lowered. "And I am sorry. It's been a tough week, and I really didn't want to come to this function. I figured if I got drunk, I wouldn't feel anything." Cal glanced up, meeting and melting beneath her suddenly compassionate blue eyes. "I hadn't counted on meeting a highly fascinating, not to mention beautiful, red-haired woman tonight." Cal forced himself back to his feet, dizziness stalking him as he took his hands out of his pockets. He gave her a warm smile. "That's all I wanted to say, Dev. I didn't mean to ruin your evening."

Dev watched him turn and slowly walk down the hall toward the elevators. He was weaving. "Wait!" she called, her voice carrying strongly. "Cal?"

He stopped and turned. "What?"

She held up the heel. "How about that coffee? I mean, you drank a lot. And you're walking like a duck."

His grin was irrepressible as he turned and came back toward her. "A duck?"

"Sort of. You had three doubles. That's a lot of liquor. Come on in."

Cal wandered through the door, taking a look around her room. He spotted the cocktail dress in a heap on one of the beds. In one corner were two green canvas bags, holding, he was sure, some of her fencing weapons. On the coffee table directly in front of him were two weapons lying disassembled with electrical wires sticking out of the bell guards of the blades. He carefully made his way around the table, unbuttoned his jacket and dropped it across the back of the blue silk settee before he sat down. He unbuttoned the shirt at his throat, loosened his tie and pulled the collar open. He hated ties. Although he was dizzy and out of sorts, his focus on Dev was all too clear. She was attractive, and he added another word—fearless. He liked the low, husky tone of her voice and listened to it as she ordered the lifesaving liquid.

"The coffee will be here in five minutes," Dev promised, putting the phone back into the cradle. Why did she suddenly feel nervous? She wasn't eighteen and this certainly wasn't a date. Yet the look in Cal's eyes instantly made Dev feel breathless...and then afraid that she might want this man one day. He was male. Totally male, the strong column of his throat exposed at the open collar, a few dark hairs peeking out from above the white T-shirt he wore beneath his uniform. She swallowed and gave him a nervous smile, coming to sit down in the chair at the end of the coffee table. Wanting to somehow quell her nervousness, Dev reached for her small toolbox near the leg of the chair and began reassembling one of the weapons.

"This is a first," Cal said, amusement in his voice.

Dev looked up briefly. "What?"

"A woman with weapons in her bedroom. Do you always keep them lying around to scare off a man who might get ideas?"

She met his smile, then forced her attention back to threading the wires through the aluminum bell guard. "So far, I haven't had to march anybody out at sword point. But," she added, measuring him with a look, "there's always a first time for everything."

"Is that warning for my benefit?"

"Take it any way you want, Major Travis."

He scowled. "Now we're back to formality." He leaned forward, reaching out, his long, tapered fingers gently wrapping around her wrist. "I'm not a wolf, and you're certainly not a defenseless rabbit. So relax, will you? You're making me nervous, and I'm drunker than hell."

His touch was electrifying, making wild tingles race up her arm. Dev's eyes rounded, and she froze beneath his hand until he released her. "It isn't every day I meet a hotshot pilot who's handsome and a playboy to boot," she muttered, returning to her work and refusing to meet his eyes.

Cal eased back, putting an arm along the top of the settee, finding himself enjoying her company. The light from the lamp made her hair come alive, and he was mesmerized by the copper, wine and gold colors. He wondered what her hair would feel like beneath his exploring hands and had to physically stop himself from satisfying his curiosity. "I might agree with the hotshot pilot label. Definitely with the handsome bit. But I'm not a playboy."

Dev hooted, throwing back her head. "Excuse me, Major. But there's no wedding ring on your left hand, and you've got all the subtle, sexy moves calculated to melt a woman right into your arms. Oh, yes, you're a playboy, all right. And very good at it, too."

His eyes glittered as he studied her. "So what's wrong with enjoying women?"

"Nothing. Not a thing. It's just that I'm not prepared to be one of your conquests, that's all."

"Well," he drawled, "I'm not stupid enough to invite myself in here, judging by the way you handle those weapons. Don't worry, I'll behave myself."

Dev lifted her chin, meeting his smile. Cal seemed so warm and open; in that moment, she liked him. He wasn't afraid to poke fun at himself. She liked his honesty.

"They're called épées," she said, slipping the pistol-grip handle back onto the threaded steel that was welded to the blade.

"They're called dangerous."

She liked his mellow laughter. After taking a screwdriver and tightening the bolt, she handed him the épée butt first. "Nah, they're not dangerous and neither am I."

Cal sat up, gingerly holding the long, triangular blade. "Correction: any redhead is dangerous."

"Just ones without freckles. See? I have freckles. Your basic, harmless type."

"In my book, no redhead is harmless."

"And I'll bet you've got lots and lots of experience under your belt with women from around the world."

The knock at the door broke their friendly mood. Dev got lithely to her feet, skipping across the room. Cal sat back, enjoying watching her. The houseboy, dressed in black slacks and a white top, brought in the coffee. He placed it on the table, bowed, then left. Dev flopped down, crossed her legs beneath the table and poured. When she handed Cal the cup and saucer, he had the oddest expression on his face.

"Why are you looking at me like that?" she asked.

Cal shook his head slightly, taking the fragrant coffee from her. "Don't mind me, Dev. I'm drunk, remember?" She was so natural and unaffected. She had a way about her that shook his deteriorating control. Dev wore no makeup, looked utterly delicious in a pair of old jeans and a T-shirt that lovingly outlined every contour and valley of her body and matched his wit at every turn. He saw her eyes darken momentarily with concern.

"It's starting to get to you, isn't it? First the dizziness, and next, you'll pass out." She wrinkled her nose. "Or worse, get sick. I hate getting sick. That's why I never drink much. Except for tonight."

You're *getting to me*, Cal thought. "Did I drive you to drink tonight?"

"You know you did."

"I haven't been very good company," he agreed.

She tilted her head. "Are you feeling worse? You're looking pale."

"A little," he lied.

"Are pilots known for understatement?"

He sipped the scaldingly hot liquid, hoping to quell the increasing hunger coming to life in him. What would it be like to kiss those full, smiling lips that quirked, pouted and compressed according to her quicksilver mood? Or to allow his hands to outline those wonderfully shaped breasts? Or...Cal took a very long breath and expelled it slowly. Well, he was drunk. And he wasn't feeling any pain now over Chief's death. He was feeling another kind of pain, a sharp ache deep inside his chest, one that he couldn't quite identify, having never felt it before. "Probably," he admitted, forcing down more coffee.

Dev poured herself some and added a hefty portion of cream and sugar to it. All the while, she was watching him. "I'm not exactly sober myself."

"You hold your liquor real well," he congratulated her.

"So do you. But I don't see how you're managing."

Dev was so flustered by the keen, incisive look Cal gave her that she nearly dropped the saucer. She quickly set it down on the table in front of her, getting back to work on the second épée. The silence became awesome, and inwardly Dev tensed, realizing he was watching her every move.

"When do you fence in this competition coming up?" Cal asked, trying to ease the uneasiness between them.

"Wednesday. I'm lucky, I have a chance to recover from jet lag before I have to go out on the strip."

"Strip?"

Dev eyed him, noticing he had a silly smile on his mouth. A mouth that was used to giving orders and having them carried out. She wondered blankly what it would be like to be kissed by a mouth like that. "Uh, we fence on a copper-mesh strip that's approximately forty-six feet long and six-and-a-half feet wide. Epée and foil are electrically scored, and the copper strip grounds us. Officially, it's known as a *piste*, but we call it the strip, instead."

Cal finished the first cup, awkwardly pouring a second one, spilling a few drops on the table. "How long are you going to be here in Hong Kong?"

"A week. I have to fence Wednesday and Friday. We leave on Sunday. What about you? How long will you be here?" She looked up, struck by how relaxed Cal looked.

"One week."

"Must be nice. A paid vacation to ports all over the world."

He grimaced, not meeting her teasing blue gaze. "Yeah, I suppose it is."

Dev picked up the bell guard. A flash of pain shot through her fingers and then up to her elbow. Her fingers became nerveless, and the bell dropped to the carpet. She bit down hard on her lower lip, instantly covering her injured wrist with her other hand.

"What's wrong?" Cal put the cup down on the table and leaned forward.

"Oh, nothing," she muttered. Damn it! She got up, holding her wrist, the pain increasing. She was so absorbed by the fact her wrist was giving her trouble again that she didn't notice Cal get to his feet. It was only when his long fingers gently pulled her hand from her throbbing wrist that she realized he was there, standing over her. His brows were drawn down as he carefully examined the injury. Her pulse jumped; her heart thudded in her breast. Dev could feel the power radiating from Cal, making her dizzy, frightening her, thrilling her. She could smell his subtle cologne, and her nostrils flared as he carefully turned her hand over.

"What did you do? Strain it? Looks a little swollen here," he said, lightly running his thumb across the affected area.

"I—I sprained it about three weeks ago." She sounded like a stammering eighteen-year-old.

Cal drew up her hand, positioning her wrist in a better light. "Yeah, there's still some bruising. You can barely see it, though." He looked up, his face inches from hers. "What happened? Did you hurt yourself fencing?"

His eyes were so wide and inquiring that Dev lost herself in them. Eyes that were at once intelligent, clear and yet filled with genuine concern. He wasn't a sham, after all; she knew it in her heart. This was another side to the enigmatic Cal Travis. Dev blinked, shaken. She reclaimed her hand and took a step away from him. "No . . . I got shoved down by a couple of union guys about three weeks ago."

"What?"

Dev's lashes flew up at his growl. "I'm a television camera operator. The reporter, Tucker, and I had to go out and cover a strike. He wanted some close-ups of the union people having words with the police, and he ordered me into the confrontation. One of the guys tried to tear the camera off my shoulder and out of my hands." Dev shrugged. "I held on to it, but me and the camera both went flying." She glanced down at her wrist. "I took a bad strain, and I've been trying to baby my wrist along ever since then so I can fence at my best in this competition."

Cal's eyes flashed with anger. "Tucker was a fool to let you that close to something like that," he snapped. "What's the idiot got for a brain? A pea?"

Dev gave him a feeble smile. "Don't be angry at him. He's always where the action is. I only banged up my wrist a little," she lied.

Cal threw his hands on his hips, assessing her. "That épée must weigh around a pound and a half. If you can't even hold a lightweight piece of aluminum with that hand, how are you going to fence?"

Dev raised her eyebrows, pleased by his insight. "Good question. I'll probably have to wrap it tightly and pray it holds up during the bouts. I'll be back in a minute. I want to get a warm cloth and wrap my wrist."

"No, sit down here. Let me do it."

"But—"

"Sit down."

Dev sat, rather shocked, watching him stalk to the bathroom. When Cal came back with the washcloth and hunched down in front of her, Dev held out her wrist. "I want you to know, I don't normally take orders from anyone."

Cal wrapped the cloth around her wrist, holding it between his hands. He raised his chin, meeting her cool blue eyes. Eyes that were flecked with gold spikes in their depths. "You're pulling back from me. I guess sometimes retreat is the better part of valor."

"You're impossible, Travis."

A grin lurked around his mouth. "Yeah, I know. And you like me that way."

A flush invaded her cheeks. "I didn't say I liked you at all!" she blustered, her flesh tingling madly where his hands rested. His touch was firm without being painful. As a matter of fact, her wrist felt better already.

"You also admitted I was handsome."

"And a playboy. Don't forget the last label. It's the most important one."

"What do you have against me enjoying the woman I want to give my undivided attention to?" he asked huskily, the vibration of his voice moving through her like a sensual drug.

Dev wanted to run. She was reeling from his decidedly masculine aura. "Nothing. Everything," she muttered, refusing to meet his eyes.

"If you were my woman, you wouldn't be saying that," he told her softly, his voice deep, penetrating.

Her defenses were up; the red light was going off in the back of her head, and she was trembling. Trembling! And it wasn't from fear. It was from the promise in Cal's intimate baritone, aimed at her. She swallowed. "My wrist feels better now."

He shook his head, removing the cloth and then refolding it around her wrist. "Why are you afraid of me, Dev Hunter?"

Cautiously, she met his frank gray eyes. "You make me feel as if I'm being hunted." She was completely unprepared as his hand left her wrist and framed her face, tilting her head slightly upward. His breath was moist against her flesh as he bent his head.

"You are...." he said thickly, his mouth slanting across her parted lips as he slowly drew her to her feet.

The breath was stolen from her body, replaced by the gentle invasion of his mouth, tasting, testing and teasing her lips. Her world shattered into a million golden fragments as Dev felt his hands frame her face, deepening the exploration, coaxing her to partake of the heat that boiled within them. She had no time to react, her hands automatically lifting to rest against the hardened muscles of his upper arms. The scent of Cal entered her nostrils, and she tasted the maleness of him. A driving hunger flared to life in her lower body, liquid fire racing through her as he continued to gently tease her lips with little nips, his tongue lightly stroking her flesh with unexpected tenderness. Her knees weakened, and Dev trembled outwardly as his onslaught continued. Somewhere in her stunned, incoherent mind, Dev recognized that if Cal had been ruthless or brutal, she would have reacted negatively. Instead, he had surprised her again. He was a man of war. Someone who was used to flexing his muscles and using his strength. But he wasn't capable of using force on her. Dev found herself capitulating to his coaxing.

Cal slowly broke the kiss, need screaming through his hardened body. "God, you're so sweet," he rasped, looking deep into her dazed cobalt eyes. "Sweet and good and all woman."

Dev blinked, languorously. If it weren't for Cal's fingers spanning her jaw, she would have slumped against him, dizzied by his kiss. She had *never* savored the utter raw sensuality of a kiss before as she had with him. Confusion darkened her eyes as she basked in his warmth. Dev saw a hint of a smile tugging at his wonderfully shaped mouth.

"Come on, I think you'd better sit down before you fall down." Cal led her over to the settee, briefly keeping his hand on her arm. He picked up the cloth that Dev had allowed to drop to the carpet when he had kissed her. Going to the bathroom, he wet it again. Dev gave him a guarded look as he walked back toward her; he saw her defenses going up. Could he blame her? As he hunched down, Cal felt a wave of dizziness race through him. Not because of her giving, vulnerable kiss, either—because of the damn liquor he had consumed. Wrapping her wrist once more, he cursed himself. Now he wanted to be sober. To be clearheaded. Dev interested him. She was different. Independent. And she didn't play games. Cal didn't regret the kiss, but he regretted how he was feeling. It had been a stupid, immature idea to drink. Normally he'd have had a few beers, that was all. No carrier pilot lasted long if he hit the bottle.

"I have a favor to ask," he began, meeting her grave eyes, "and I know you'll probably think I'm playing a game when I ask you."

Dev's arm tingled where Cal's hand rested. Her voice was soft when she answered. "Are you feeling bad?"

A mocking smile lingered on Cal's mouth. "Not from kissing you, believe me. It's from the scotch." His brows drew downward. "To make a long story very short, Dev, I've had about seven hours' sleep the past four days. All that liquor and I'm ready to keel over."

"You'll never make it back to your ship."

"No, I won't." He glanced toward the beds. "If you could let me just kick off my shoes and sleep for a few hours—"

Her eyes flickered with concern. "Four days? Cal, what happened? I mean—"

His mouth thinned. "I can't talk about it, Dev. Trust me, all right? Just let me get a few hours and then I'll leave. I promise I'll keep my hands off you. No games, my red-headed witch."

She studied him for a moment. Her instincts always ran true, no matter how the rest of her was feeling. She searched Cal's face, noticing that the skin was drawn tautly across his flesh, dark shadows beneath his eyes.

"Okay. Go lie down. I'm tired, too. Do you want a shower? The hotel supplies robes—"

Cal slowly stood up. "No. I've taken enough advantage of your generosity already, Dev. If I can grab a few hours, that's all I'll need." He walked over to the bed, turned the lamp off and sat down. Dev watched as he took off his shoes, then stretched out, his hands behind his head. She got up, moving to the hall and shutting off another switch, which darkened the entire suite. Her lips still tingled from the coaxing fire of his kiss, and dazedly, she wandered into the bathroom to have her bath. The evening was turning out to be incredible in so many ways.

Dev languished in the orange-scented bath salts, her thick mane piled on her head. If someone had told her she would be meeting a devastatingly handsome man, a marine corps fighter pilot, she would have roared with laughter. And then to have him in her room, sleeping in one of the beds! If Sarah ever found out, her twenty-year-old eyes would widen to saucer proportions, and her mouth would drop open. Dev smiled. *Cal Travis, you are something else. A breed apart. An interesting man. A fascinating human being.* She mulled over the facets of him that she had glimpsed that evening. Putting them all together, Dev confirmed her belief that something tragic had happened lately to Cal. After he had kissed her and she had opened her eyes, Dev had seen grief in his gaze. Raw anguish that hadn't yet been expressed. She sighed tiredly, rising from the water and stepping onto the rug, wrapping the thick white towel around her and drying off.

Slipping into her lavender-sprigged, knee-length gown, Dev quietly opened the door, shutting off both the bathroom and hall lights. She waited a few moments, allowing her eyes to adjust to the gloomy darkness. A slight smile chased across her lips: she could hear Cal's occasional soft snore breaking the silence. Padding barefoot into the main room, she noted that she had left the gauzy blue panels drawn across the huge wall of windows. The lights of Hong Kong shed a luminescence into the room, making it easy to see where she was walking.

Dev hesitated after pulling back the covers on her own bed, turning to look at Cal. He had rolled onto his side, legs slightly drawn up toward his chest, arms around the pillow he had laid his head on. In sleep, he looked vulnerable, and her heart gave a funny lurch. No longer did the corners of his mouth pull in as if he were experiencing some pain known only to himself. Dev felt sudden compassion for him and, walking around the bed, drew a lightweight blanket up across his body. Several strands of his dark-walnut hair had dipped down across his brow. She leaned over, coaxing them into place with her fingers.

"Good night, Cal," she whispered. "I hope you've escaped all that hurt I saw in your eyes." Dev straightened up, her own eyes fraught with worry. She recalled the only time in her life when she had gotten miserably drunk and on a great deal less than what Cal had probably consumed. Dev gnawed on her lower lip for a while before going back to her bed and slipping between the cool, crisp sheets. If Cal hadn't slept much in four days, he wasn't going to be getting up in a few hours feeling fit. Or even human. Dev found herself hoping he would sleep through the night and be around when she woke up in the morning. Her dreamy side wished that. Her realistic side chided her: Cal would get up in a few hours and quietly walk out of her life, never to be seen again. She snuggled into her pillow. Despite everything, she liked Cal Travis. Despite his obvious love of himself, he did have some facesaving traits that endeared him to her. On that thought, Dev spiraled into the welcoming folds of sleep.

CAL MOVED RESTLESSLY in a stupor that straddled sleep and the nightmarish reality that haunted him. He twisted his head to one side, feeling a rivulet of sweat running down from his temple, across his jaw. His mouth moved, unintelligible words torn from him. Chief was smiling. Even though his friend wore the mandatory oxygen mask, Cal could always tell when his copilot was smiling because the corners of his chocolate-brown eyes crinkled. He smiled back beneath the rubber of his own face mask. They were running through the last compulsory checks on their A-6 Intruder jet. It stood poised in front of the catapult that would soon sling them like an arrow off the deck of the carrier and into the pink dawn.

"Hey, you know you have to see my sister, Kaya, when you make it to test pilot school," Chief teased him, flipping on a few more switches with his gloved hand.

Cal leaned over, his gray gaze making a final sweep of the instruments. "Told you I would."

"I'll scalp you if you don't, buddy," he teased goodnaturedly, giving Cal a light punch on the right shoulder.

"I promise. I promise." Cal looked over at his friend, with whom he had flown for over a year and a half. Joe was a full-blooded Hopi Indian, one of the first Hopi to make it through the rank and file to become a fighter pilot. Maybe it was because they were both taciturn, revealing little of themselves, that they had initially been drawn to each other. Cal wasn't sure. What he was sure of was that Chief, his teasing nickname for Joe, was the very best of the fighter pilot breed. They were top scorers in competitions around the world in air-to-air and air-to-ground target practice. Cal and Chief were inseparable.

"My sister's pretty. So just keep your hands to yourself, Travis."

Cal laughed, bringing the canopy down and locking it. His long fingers folded over the dual throttles. "If she wasn't your sister, she wouldn't be safe."

Chief gave him a dangerous look laced with amusement, throwing him a thumbs-up sign. "I know. Okay, check complete. Let's get this baby airborne, I want to play eagle."

The hookup man on deck, crouched beneath the A-6 Intruder, handed the plane off to the catapult officer, who stood a few feet off the wingtip. The cat officer thrust his right hand, two fingers extended, into the air and waved it in a rapid rotating motion. Cal scanned his instruments and moved the control stick forward and back, from right stop to left stop. He saw four other deck-crew troubleshooters rapidly moving down the expanse of his aircraft, searching for leaks, proper engine function, control movement or anything abnormal. When one of the crewmen gave a thumbs-up, the cat officer looked down at the hookup man, still kneeling by the aircraft's hook that was now linked to the steam catapult.

Automatically, Cal asked, "Harness tight?" The raw power of the catapult, hurling the A-6 off the deck at one hundred eighty miles per hour, could snap a neck. The crisscross of harnesses kept Cal and Chief tightly strapped to their individual ejection seats, pinned in one position. Cal always had bruises on his shoulders from the straps biting deeply into his flesh.

"Yeah. Tight enough to make a pig squeal. Brakes full power," Chief replied.

Cal saw the hookup man scurry away from beneath their A-6. Immediately, his gaze moved to the yellow-vested cat officer. Cal snapped off a salute, preparing himself for the release.

"We're going to get the signal," he said, watching as the shooter, who stood over the catapult console on the edge of the deck, raised both arms skyward. The cat officer took a wide stance, his left hand in the air, two fingers extended. He returned Cal's salute, then suddenly dropped to one knee, signaling the shooter to press the button that would send them down the deck.

Cal heard the call from the control tower that sat above them. The dawn was turning a brilliant red and pink; the South China Sea was placid on that beautiful late October morning. But Cal didn't notice. He was locked into one of the most dangerous maneuvers ever to be performed by any pilot in any jet—takeoff from a carrier. The jet began to scream, trembling and howling like a banshee around him and his copilot as he arced the throttles to full power. Then, at a hand signal from the navy crewman who stood five yards away from the wingtip of the jet, he knotched them into afterburner range. Cal braced himself, unconsciously pressing his helmet back into the seat and keeping his neck relaxed. His fingers tightened imperceptibly around the stick.

The wrenching jerk of the catapult driving the screaming jet down the expanse shattered the aircraft's immobility. There would be five seconds of thousands of tons of catapult pressure pushing the jet, giving it enough speed to safely hurl it off the carrier.

It was then that Cal heard an explosion. The jet suddenly lagged beneath them. His gaze snapped to the engine manifold pressure. The engines were screamingly alive. The catapult! So many thoughts sheared through his steel-trap mind. He had decisions to make: slam on the brakes and shut down the engines, try to stop before they hit the lip of the deck and slid over the edge of the carrier or— No, it was too late! Too much yardage had been eaten up. His hand pressed against the throttles, willing the engines that were shrieking around them to have the power to lift them. Too late! Too late! His eyes bulged as he saw that the manifold pressure wasn't enough to lift the jet's tonnage off the deck. His breath froze in his throat. He heard Chief's curse.

The A-6 screamed off the carrier, but Cal felt the jet drag, and he kept the throttles to the fire wall, working the sluggish rudders to turn the aircraft out of the path of the carrier. If they dropped below the bow and crashed, the ship would be heavily damaged. Teeth clenched, his body straining against the harness, Cal wrenched the stick to port, praying the jet would make the turn before they hit the gray-green water coming up fast. And then . . . water spewed in avalanching sheets around them as they hit the ocean's surface. Cal wrenched back with all his strength, keeping the nose of the jet up so that they wouldn't tunnel in, giving them precious seconds to break free as the jet's stubby wings kept them on top of the water. His teeth ground together. Pain soared up through his left hand as the stick was ripped out of his fingers.

Frantically, Cal and Chief worked open the jammed canopy. Steam shot skyward as seawater rushed into the hot engines. Water gurgled and burped into the cockpit. Cal's hands trembled badly as he worked to unsnap all his harnesses. He glanced over at Chief. He was doing the same.

"I'm in trouble, I'm in trouble," Chief yelled.

Cal released the last hitch on his harness, twisting. Water slopped in over them. He felt the jet's nose begin to drop. It would be a matter of seconds before they were swallowed by the ocean. Cal tried to help Chief get the lap harness released. The thick, heavy, leather lap belt was held by a stout aluminum device. Water washed up to their chests.

"It won't come...." Cal said, gasping. He twisted back again, pulling his survival knife from his belt, throwing off the sheath.

"Jump, Cal!" Chief cried hoarsely. The jet was sliding in, wing down. Sliding into a cold, watery grave.

Cal cursed, sawing into the confining leather belt. "No! Shut up, damn it!"

Water closed over them. Cal took a deep breath into his lungs, clinging to the belt as the jet sliced downward with frightening speed. The knife made huge, gaping tears across the leather. Cal felt his chest expand as if it would burst. Two more cuts . . . God . . . just two more and Chief would be free. The aircraft suddenly rolled over. As it did, the action wrenched Cal, who had nothing holding him in the cockpit other than one hand on the leather belt, free. His gloved hands clawed outward as he felt himself tumbling, trying desperately to grab for the cockpit frame. Fire arched through his chest. Water funneled up into his nose and down into his throat. He was going to drown. Chief! Oh, God, Chief! Cal struck out toward the surface that seemed so far away, blackness closing in on him. Only one thought screamed through him: Chief was going down with the jet. He would drown. He'd die. Oh, God, no . . . not Chief! Not his best friend.

"Cal, Cal, it's all right . . . shh, it's all right. You're safe . . . safe." A soft voice crooned to him.

Cal shuddered, still hooked into the nightmare of survival that haunted him, as he broke the surface of the gray sea. Gasping, he vomited up the sea he had swallowed, flailing weakly to stay afloat. Instinctively, he pulled the cords on his life vest and it inflated immediately, holding his head and shoulders above water. He cried out Chief's name, oblivious to the rescue helicopter that had been launched immediately after the accident. He felt cool hands on his face, fingers gently combing through his hair, and he sobbed. Chief was dead. The only real friend he had ever made was dead. Heading fifty fathoms down in a jet while he floated on the surface, rasping and swallowing the life-giving oxygen.

"You're safe now, Cal. Relax. Come on, you're going to be all right...." Cal felt movement. It wasn't the movement of the ocean that embraced him. He forced open his tightly shut eyes, aware of sweat running down his taut face. Dark. It was so dark. Cal felt the moist warmth of a cloth against his face. Heat. It felt so good and he was so cold. Icy cold in the water. Automatically, he began to relax. Someone was gently running a hand across his trembling shoulders, and he visibly responded to these tentative ministrations. Where was he? Where?

"Chief?" His voice came out in a raw whisper.

"No. It's me, Dev. Just rest, Cal. You've been through a lot. Just close your eyes and rest. You're safe. I promise you...."

Her voice was so close, so rich and husky. Cal closed his eyes, trusting her. Trusting her hands that were easing the coldness and terror out of him.

"But... Chief..."

"He's gone, Cal. You couldn't help him. But you're alive. Alive. Come on, try to rest. You're so tired."

A huge pressure welled up like a fist within his chest, and Cal turned his face, burying it in the soft warmth of her. He shut his eyes tightly, fighting the pressure, trying to wrestle with the grief and loss. The instant her trembling hand settled on his hair, he blindly reached out, his arms sliding around her body. He felt scalding tears pummeling the back of his eyes, and he felt her arms embracing him. Holding him and rocking him. The pain was like a fist ripping through him, and a low, tortured sob tore from him, sending a shudder through his entire body. The sounds were so foreign to him, so strange. But he couldn't help himself. Animallike sounds shattered him, expressing the loss, and all the while, she held him. Held him and murmured soft, unintelligible words meant to heal.

3

CAL FORCED HIS EYES OPEN to mere slits. His head was throbbing like a kettledrum, and his mouth felt as if an army had tramped through it. His scowl deepened as he realized someone was sitting very close to him. He forced his lids higher, his vision unfocused. Light was cascading from a hall, slanting into the room, backlighting the unruly auburn hair that framed her concerned face. Her eyes were cobalt as she sat there in silence, leaning across him, her one hand resting near his hip.

He moved his mouth, trying to form coherent words. He felt drugged and incapable of speech. "Where?"

"You're in my hotel room, Cal. The Shangri-La Hotel. Remember?" Her voice was low. He was grateful for that; each sound multiplied and reverberated through his pounding skull. His eyes slitted again as he tried to piece together the jumble of events, separating the present from the accident. And Chief. Giving him an understanding smile, she sat up, removing her hand.

"You've had a rough twenty-four hours, Cal."

He forced his limited attention back to her. Back to her kind and beautiful face. He knew her. Yes, Dev was her name. Wasn't it?

"Dev?" His voice was raw as if he had been screaming at the top of his lungs for hours. Had he?

"Touché, Major Travis. You're starting to remember, I see. How about some water? You've been very sick. I think you're close to dehydration."

The information was too much for him to assimilate. Twenty-four hours. What was she talking about? And sick? Why? The water sounded heavenly. "Yeah...water... please...." It hurt to talk. Croak would be a more appropriate word, he thought blearily. He watched through blurred vision as she rose and went over to a table. What was she wearing? White knickers and socks and a red T-shirt? That didn't make sense. He closed his eyes, dizziness making him nauseated. The moment the cool dryness of her arm slid beneath his sweaty neck and she supported him with her body, Cal reopened his eyes. He rested his head against the softness of her breast and shoulder as she pressed the glass to his lips. The coldness soothed his raw throat, cleansing his mouth of the bile taste. He sucked up the water thirstily, some of it dribbling from the corners of his mouth.

"There's more," Dev said, setting down the glass and then blotting Cal's mouth and stubbled chin. She poured another glass; he stared at it like a man who had been in the desert and was about to die from lack of water. Finally though, his thirst was satisfied, and dizziness forced him to close his eyes once again. He heard the steady beat of her heart, nuzzled his bearded cheek into the hollow between her breasts and took a deep, shuddering breath.

"Feel a bit better?" she asked, holding him.

"A little."

Dev gently laid him back down, pulling the blankets up across his naked chest. "Go back to sleep, Cal. I'll be here if you need me."

Her voice was like thick, soothing honey pouring over him, somehow easing his spinning head and exhaustion. He looked up into her eyes, lost in their luminous softness, and felt safe from the storm's remnants. Cal wanted to say "Thank you," but total fatigue dragged him back into the healing realm of sleep.

SHE WAS SITTING BY HIM when he awoke the second time, her eyes filled with worry. She was chewing on that full lower lip that he sharply remembered kissing. Cal was dully aware that it was barely dawn, the sky lavender through the panels drawn across the windows. The low lighting from the hall shadowed her pale face, and he wondered why darkness lingered beneath her glorious blue eyes. "How do you feel?" she ventured softly, placing a hand on his shoulder.

Cal felt the dry warmth on his cool, damp flesh. It felt good. Stabilizing. "Like hell," he answered, finding his voice a rasp.

"Do you remember where you are?"

Memory of the room and of Dev eventually congealed in his sluggish brain. Cal felt as if someone had taken a bottle brush to his mind and wiped it clean of everything other than Dev's haunting voice. Cal moved his gaze back up to her. "I think I do. You look tired."

Again that slight smile. Her hair curled around her head and shoulders. She looked like a winsome child. "It can't be because I've been playing nursemaid to you for almost thirty-six hours. I have to hand it to you: when you want to get drunk, you really go all the way, Major."

Cal frowned. "Thirty-six hours? What are you talking about?" He struggled into a sitting position, his head throbbing. The sheet and blankets fell away, revealing his powerful chest and hard, flat belly. He looked down at himself and then up at her, questions in his gray eyes.

Dev shrugged apologetically. "The first twenty-four hours you were sick. You sweated a lot. I had to take off your clothes because they were soaked. The next twelve hours you slept like a baby. No nightmares . . ."

His mouth tightened at her whispered words. "Nightmares?"

Dev's expression grew soft. "Yes. You kept reliving the accident, Cal." She couldn't meet his narrowed gaze. "I'm sorry about Chief. My God, you almost died, too, trying to save him." Dev shyly reached out, her hand sliding across his, her voice quavering. "How tragic...."

Cal groaned and pulled his hand away from hers, covering his face. He leaned back against the headboard, bringing up his knees beneath the covers. "Damn it," he muttered thickly.

Dev rose, sensing that he didn't want her near him. That hurt her. In the past day and a half, she had grown close to Cal as he relived the raw grief. He had found release in her arms. "Listen, I've got to go jog three miles. Part of my daily exercise routine. I'll be back in a little while." Nervously, she slipped into her jogging shoes to complete her outfit—baggy pink sweatpants and shirt. Dev felt his eyes on her as she straightened up, a knot forming in her shrinking stomach. As Dev met his predatorlike gaze, she pulled on a red sweatband. "The hotel supplies razors and that sort of thing if you feel like getting cleaned up." Grabbing her wristwatch and a key for the room, she quietly left the stilted silence, glad to escape Cal's wariness.

Cal sat there in bed, feeling utterly embarrassed and angry with himself. Dawn was creeping over the horizon behind the island of Hong Kong, the golden rays reaching and stretching out in brilliant arms. Dawn. The time of their accident. Of Chief's death. He rubbed his face, aware of the sharp stubble of his beard. Then he became aware that he needed a shower. Badly. His head ached but not so severely as to stop him from getting up. Throwing back the covers, he noted with chagrin that he wore only his briefs. As he slowly got to his feet, he looked around for his uniform. The room was neatly picked up with the exception of Dev's épée still on the coffee table. Grumbling to himself, Cal stared at the clock on the bed table—5:30 A.M. What day was it? He found his aviator's watch on the stand next to the clock. Wednesday morning? No. Impossible! He glared at his watch in his open palm. The party had been Monday night. Where—

"Damn it," Cal muttered, stalking off toward the bathroom, ruthlessly combing his spotty memory for details. The scalding-hot shower washed away the sweat of fear from his body. It improved his mood about one degree. The bathroom was steamy and warm as he wrapped a thick white towel around his waist and then shaved. Borrowing Dev's tortoiseshell comb, Cal tamed his wet hair into place, looking a hell of a lot better than he felt. His mood deteriorated even more when he couldn't find his uniform anywhere. He searched each closet and found many white fencing uniforms, a few dresses and slacks but no uniform.

Disgruntled, Cal shrugged into one of the thick terry-cloth robes the hotel provided and padded into the room. He called down for coffee, then went over to the windows and stared stonily out. Several junks floated past the hotel. The cobblestoned shore nearby was lined with many of Hong Kong's citizens going through their morning t'ai chi ch'uan exercises. Then he spotted Dev off in the distance, jogging back toward the hotel along the wharf. Some of his anger dissipated as Cal watched her stride with long-legged confidence, her auburn hair captured in a ponytail, drifting out behind her with each rhythmic step. As Dev drew closer, he could see the flush to her cheeks, thinking that she looked beautiful. Scowling, Cal turned when the houseboy announced himself. Coffee had arrived. Thank God.

Dev knocked before she opened the door to her room, just to make sure Cal had had time to dress. Her heart was pounding strongly in her breast, and that wasn't from the workout. She closed the door and walked down the hall. At the end of the hall, Dev halted, her lips parting.

"Oh." She stared stupidly across the room at Cal, who was sitting on the settee, coffee in hand, observing her. Instantly, she flushed and pulled the damp sweatband off her brow.

"It looked like you were having a good run."

Dev walked over to the bed and sat down, unlacing her shoes. She was surprised at the quiet quality of Cal's voice. Was he angry? He was a man of immense pride, she suspected. Yet he had spent the past day and a half in her room, helpless as a baby, having to rely totally on her for care. Dev didn't imagine Cal leaned on anyone for anything. Especially a stranger who had witnessed him suffering a deep, personal tragedy. She licked her lips, tasting the salt of perspiration on them as she leaned over.

She nudged off her shoes, giving him a shy glance. Cal looked devastatingly handsome, though weary. His face was free of the dark, bristly growth of beard, his gray eyes were probing and the planes of his face were relatively free of tension. He smiled a little, making Dev relax slightly. She prayed that the tenuous middle ground she felt they both wanted would grow between them.

"Got time for a cup of coffee?"

Dev's heart lurched at the husky quality in his voice, and her spirits rose. Cal wasn't angry with her. For all his ego, he wasn't going to take his embarrassment out on her. She rewarded him with a genuine smile. "Let me take a shower first."

"Sure."

Cal watched her walk to the bathroom, impressed, even mesmerized, by her graceful carriage. He sipped the coffee, relishing the taste. He had seen the unsureness in Dev's eyes as she had come into the room. Suddenly, all the embarrassment and anger he might have aimed at her dissolved. Dev didn't deserve that from him, no matter how ashamed he felt. Oddly, Cal found himself wanting to reach out, to continue to bask in her company. Whether he liked it or not, Dev had shared one of the most brutal moments in his life with him. And Cal had never shared any of his deep emotional responses with anyone. Except Chief. But not to the degree he had with Dev. Ruminating on that, he contented himself with watching the traffic increase in Victoria Harbor as the sun rose and the morning stirred to life.

Dev emerged from the bathroom in a pair of white polyester knickers, white socks and a pink T-shirt that lovingly emphasized her breasts and flat stomach. Her hair was piled in a loose knot on top of her head, tendrils curled temptingly around her temples as a result of her shower. Dev smiled and flopped down opposite him, legs crossed beneath the table.

"I think I'm going to live now," she said, pouring herself some coffee.

"I'm thinking about it, too," Cal offered wryly, watching her slender hands slide around the china cup.

"You look a hundred percent better." Her blue eyes sparkled as Dev drew the cup to her lips. "You look handsome again."

He smiled. "I don't feel very handsome." He met and held her gaze. "I've been remembering some of what happened, Dev." His voice dropped to a husky whisper. "The past day and a half have been a living hell for me and not much more than that for you."

Dev placed the cup on the table. "I know you're feeling awfully vulnerable and emotionally raw right now, Cal."

"I feel brittle. I think if someone yelled at me right now, I'd shatter. I've never felt like this before," he muttered.

"Only when you lose someone who's very close to you does that happen."

Cal took a deep breath, closing his eyes and shaking his head. "You know what I find phenomenal?"

"No. What?"

"Us. You and me. I'm a stranger who crashed into your life, made an ass out of myself, embarrassed the hell out of you in front of my friends and yet you stuck it out with me." He opened his eyes, his turbulent gaze settling on her. "You had every right to kick me out of your room Monday night. Why didn't you?"

Dev swallowed against a forming lump. "Because you were hurting."

Cal stared at her. "The women I know would gladly have booted me out and told me to catch a cab and go back to the carrier to get sick."

"You'd had too much to drink, Cal. I didn't think you could have even made it downstairs to get a taxi. What I hadn't counted on was your tragedy." Dev lowered her lashes. "Now I understand why you wanted to get drunk and why you didn't want to be at the party on Monday." She clasped her fingers in her lap. "You were hurting. And—and when you started crying—"

Cal stared disbelievingly at her. "I what?"

"Cried. What's wrong with that? I was crying right along with you after I pieced together what had happened."

He stared at her.

"I couldn't stand by and not help you." Dev raised her head, drowning in his gray eyes. "You needed help. I couldn't kick you out." And then a small smile touched her lips. "Besides, you weren't a total bastard. You came and apologized to me for your behavior earlier, and you also brought me the heel."

A vague memory stirred in Cal's shocked mind. Yes, he remembered being held, rocked to and fro like a child in the arms of its mother, sobbing. And Dev's softened weeping as she held him tightly to her. Cal swallowed hard. "I've never cried."

Dev frowned, searching his face that was lined with denial. "I see. Is that a maxim of the marine corps or fighter pilots in particular? You're real men? Real men don't cry? Don't show any emotion?" Dev's voice lowered. "Well, in my book, any man who exhibits that kind of behavior is emotionally constipated. I see nothing wrong with showing and displaying how you feel. As a matter of fact, it's kind of nice to be able to share someone else's feelings. Women do it all the time. A man has a heart and can feel just as we do. Why shouldn't he cry when he's in pain?"

Cal shot to his feet. He winced, the quick rise costing him dearly. He turned away from Dev, glaring out across the harbor. Sunshine spilled blindingly into their room, caressing him with its warming rays. He was angry. Angry at her. No, at himself. His hands clenched at his sides. He wasn't used to expending himself emotionally in any woman's company. And yet, he vividly recalled how Dev had held him in her strong embrace, giving him the solace he sought as he gripped her tightly, his arms wrapped around her slender, giving body.

"Cal?"

"What?"

"Please, sit down and talk with me. I don't want you angry at me. Or at yourself. I don't know much about military pilots. Maybe your kind has to shove their emotions into a little box in order to function. What we shared was—special. Too special to let it be destroyed by pride on either side. Your feelings were—are—real. You must have loved Chief like a brother to be that torn up. I was privileged to share that with you."

Cal turned, looking down at Dev. His heart wrenched in his chest, warmth flooding through him. Slowly, he unknotted his hands, sitting back down. He poured himself more coffee.

"I'm not used to baring my soul, Dev. To anyone. Ever."

Dev nodded. "I kinda got that feeling."

His gray eyes glittered. "It's dangerous."

"Why?"

"Because people take advantage of people who let their guard down, that's why."

She laughed softly. "That's not true! I'm the exact opposite of you. No one has taken advantage of me."

"Correction. You're special," he grudgingly admitted. "That's why you can do it and get away with it."

Delighted with Cal's effort to talk honestly with her, Dev tried to remain serious. She wanted to throw her arms around him, hug him fiercely and kiss him. He was vulnerable right now. "Well, you're special, too," she confided huskily. "Is it your job that forces you to hide your emotions, Cal?"

He shrugged. "You certainly can't sit in the cockpit of a fighter crying like a baby when something goes wrong."

"That's understandable. But a few minutes ago, you said you've never shared your deep feelings with women. Did someone hurt you so badly that it was easier just to close up instead of risking your feelings again?"

Cal shook his head. "No, not really. My sister Storm is like you. She's a coast guard helicopter pilot. When we were kids, I used to watch her take it from all sides. She started flying with my father when she was only ten. The boys at school were jealous as hell of her. They used to really abuse her verbally, call her names. My brother Matt and I took on the bullies when they went too far. Storm would cry. I stood there watching every insult and name they hurled tear Storm apart. I couldn't stand to see her cry because I knew how much they were hurting her.

"Storm never changed. She kept wearing that damned heart on her sleeve even after she joined the coast guard. I told her she was crazy, that she should button up her emotions and not let anyone know he'd gotten to her." A slight smile came to Cal's mouth. "She told me to mind my own business, that she could handle herself now. Even to this day, she's an emotional barometer."

Dev leaned forward, resting her elbows on the coffee table, holding his warming gaze. "And yet Storm survives."

"Yes, she does."

Dev grinned. "More power to her. So do I. But tell me something, Cal."

"Anything."

"Tell me that you don't feel better this morning after crying. After letting go of all that grief."

She was right. Cal pursed his lips and lifted his head, looking out the windows, seeing nothing but feeling a lot. "It's the damnedest thing, Dev. I do feel better. I'm empty as if all that load of pain I was carrying around in me since the accident has disappeared."

Dev's eyes became luminous with tears that she quickly blinked away. "And did it feel good at the time to just let it all go?"

"What little I remember, yeah."

"Well, that's what Storm or any of the rest of us experience. Tears are cleansing. They're healing, Cal."

He turned his head, absorbing Dev into him. "*You're* healing, lady," he responded in a gritty voice. "I don't remember everything, but I do remember your voice, your arms, how soft you felt. How strong you were for me." Cal gave her a bashful look, unable to put much more into words. The fact that her cheeks flushed endeared Dev to him even more. She could have taken advantage of him in many ways this morning. She could have been justifiably upset with him, rude, stinging, caustic. But she was none of those. "I'm going to throw caution to the winds, Dev, and ask you something I have no right to."

"All right, ask me."

Cal wanted to reach out, to lean across that table and caress her velvety cheek. He wanted to love her. Thoroughly. Completely. Another new feeling jolted through him. He had gone to bed with his share of women. And he had pleased himself, then pleased them. Now he ached to fulfill her, to give to Dev in return for what she had already given him in honesty, care and compassion. For the first time in his life, Cal wanted to give to, not take from, a woman. And not out of gratitude, either. That realization shook him to his soul.

"I don't have to be back on duty aboard the carrier until Sunday. I want to be with you. To share this time we have, Dev. What do you say?"

She sat back, taking in his tone of voice. Her pulse was beating erratically, and her heart . . . oh, God, her heart was blossoming like a flower. Dev tried desperately to sort out her feelings. "Cal, I'm not that kind of woman," she began, her voice hesitant, "I'm not good at handling an affair. I believe in commitment."

He shrugged lazily. "So I'll get another room here at the hotel. Look, Dev, I didn't mean it that way." Liar. He wanted her as he had never wanted another woman in his life. Cal felt the heat of desire uncoiling deep within him. But even more unsettling, he felt a sharp ache in the region of his heart. Those two sensations coupled to make him just that much more assertive in getting what he wanted—Dev. "Let's spend the time together."

"I have the fencing competition, Cal."

"That's a part of Dev Hunter. I want to know all about her. I want to explore her," he countered softly.

All her excuses were crumbling. Cal scared her. Dev knew by her reaction to his kiss that she was vulnerable. She didn't want to be, but there was that inexplicable chemistry binding them. "You might get bored, Cal. A lot of people don't like fencing."

"That's probably because they haven't taken the time to understand it." Cal gave her a devastating smile. "Are you politely trying to tell me 'no'?"

Miserably, Dev shook her head. "No. It's just that, well—"

"Is there someone back home, Dev?"

"Between my job at the television station and my commitment to fencing, I don't have time for a real relationship. At least not right now."

Cal took a deep breath. Good. He watched her as she laced her fingers in her lap. "What is it, Dev? Why are you nervous?"

Dev looked up, her eyes dark with confusion. "You scare me, Cal."

He scowled, taken aback. "I do? In what way?" He ruthlessly culled his memory to find a source for her fear and found nothing.

"You're a predator, Cal. I'm old enough to have seen all types of men. And I recognize your kind. You have the looks, the suave lines, the macho image. Everything designed to lull any woman into your arms. And your bed."

Cal grinned. "I like your honesty, Dev Hunter. So I won't lie to you. Yes, I find you provocative. Maybe that's why I want to spend the time with you. You're not like other women I've known."

She slowly got to her feet. "Do me one favor, Cal?"

"Sure."

Her voice lowered. "Don't hunt me. I'm not some prey to be trapped with your words and your come-on. Don't use me like you have other women. Your kind of man lives for the chase. Once you get a woman into bed, that's it. You get up, walk away out of her life." She chewed on her lower lip, unable to hold his sharpened gray gaze. "I—I couldn't take that, Cal. I'm just not built that way emotionally." She forced her chin up. "Be my friend, instead. Be someone to share laughter and bad times with for the next few days."

A friend. He'd never had a woman as a friend. And he certainly felt more than friendship for Dev. Her quietly spoken plea tore into him. "I sure as hell have an image problem to overcome with you, don't I?"

Dev wandered over to the closet, pulling out her white fencing shoes. "There's nothing to apologize for, Cal. We just see relationships differently." She sat down on the bed and pulled on the shoes. "But there is a middle ground, you know.

Friendship. And a wonderful friendship can be like a good marriage—fulfilling to both parties."

Cal nodded, grinning. "This will be a first—a woman for a friend. Okay, I'll try it."

Dev stood, giving him a winsome smile. "Maybe you aren't a playboy, after all," she teased, coming over. Leaning down, she wrapped her arms around him, hugging him quickly.

Before Cal could respond, she straightened up. He was pleasantly shocked by Dev's spontaneity. She was willing to trust. And it was that trust that reined him in. She deserved his respect first, not his lust. But sooner or later, one way or another, she would be in his bed. Beside him. Where she belonged. "Playboy or not, I need some clothes."

"Yesterday I had the houseboy take your uniform down to get it cleaned. It was so damp with sweat, Cal. It should be back anytime now."

"Where are you off to?"

Dev walked over to the corner and slung one of the large canvas carriers that held her weapons across her shoulder. "Practice at 7:00 A.M., Coach's orders. The strips have been laid in the central ballroom downstairs. Why? Did you want to come and watch?"

"How long will you be gone?"

"Two hours. I have to do a series of fencing exercises and then go at least six or seven bouts with the other men and women who are fencing in my particular weapon."

Cal frowned, remembering something else from his brief time with Dev. "What about your wrist?"

"I'll have to baby it. Well, will you be down?"

"I'm going to get my uniform first, go back to the carrier and get some civilian clothes and then come back to the hotel." He looked at his watch. "Which will probably take less than two hours. How about if I take you to breakfast after your practice? I'll meet you down in the ballroom."

Incredible elation flowed through Dev. "I'd love that."

"Dev! Get more aggressive!" Jack Gordon, her coach, ordered from the sidelines.

Sweat rolled down her cheeks, and Dev cursed under her breath. She stood in a fencing position: right leg extended and both knees deeply flexed, her left arm behind her. The leather glove she wore on her right hand was wet with her sweat, her fingers slipping slightly on the aluminum pistol grip of the handle. She was facing Steve Bauer, the national épée champion from the United States. This was her last bout of the morning, and it was the toughest one. Steve was six-foot-two and built like a string bean. Great for an épée fencer, tall, thin and a tough target to hit with the point of her épée. Automatically, Dev locked her right elbow, keeping her arm extended, the épée blade aimed at Steve's white-suited chest.

The score was three to two in Steve's favor at the end of the first five minutes of the bout. There was only one minute left. Dev had to score at least one more touch to even out the score. Her competitiveness wouldn't allow her to lose. She advanced swiftly, cracking her wrist, sending the solid part of her épée blade against Steve's. For a split second, Steve's blade was snapped centimeters out of line and Dev lunged. The tip of her épée point depressed. An electrical impulse shot through the blade, down the body wire plugged into the bell of her handle, to the circuit that was snapped to a special loop on the back of her uniform, to the reel that sat at the end of the strip. An electrical cord was then plugged from the reel to a set of machines with red and green lights. The instant her tip found his body, a red light went off.

"*Halte!*" the director called.

Breathing hard, Dev straightened, looking over at the machine through the wire mesh mask that totally covered her face. She grinned recklessly, sweat trickling down inside her uniform, making her want to scratch those places that itched.

"Damn," Steve growled.

"Touche droite," the director called to the scorer behind the machine. Touch right. *"En garde."*

Dev got behind the mandatory guard line, assuming her fencing position again as Steve did.

"Etes-vous prêts?" the director asked. Are you ready?

"Oui," they both responded. Yes.

"Allez!" he ordered. Play!

Dev knew she had less than a minute to score a winning point. And Steve was stalking her, waving his épée languidly at her, feinting, pressing and testing her. She was breathing hard, blinking away the sweat that kept running into her eyes as she retreated. Steve was known for his flèche attack so Dev prepared herself. She watched his hips. Sure enough, Steve exploded on her. The flèche was one of the most violent attacks in the fencing repertoire. Steve pushed off from his left foot, his entire body catapulting forward at an impossible angle, his épée moving toward her with startling speed. Dev held her ground, praying her wrist would take the punishment as she parried left to deflect the tip of the oncoming épée. Blade met blade. It was enough of a parry, and as Steve passed on her left, Dev twisted, sliding the point of her épée up into his hip, scoring the point.

The buzzer rang, indicating the bout was over. Dev slipped out of the mask, giving a yell of triumph and jumping up and down. Steve took off his mask, grinning sheepishly as he came back on the strip. Dev extended her left hand, shaking his, something all fencers did after every bout.

"You got lucky, Dev," Steve said.

"Ha! If you hadn't broadcasted that flèche from ten feet away, I wouldn't have been so well prepared."

Steve leaned over, giving Dev a peck on the cheek. "Next time, I'll nail your foot to the floor with a toe shot, Hunter," he threatened good-naturedly.

Dev smiled and waited patiently while Jack unhooked her from the reel cord that was snapped to the back of her uniform jacket. She tucked her mask under her right arm and transferred her épée to her left.

"How's the wrist, Dev?" Jack wanted to know.

"Sore. But so far, so good."

Jack nodded his balding head. At fifty, he was an Olympic coach and had his own fencing *salle* in Los Angeles where Dev trained four times weekly. "Okay, but go back and soak it for a while. And before the meet tonight, I want to examine it again."

Dev wiped her sweaty face with the back of her arm. "Okay, Coach." She left the strip, heading toward the far wall where everyone's bags of equipment had been placed. She threaded between the copper strips filled with fencers from many countries engaging in free play. The pleasant sound of steel blades meeting, shouts of directors, protests and groans from the volatile fencers, all combined to make her smile. She loved fencing. Dev was so busy avoiding judges and directors who had to move quickly with the fencers that she didn't see Cal. He approached her from the side and met her just as she stepped free of the strips and activity.

"I'm impressed, Dev."

She jerked her head to the right, her eyes widening beautifully. Cal Travis simply took her breath away. He stood there, a lackadaisical smile softening his hard features, his gray eyes warm, hands resting languidly on his trim hips. He was wearing a pair of dark-brown slacks that outlined his well-muscled thighs to decided advantage as well as a gold plaid shirt that emphasized his chest, the long sleeves rolled up on his forearms. Dev swallowed, swept off guard by his intense masculinity. The gold plaid brought out the highlights in his short hair and accented his deep tan. Pleasure shivered through her as she stared up into his smiling face. No longer was he tense or pale. The shadows that had lingered beneath his eyes were gone. The man who stood before her was utterly self-assured and strongly appealed to the female in her.

"God, you scared me!" she whispered.

Cal shifted his weight to one foot and watched as Dev carefully laid the épée down beside the canvas fencing bag. "You didn't look scared," he teased in a low voice, taking the fencing mask from beneath her arm. "You know, in some ways this is like the helmet I wear."

Dev smiled, pulling the Velcro apart on the left side of her white, long-sleeved, polyester fencing jacket, shedding the garment. "Yeah? How?"

"Good protection for your head. There's plenty of foam rubber padding on the inside of the mask; it rests against your face to absorb the impact."

"You need it, no doubt," Dev answered, untying the laces to the heavy cotton vest she wore beneath her jacket.

Her pink T-shirt was dark with sweat, clinging to her shapely form. He saw aluminum cups in the vest. "What are these for?" he asked.

Dev removed one of the aluminum cups. "They're called breast protectors."

He took it, examining it carefully. "There must be five or six dents in this one."

"Fencing is a controlled-action sport, Cal," Dev said, pulling a towel from her fencing bag and placing it over her head. Next she took a pink sweat jacket and slipped it on, not wanting to catch a chill.

"Controlled?" he snorted, eyeing the indentations in the heavy aluminum cup. "Do you know what would happen if you weren't wearing these?"

She grinned, kneeling down and slipping her épée into the bag along with her soaked uniform. "I'd probably be minus a breast."

He didn't like the whole idea. "And you actually like this sport?"

Dev rose in one fluid motion, sliding the bag across her shoulder. Cal promptly took it from her and placed it on his shoulder. She liked his protectiveness toward her. "Love it. It's a great way to take out all your inhibitions—on the strip. If I'm mad at Tucker, the reporter, I can pretend he's my opponent, and I have the pleasure of nailing him with my épée."

Cal wasn't so sure. He took Dev's elbow, guiding her toward the exit. "You were fencing against a man who was taller and heavier than you. When he hits you, it's got to hurt."

"Bruises are a part of the game. I've never had worse than that in the ten years I've been fencing. Okay? Quit brooding over me like a mother hen." She smiled, her hair clinging damply to her brow. "Let me get a quick shower, change and then we can eat. I'm starved!"

Cal nodded. He was starved, too. For Dev. Food still didn't appeal to him. "After two hours of fencing, I can see why."

Dev hooted. "Wait until you see how much I eat after the tournament tonight! You burn up so many calories on the strip. I'm constantly dehydrated. There isn't a fencer alive who doesn't drink Gatorade to replenish the lost water supply."

He gazed appreciatively down at Dev. "I like your style, lady, whatever you do."

"Thank you, kind sir," she said, curtsying. They caught the elevator, and Cal punched the button for her floor. Dev leaned back, resting against the wall, watching him. "Did you get a room?"

"Yes. I'm up on the fifteenth floor. 1501."

"Great." Dev sighed, closing her eyes for a moment, a smile lingering on her mouth. "I always feel so good after I've had a workout on the strip."

One eyebrow rose as Cal absorbed her happy state. "You looked like you were enjoying yourself out there," he agreed.

"How long were you there?"

"About fifteen minutes."

Dev opened her eyes. "Why didn't you come on over? You could have sat down behind the scoring table."

"No, I liked watching you when you didn't know I was there." A mysterious smile played on Cal's mouth. "You're one hell of a woman, Dev Hunter. One of a kind, in my book."

THEY SAT in the restaurant on the fourth floor of the sumptuous Shangri-La Hotel in an alcove with a window. Sunshine spilled across Dev's shoulders, highlighting her recently washed and now curling hair as it framed her flushed face. Occasionally, she glanced up from the meal of scrambled eggs, a rasher of bacon and whole wheat toast that she was tackling. Cal sat with a cup of coffee in hand and that same smile on his face. Dev felt at once thrilled and slightly on guard. Her wariness didn't take away from the happiness she felt simply sharing time and space with him.

"Did anyone give you a hard time when you went back aboard the carrier? Like your friend Scotty?"

"No. Matter of fact, they were all jealous, if you want the truth." Cal found himself wanting to stare at Dev. She wore a flattering madras sundress of lavender, pink and green attached at only one shoulder, displaying the slender column of her neck and her delicate collarbone. Ivory shell buttons went down the front of the dress, a wide lavender sash emphasizing her narrow waist. The colors enhanced her blue eyes and auburn hair that tumbled across her bare shoulders in provocative abandon. Pink pearl earrings brought out the natural color of her full lips.

"I suppose all your buddies think you've 'scored'?"

"Shame on you," Cal teased, meeting her concerned gaze. "I told them I had met and fallen head over heels in love with a woman who wielded a sword. They said they couldn't recall anyone over in the Wanchai District with that particular S and M talent."

She colored fiercely. "Damn you, Cal Travis!"

He laughed fully. "I'm kidding you. Scott was worried," he admitted, "because he knew how close Chief and I were. He thought I'd been hit over the head, robbed and left for dead in some back alley over in Hong Kong. They were kind of glad to see me make an appearance."

Cal turned the coffee cup slowly around in his lean, tapered fingers. "Carrier pilots are a pretty tight bunch, Dev. There are very few pilots who can land or take off on a postage stamp in the middle of a wild, heaving ocean. We all know the dangers, and we're protective of our own kind." Then he smiled. "You realize marines take care of their own, don't you? Doesn't matter whether you're the wife, girlfriend or child, if you're part of a marine's life, any other marine will help you in any way he can. It's the buddy system."

"Interesting." Dev digested the idea. "It's that way up to a point with fencers. We're very team oriented, always cheering on whoever's up on the strip." She returned his smile, picking up her cup and taking a sip of coffee. "And you're right, it's a nice feeling having that extended family."

Cal's brows drew down; he stared hard at the cup in his hand. "So tell me, was I a miserable bastard to take care of all that time? I still don't remember much except for bits and pieces here and there."

"How about if I leave out the gory details and say that you were sicker than any dog ever deserved to be? You'd sleep for a while and then start moving through that nightmare sequence. I got pretty good at timing how long you'd sleep before one of those cycles would hit."

Cal grimaced. "Did you get any sleep on Tuesday?"

"Some. I had to make practice that morning or the coach would have skinned me alive. I just prayed you'd sleep until I got back." Dev flashed him a smile. "Fortunately, you did.

I ordered my meals in for the rest of the day and stayed with you."

"You deserve a medal for service beyond the call of duty," he growled, embarrassed.

"Don't worry about it."

"I'm not used to being helpless, Dev."

"I know that. Proud men never are."

Cal raised his chin, meeting Dev's frank eyes. "Just how in the hell do you get so knowledgeable about a person in such a short time?"

The waiter came, took away Dev's plate and poured more coffee. Dev relaxed. "Observation. Experience. Is there any other way?"

"I have observation and experience, too, but it wouldn't match the kind of knowledge you gained of me, considering we haven't spent much time together."

"Maybe it's just me," Dev said, smiling.

Cal leaned forward, his gray eyes almost colorless, as he studied her. "Let's talk about you."

"Easy, Cal . . . you're stalking me."

"Yes, I am."

Heat rushed into Dev's cheeks, making her look even more delicate in that moment as they stared across the table at each other. Dev licked her lower lip, wrapping her hands around the coffee cup in front of her. "I was born in Los Angeles twenty-eight years ago."

"All right, that's good for a start. Go on."

"Why don't you just ask questions?" she demanded with a flash of temper.

"Because I might miss something, that's why. So you're from the land of sunshine. What else?"

Dev moved uncomfortably beneath his inspection. "I grew up there."

"Brothers? Sisters?"

Her lashes lowered. "My mother gave me up for adoption when I was born," she admitted softly.

"Why, for God's sake?"

"Don't be angry, Cal. That was a long time ago."

Cal snorted. "I don't understand women giving up their babies."

Pain shadowed her eyes briefly, and Dev forced a slight smile. "I don't, either. But that's water under the bridge."

"So you were adopted?"

"Yes. My mother died when I was twelve. Dad was a fencer for many years and was responsible for getting me into the sport. He's a wonderful man."

Cal had a tough time tempering his inner rage as he watched Dev. As open and loving as she was, how could she have withstood that total rejection? And yet Dev had. And she was whole. Functioning. Giving, not taking. Not defensive, shielding herself from possible present or future hurt. With a shake of his head, Cal found himself starving for more information. "Where did you get your interest in cameras and television?"

"Dad owned his own television repair business, and I used to pay attention while he repaired them. I guess it rubbed off on me. I had a natural curiosity about electricity. When I graduated from high school, I went to UCLA and got a degree in electronics."

"Then what are you doing carrying a Minicam, getting knocked around by a bunch of angry union strikers?"

Dev grinned. "I like being where the action is, Cal. My degree got me into the television station that I work for. When Tucker's cameraman had a car accident shortly after I was hired, I volunteered to take over. Eventually, Tucker's cameraman went on partial disability, and I kept the job. I love it. I get to see a lot of things. People interest me."

Cal wasn't so sure he liked her in either that vocation or her sport. "Maybe you should have gone after a degree in psychology, then, and stayed off the streets. It would be a hell of a lot safer."

She chortled. "You're such a throwback to the age of chivalry, Cal Travis! Protect the damsels in distress, slay the villains and keep the children safe." Dev reached out, her fingers covering his. The action shocked both of them, and she quickly withdrew her hand.

Cal smiled to himself; she was a toucher. At least he could detect that much in a person. Some just liked to reach out and make contact. Dev's action wasn't sexual in its overtone, but it meant a great deal to him. Despite their harrowing meeting and his ordeal that she weathered with him, she liked him. Good. His gaze flicked to her parted lips, and he wanted to kiss her again. Hard. Demandingly. He wanted to feel her go soft against him as she had done before. He wanted to possess her, love her. Gently, Cal put those thoughts aside, realizing Dev was staring at him, a hint of panic in her eyes.

"So you see me as a chauvinistic knight?" he teased, easing the brittle tension that was strung almost palpably between them.

"If you want the truth, I sort of like your protectiveness toward me. It's a refreshing change. At the television station, I think they sometimes forget how demanding the work is, that a Minicam operator could use a break occasionally."

Cal traced a pattern on the damask tablecloth with his finger. "What do you mean?"

"If we cover a fire or something traumatic, I always cry my eyes out afterward. Tucker sometimes gets irritated with me if word gets back to him. But that's his tough luck. I'm not going to stop feeling just because he gets uncomfortable when a woman cries a little."

A grin edged Cal's mouth as he studied her. She was so heartstoppingly refreshing. "You live out in L.A.?"

"Yes, San Bernardino. It actually sits to the northeast of L.A."

"How far is that from Edwards Air Force Base?"

"About an hour and a half by car. Why?"

"Because that's my next assignment. Come late December, sometime after Christmas, I'm being transferred from carrier duty to the U.S. Air Force Test Pilot School facility out there to become a test pilot."

Her heart began a slow pound as she studied Cal. "Why are you telling me this?"

"Because I have every intention of seeing you once I get on base. An hour and a half's drive is nothing. That is, if you want to see me."

Dev couldn't still her racing heart. One part of her was thrilled to know that Cal would be close to where she lived and worked. Another part of her wasn't sure. Time would tell whether Cal's being in her backyard was a blessing or a curse. "Why don't we let this week help determine that," she said.

"Good idea. Well, you about ready to go?" he asked, sitting up.

"Go? Where?"

"To play tourist. Let me be your guide. I've been in Hong Kong so many times over the past few years that I know this area like the back of my hand."

Dev was about to sign the breakfast bill, but Cal took it. She smiled. "Thank you. I'll let you treat this time."

He rose. "Just being my knightly self," he teased. Cal held out his hand to her. "Ready, my redheaded witch?"

"I'm not so sure." Dev laughed and stood. His outstretched hand looked so lean and confident; her own hand was damp and cool. She thrilled to his pet name for her. No one had ever called her a witch before. Not with that kind of sensual implication. The way the word rolled off his lips accompanied by that low growl made Dev feel special. Very special.

Capturing her fingers, Cal drew her alongside him as they walked toward the front of the busy restaurant. "What's this?

The premier woman épée fencer in the U.S., afraid of a little adventure?"

"I like adventure," she parried.

"But not necessarily adventure with a man?" he taunted, his voice a whisper near her ear.

Dev glanced up, drowning in his gray eyes, melting beneath that sultry, hooded look that made her pulse rate continue to climb. "I'm sounding paranoid, right?"

"Right." Cal paid the bill. They took the escalator to the lobby, and he escorted her out into the humid ninety-degree weather and sunshine of Kowloon.

This was the first chance Dev had had to see part of mainland China. The late-morning crowds met and mingled on every sidewalk and crosswalk. She was glad Cal was holding her hand since they were jostled from every side by the people rushing around them. The air was heavy with the odor of freshly fried fish, fresh vegetables in an outdoor market, fumes from any number of red double-decker buses. Bicyclists zoomed by them by the hundreds like kamikazi pilots bent on self-destruction. Kowloon was spellbinding. Dev's heightened senses were dizzied by the high rises all around them and by the tiny shops strung together like boxcars in between the taller buildings. There wasn't an inch of space free; either a street vendor was hawking his leather wares, or a stall sporting colorful silk, perfume or hand-knotted rugs was wedged in.

For the next three hours, they just walked and held hands. While Cal helped her discover the lush oriental mystery of Kowloon, Dev felt the chemistry intensifying between them. And she couldn't help but admire Cal's powerful chest, his broad shoulders thrown back cockily and his flat stomach where his shirt clung because of the humidity. He was so brazenly male. She didn't try to fool herself: she had enjoyed looking at his lean, athletic body when she had taken his uniform off early Tuesday morning. Cal was in magnificent shape, which made her insides curl with a delicious feeling. The shape of his mouth mesmerized her, too—how he formed his words, those quick smiles, the wry grimace that would sometimes pull down one corner of his mouth. She vividly recalled his gentleness with her when they had shared that first kiss. And now, despite her speech about being just "friends," Dev wanted more from Cal. Much more.

By 1:00 P.M., the heat of the day weighed down on Kowloon. Imposing cumulus clouds rose above them, threatening a shower. Cal led her to the bright-green Star Ferry, and they took the boat, along with hundreds of other passengers, across Victoria Harbor to the island of Hong Kong. Once they landed, Cal suggested lunch at the very popular and exclusive Mandarin Hotel. Dev gawked like a tourist as Cal led her into the lobby filled with luncheon patrons. A maître d' had them seated at a small marble table with sumptuous, red velvet-upholstered chairs. On either side of them stood huge potted palms. The table was near a window so that they could watch the ceaseless traffic move by the hotel.

Dev smiled, resting her chin on her hands, meeting Cal's gaze. He was happy. She could tell by the dancing quality in his intelligent eyes and smile that played around his mouth. "This is all so exciting," she confided. "I've never done much traveling except to fencing meets. This is the first time I've been out of the country. There's so much I could learn about the Chinese."

Cal ordered them cold lemonade and then returned his attention to Dev. The humidity had curled her auburn hair even more, giving it a soft, mussed look. He longed to slide his fingers through those tresses, gently massage her scalp and hear her purr beneath his ministrations. His sister-in-law Kai also had red hair. But that was where the resemblance ended. "Now you can see why people like to travel. It gets in your blood after a while. And you're right: you can learn a lot by observing. I like the Chinese. They're some of the most industrious people on earth."

The waiter brought the tall glasses of lemonade, and Dev discovered just how thirsty she was. She slid her fingers down the cool, sweaty glass, her gaze leveling with his. "So tell me, is the traveling bug in you? It must be."

"I like what I do. But traveling is secondary to flying, Dev. Flying is everything."

She tilted her head, playing with the straw, pushing the ice cubes around in the glass. "Seems to me that was one of the first statements you threw at me: my plane is my mistress and the marine corps my mother," she mimicked and they broke into laughter. "Why don't you just say, 'I'm a confirmed bachelor with wanderlust in my soul'?"

Cal grinned, raising his glass in salute to her. "Touché, Ms Hunter."

Dev got serious for a moment. "Why haven't you married, Cal? You certainly have all the attributes any number of women would be attracted to."

Cal lost his amused look. "Flying comes before everything, Dev. And knowing that, how can I expect a woman who's wanting equal or more time to play a secondary role? No, I don't think it would be fair to ask that of another person so I make it very clear to the woman I'm involved with at any given time where she stands with me."

Dev felt a pang of hurt but didn't show it. "It's always been that way, Cal?"

"So far, yes."

The waiter came over and they ordered lunch. Afterward, Dev asked, "How long will you be stationed out at Edwards?"

"Initially, at least nine months for the test pilot schooling. After that, who knows? I've heard the navy is getting ready to start testing a new fighter in about a year, and if that comes through, I might be lucky enough to stay at Edwards and become part of that testing team." He flashed her a confident smile. "Testing is the ultimate goal for me. I've been working all my military career for this assignment."

"I'm happy for you, Cal. I think it's wonderful that you can fulfill your dreams."

"What about you, Dev? What are your dreams?"

She shrugged shyly. "I'm afraid you'd find them terribly mundane and boring next to yours."

"Try me."

"Apart from my fencing, I want to marry someday and have a marriage like my father had. He always said they worked hard at communicating and compromising so that he and Susan could grow together. What they shared wasn't a figment of someone's romantic imagination."

"And yet you're twenty-eight, and you still haven't found the right candidate?"

She wrapped a silken curl around her slender finger, giving him a wry smile. "A lot of guys I meet are threatened by my independence, Cal. They want to corral me and keep me captive in the world they think I should live in." A sadness came to her voice. "I haven't found anyone who is happy about the way I am and supportive of all that I want to be."

He snorted. "Just like the women I meet. They all want to change me in some way."

Dev brightened. "Maybe we're just two oddballs, Cal Travis. Too stubborn, independent and goal oriented for anyone."

"Well," he drawled, giving her a heated look, "maybe we deserve each other then. I like you just the way you are. And so far, you've respected me and where I'm at."

The waiter came with their lunch. Dev flashed Cal a teasing smile. "If you're as good as you say you are at flying, then that should be your world, Cal. We need good pilots like you."

Cal found himself not tasting the salmon mousse salad. Instead, his eyes were filled with Dev. His instincts told him she really did understand his need to fly. Even if she was a civilian with little knowledge of the military, she intrinsically understood. And that made him just that much more fascinated with Dev. After lunch, as he walked hand in hand with her down a busy street, Cal leaned over, pressing a kiss to her hair.

"You know what you are?" he said huskily, smiling.

Dev caught her breath, wildly aware of his masculinity as he walked slowly at her side. The brief kiss had caught her off guard. "What?"

"You're an eagle, Dev Hunter. And like an eagle, you fly solo and you fly high." Cal's fingers tightened on hers; his voice grew gritty as he held her widened gaze. "And like an eagle, you have only one mate for the rest of your life."

"DEV?" JACK CALLED. "You about ready?"

Cal stood back, arms across his chest as he watched Dev hurriedly slip on the protective padded vest. Her hair, once free and long, had now been tamed into a ponytail. Even in a red T-shirt and white knickers, Cal thought she looked elegant as she trotted over to her waiting coach. He lifted his head, looking around the huge ballroom.

The best fencers from around the world were utilizing the last few minutes before the international competition to warm up and practice. The tension level was sizzling, reflected in Dev's stance. He was fascinated by the change in her. All afternoon she had been a delightful companion. This evening she was down to business. A smile quirked his mouth. Well, wasn't he the same way? Outside of the jet, he partied and celebrated with his squadron mates. In the cockpit, his brain ruled his precision-trained body and reflexes.

She came back, and he saw worry in her eyes. "What's wrong?"

Dev reached down, climbing into her fencing uniform and deftly closing it with the Velcro. "Oh . . . nothing," she murmured, as if thinking of something else.

Dev pulled on the well-padded leather glove over her right hand. The top one-third of the glove was made of tight elastic that clung to her forearm and kept the sleeve from hanging and thereby becoming a target for the point of someone's épée.

"Is it your wrist?"

She touched the red headband she wore across her brow. "It's sore but usable."

Cal reached out, drawing Dev around to him, his fingers gently massaging her tight shoulders. He could feel the tautness of her muscles beneath the thick padding. "What is it, Dev?"

Her lips parted at the intimacy of his voice. "There're going to be four preliminary bouts this evening with twelve women in each. That means I have to fence eleven people tonight."

"Eleven bouts with that wrist?" he asked in a disbelieving tone. "My God, that's a lot." Cal remembered what Dev had told him before: a bout could last up to fifteen or twenty minutes if no one scored the necessary five points to win. Each time a halt was called, the clock was stopped. And each time the director said *"Allez"* to begin the bout again, the clock was punched and the fencers timed. He mentally calculated the possible time factor, his eyes widening. "No wonder you're in such great shape." He ran his knuckles gently across her cheek. "Will you be able to do it?"

Dev nodded. "I will, but my wrist might not hold up. Did you see those two Italian women over there to your left? One is five-foot-ten and the other is six feet tall. And they both weigh closer to a man's weight than a woman's. They're going to have the arm reach over all of us, and that means I'm at a real disadvantage. Now you can see why all winning épée fencers are tall with long arms and legs."

Cal nodded, watching her upturned face. "You can do it," he coaxed her in a low voice. "Just remember, you're an eagle. You fly higher and better and farther than any of them. . . ." He leaned down, kissing her. Her mouth was soft and inviting beneath his tentative exploration. She tasted sweet, wholesome and yielding. He felt her tremble, felt her melt, her willowy body resting lightly against his. He framed her face with his hands, drawing away, drinking deeply of her. Raw need quivered through him; simultaneously, Cal felt fiercely protective toward her. His thumbs traced the arch of her eyebrows. "You just be careful out there."

"Dev! Let's go! You're up next on strip number four," Jack called.

Dev blinked, her body simmering. In a daze, she pulled from Cal's embrace and picked up her épée, walking quickly down the sideline to where her coach stood.

Cal swallowed, his eyes narrowing as he watched Dev. An explosion of feeling was catapulting though him. He wanted her. More than just in a sexual sense. He was thirsting to drink in her every facet—he'd never felt this way about any woman in his life. Scowling, Cal picked up her fencing bag and a towel, making his way toward the other side of the huge ballroom where she would be fencing.

Dev fenced from 7:00 P.M. until well after eleven, and Cal gained respect for her and the sport of fencing as a result. Women from around the world, all experts with the épée, met and fought in carefully choreographed bouts beneath the watchful eye of a director and scoring machine. Cal's heart almost burst with pride as Dev fought her way through those first ten grueling bouts. Between each bout she would join him, sitting on the floor, knees drawn up, her arms resting on them as she watched the others fencing. She taught Cal how to discern their strong and weak points. In foil, she told him, only the torso area was scored upon. In épée, the entire body became a target.

In his eyes, Dev was the most beautiful of all the female competitors, with her auburn hair spilling over the stark whiteness of her uniform, her lips a ripe, natural red, her blue eyes narrowed and her body endowed with a cheetahlike grace. His heart beat harder each time she fenced.

Dev was tiring in the next bout, but so was everyone else. It was unusual, she had told him, to have so many fencers in a preliminary round. This couldn't be helped because it was an international competition, and they had only so many days to complete the meet. Dev's face was flushed, her cheeks a vital pink color, flesh glistening with sweat, the uniform she wore dampened long ago because of the strenuous workout. More than once, Cal had retrieved a new bottle of Gatorade for her to drink so that she wouldn't become dehydrated. Now he understood why she had no flesh or fat on any part of her body; he longed to run his hands down her slim limbs and feel her femaleness against him.

"One more to go," she rasped, sliding down beside him. Gratefully, she took the towel from Cal, mopping her face.

"How's the wrist?" he asked, resting his hand on the knee closest to him. After their kiss, there had been an unspoken warmth between them. Dev always sat close when she rested between bouts, her arm and leg against Cal's, head thrown back and resting against the wall, exposing the slender curve of her throat.

"Really getting sore."

"Take off the glove and let me look at it."

Dev barely opened her eyes but did as Cal asked.

Cal frowned, noting the swelling. He gently ran his thumb over the area, watching as Dev winced. "Don't you think you'd better tell Jack about this?"

"No." She opened her eyes. "Cal, he's liable to stop me from fencing in the finals. I've worked so long and so hard toward this meet. I'm representing all the U.S. women fencers who have fought for the right to fence in épée. How can I let them down?''

He released her wrist. "At least let me wrap it, okay? You need some support for it, Dev.''

She pouted. "How do you know so much about strains?''

"When I was a young kid, I worked at a racetrack to earn money for flying lessons. The trainer I worked for taught me a lot about sprained and strained ligaments, muscles and tendons in the thoroughbreds he raced." His voice turned to a rasp. "Or torn ones. I know what I'm talking about, Dev. Let me wrap it. What if you twist it the wrong way? Or this last Italian fencer really hits you hard with the tip of that épée? These muscles are already hurting; they're swollen with fluids. And you've got to be in pain.''

Dev squirmed uncomfortably. "You're too damn smart, Travis.''

He grinned and put his arm around her for a moment, giving her a quick embrace. Reaching over, Cal rummaged through her fencing bag and found some one-inch-wide adhesive tape. Taking out a small penknife from his pocket, he pulled her wrist back over, resting it across his thigh. "I'll tape it just enough so that you survive this Italian giant and make the finals. Okay?''

She smiled gratefully and rested against his shoulder. "You're one hell of a nice guy, Cal Travis.''

He snorted and began to gently wrap her wrist. "Didn't you know all lone eagles are nice to each other?''

"I wasn't even aware of an eagle's habits until I met you. Much less that eagle metaphors could be so nice." She sighed, absorbing some of his strength, closing her eyes and leaning against him.

Cal inhaled her scent, a hint of jasmine laced with her sweat. The feathery bangs that hung across her eyes were wet and clinging to her skin. "Am I nice?" he teased, completing the taping.

"You know you are."

"Just wondering."

"You're so conceited," she prodded, enjoying his closeness.

"I like you. Does that make me less conceited if I like someone other than myself?"

Dev raised her head, giving him a look filled with humor. She slowly worked the sweat-stained leather glove back on her right hand. "I guess that takes part of your conceit away, jet jockey."

The buzzer rang, signaling that it was time for Dev's last bout.

Cal got to his feet, resting his shoulder against the wall, watching as the two fencers were hooked up to the electric reels. The Italian woman, Bianca Santullo, was built like an oversize pit bull, in his opinion. She had a thick, heavy body, a short neck and powerful shoulders. Her brown hair was drawn severely off her forehead, and Cal watched as Santullo pinned Dev with her penetrating black eyes. Dev seemed fragile in comparison so that he became worried, taking his hands out of his pockets, tensing as the director stood a few feet from the center of the strip and gave the fencers permission to fence.

Having watched ten bouts in a row and benefited as well from Dev's explanations, Cal recognized Bianca's advance. The Italian's power was obviously superior; Dev's blade was knocked out of alignment more than it should have been, leaving her exposed to attack. The two fencers tested each other, trying to find out how the other would react to a genuine attack. In Cal's mind, the only advantage Dev had was she was a hell of a lot quicker and more agile than Santullo, who moved sluggishly in comparison. The two fencers were evenly matched in their degree of skill. Suddenly, he saw Dev lunge, her blade point dropping in a split second, touching the Italian's foot. The red light went on, indicating a hit.

Cal grinned and relaxed a little. Dev had talked about toe touches and how difficult they were to achieve. Ideally, the fencer lunged forward, kept her eyes on the opponent, the blade aimed at the chest, then cracked her wrist at the last second, allowing the tip of the épée to plunge down. If all went as planned and the fencer was accurate, a toe touch was possible. He saw Bianca grow angry behind her mask, glaring as Dev turned and calmly walked back to the white on guard line painted on the copper strip. Dev flexed the blade of her épée, and Cal saw a smile on her parted lips. She had the Italian's number, all right. Dev was going to use her lightning speed and reflexes to win against Bianca.

Fifteen minutes had sped by and the score was four to three in Dev's favor. Cal stood with his feet slightly apart, watching apprehensively as a furious Bianca pressed her attack against Dev. Cal saw Dev's right arm weakening at an alarming rate; he knew she was in trouble. Her épée was no longer aligned with the rest of her extended arm. Each time Bianca snapped her blade against Dev's, Cal saw Dev wince. He jerked his attention to her coach. Jack noticed the change, his fists balled at his sides.

Suddenly, Bianca gave a bloodcurdling scream and flèched, her two-hundred-pound body hurtling forward like an out-of-control freight train. Cal sucked in a breath, his teeth clenched.

Dev tried to parry the thrust of the oncoming épée. Pain shot up to her elbow, her fingers suddenly nerveless. Before Santullo's point jabbed deeply into her chest near her collarbone, Dev's épée fell from her hand, dangling by the body wire from her wrist.

"*Halte!*" the director cried. "No good. No score," he rapidly told the scorekeepers.

Bianca came stalking back, shrieking a protest in Italian. Cal was the first to reach Dev, who had knelt down on one knee, holding her wrist. Jack got there seconds later.

"Time out, Mr. Director!" Jack called.

Dev sobbed, gripping her wrist. She bent her head, fighting back the rush of pain as Cal tried to pry her fingers loose from her injured wrist.

"Oh, damn, damn," she cried softly.

"Let us see," Cal breathed.

Jack pushed her helmet back off her head. "Take it easy, Dev. Come on, take some deep breaths. Thatta girl."

Cal worked the glove off her right hand, his gaze moving to her wrist. Jack's mouth set grimly as he saw the tape.

"Why didn't you tell me, Dev? Damn it."

"It was my idea," Cal told him quietly, looking up, meeting Jack's angry gaze. "I told her to wrap it."

"I'll be all right," Dev said, gasping. Her eyes were narrow with pain. "Just let me wrap it, Coach. I'll get one more point on her. I just twisted it the wrong way, and my fingers went numb for a second. Please...."

Cal saw the swelling pushing up above the taped area. "Like Monday night?" he asked her, remembering when she had dropped the bell guard.

Dev bit down hard on her lower lip. "Yeah. Jack, you've got to let me finish. Tell him, Cal!"

Cal related the incident. All the while, he gently held her wrist as they hunched over her on the strip. Jack glared up at the Italian fencer who had raised her helmet and was smiling triumphantly.

"Damn it, Dev, she's a tank! We can call the bout. You've got enough wins to make it to the finals on Friday."

"No!"

Cal felt her anguish. Dev's skin was drawn tautly across her flaming cheeks, the corners of her mouth pulled with pain.

"She damn near put a hole clean through you," Jack breathed, touching the area near her left collarbone. "If you get up, she's gonna try and finish you off by using simple brute force, Dev. And you know that. That girl has finesse and skill to win bouts in épée, it's true, but she uses her strength in particular to wear her opponents down."

Dev drew in a breath. "I don't care! I know her weaknesses. I can do it, Jack. I can do it." She turned, her eyes pleading with Cal. "Get the tape. When I get my glove back on, tape the handle of the épée to my hand and then tape my wrist tight. Jack?"

"All right, Dev. I know how bad you've been wanting this competition, but if—"

"I'll be all right!" she said softly. "Cal, get the tape, will you?"

Dev forced herself to calm down as Cal stood there on the strip, tightly wrapping the aluminum pistol grip of the épée to the palm of her hand and glove. With each wrap of the tape, her throbbing wrist felt better.

Cal glanced down at her, meeting her blue eyes. "How's that feel?"

His voice stabilized her. "Wonderful."

"You're in a lot of pain."

"It comes with the territory."

His gray eyes glittered, and he brushed his knuckles against her damp cheek. "How about if I kiss it and make it better?"

Dev closed her eyes momentarily. "You've got a deal, jet jockey."

"How are you going to play that moose who wants to break your sweet neck?" he asked huskily, taking his penknife to cut the tape from the roll.

"Sometimes it pays to pretend to have a broken wing," she said, glaring at Bianca. "I'm going to let her think I can't stand up to her. She'll get cocky and hopefully sloppy in her attacks. That's when I'll nail her."

Cal gently pressed the tape to the inside of her arm. "An eagle with a broken wing. Interesting." His voice deepened.

"Be careful, Dev. I want you in one piece and alive when you come out of this fracas. Okay?"

She lifted her head, giving him a warm look meant solely for him. "I could kiss you, Cal."

"You play dirty, lady. I can't kiss you now in front of everyone, and you know it," he complained, grinning.

"Hold the thought. You'll get the kiss later."

"You've got it, my redheaded witch. Just be careful. . . ."

Bianca came after Dev like a tank chewing up terrain, relentlessly attacking her. Dev kept falling back, allowing the woman to beat her blade out of line. But each time the Italian lunged to get her, Dev was half an inch farther away than the tip of her épée. She felt more confident about her wrist, the tight taping giving her weakened muscles needed support.

"*Halte!*"

Dev froze, realizing she had passed the yellow warning line off the end of the strip. The director ordered her to put her right toe on the line. If she even stepped on the red rear limit line that was only twenty feet behind her, a point would be scored against her and Bianca would win.

Bianca was grinning like a hungry bear, flexing the tip of her épée, getting ready. Dev took a better grip on the handle of her blade, assuming the *en garde* position.

"*Etes-vous prêts?*" They both nodded, stares locked, bodies tensed.

"*Allez!*"

Bianca shouted, flèching. Her huge, ponderous body launched forward. Dev had seen her hips move, so at the same instant she lunged forward. The explosive action of the Italian met the point of Dev's épée before Bianca could hit her in return. Bianca knew she had been hit first, but out of anger and frustration, she jammed her blade down in a twisting motion meant to hurt Dev as she passed by her. The point landed against Dev's left shoulder, driving her backward. The other woman's épée bowed and curved. Suddenly, it snapped. The point flipped up, flying off Dev's jacket and high into the air. Dev heard Jack shout. Saw Bianca's annoyed features rush by her. And then she slammed onto the strip. Dev forced herself to remain relaxed as she went end over end, tangled in the reel wire, her épée swinging wildly, still taped to her hand. All her concentration was on keeping her wrist from receiving further injury.

It was only after Dev was pulled to her feet by Cal and she saw the horrified look on his face that she realized the broken blade of Bianca's épée had penetrated all her layers of protection. Her skin was grazed, a streak of red blood eating up the white of her jacket. She felt Cal's iron grip on her arm.

Dev gasped. She saw the Italian coach arguing heatedly with Jack. Bianca stood at the end of the strip being unhooked by a fellow fencer, a smirk on her face.

"That bitch meant to kill you," he breathed savagely.

"Jack will take care of it. Please, just get me unhooked, Cal. I'm all right. It's just a scratch. Honest."

Cal was torn between leaving Dev, who was weaving in his arms, and joining Coach Gordon, who was getting into a heated argument with the other coach. He was alarmed by how much blood was staining her uniform, and that made his decision for him. "Come on," he muttered softly, "we're getting you to a doctor."

5

"I'M ALL RIGHT. Really, I am." How many times had Dev repeated that statement? A hotel doctor had treated the three-inch laceration above her left breast. All her friends and even fencers from the Canadian team had visited Dev, murmuring their apologies, making sure she was going to be fine. And through it all, Cal had been there. He had gripped her arm, placing himself like a shield in front of her as the first deluge of photographers and reporters, hungry for a sensational story, attacked her as she tried to get out of the ballroom. In the doctor's quarters, Cal had kept the press at bay with an icy glare and a few well-chosen expletives that could be understood in any language. The reporters had been cowed, finally giving her some peace.

The doctor smiled, helping her on with her sleeveless cotton vest. "You'll be stiff and sore in the morning. But little else," he said, tying up the cotton laces.

"Thanks, Doctor." Dev slid off the table. "Can I get a shower? I'm so dirty and I smell pretty bad."

"Of course. Just wash around the laceration. I've given you a tetanus shot so it should be fine."

Taking her bloody T-shirt and fencing jacket, Dev walked out into the waiting room. Cal was standing guard at the door and turned as if sensing her presence. She smiled gamely and walked over to him.

"Any idea how to dodge the rest of these reporters?" she asked.

Cal studied her beneath his hooded eyes. Dev was getting paler by the minute. Wisps of hair hung damply around her eyebrows and temples, the majority of it still caught up in the ponytail.

"They'll give ground," he promised as he slid his arm protectively around her waist.

She leaned momentarily against his shoulder, grateful for his care. "I would never have believed you," Dev murmured.

Cal put his hand on the glass door to shove it open. "About what?"

"About marines taking care of others. Thank you."

He slid her an intense look, sensing her exhaustion. "I care about you, Dev, and I'll be damned if anyone is going to hassle you. Come on, I'll take you up to your room, and we'll get you settled in for the night. Jack said for you to sleep in tomorrow. You get to miss morning practice."

Dev laughed softly, ready to place herself in Cal's protective hands. "But I'll have to make it up tomorrow afternoon. I know Jack."

In no time, Cal had cut a swath through the press and had her on an elevator heading up to her floor. Dev leaned against him, closing her eyes.

"You're so strong," she said, her words sounding slightly slurred. It must be her imagination, Dev thought. She sounded as if she were drunk.

Cal pressed a kiss to her hair. "I know someone who was strong for me a few days ago," he countered huskily, concerned about her. Dev was starting to experience the adrenaline letdown after the accident. His hand tightened slightly on her shoulder as the elevator doors slid open.

"I'm okay," she insisted, pulling from beneath his arm.

"Yeah, I know. That's what you've been telling everybody," he muttered wryly, remaining at her shoulder as they walked down the long, carpeted hall.

"It's just a silly scratch, Cal. I'm not the only one who's ever gotten an épée broken against them. It happens in foil, too. At the last Olympics, a fencer broke his weapon, and it ran straight through the other fencer, killing him. Can you imagine? God, that would be horrible. I think I'd quit fencing after that."

"Well, Santullo wasn't trying to kill you, but she wasn't making any bones about guaranteeing that you wouldn't be in the finals, either. I hope like hell that Jack gets that protest invoked to kick her out of the meet."

Dev laughed and shook her head. All of a sudden, she felt giddy, flighty and shaky. What was going on inside her body? She couldn't control her reactions. Hadn't she been calm, cool and collected throughout the entire incident? "They'll dismiss the protest, Cal. Bianca was riposting. No one, not even the director, can prove beyond a shadow of a doubt that she was deliberately trying to injure me. She had flèched and was simply carrying through. No, believe me, I'll be facing her in the finals on Friday."

"I'd like to face her in a dark alley."

Dev laughed softly. "If you stick around fencing for any amount of time, Cal, you'll find there are several types of fencers. Some use brute force to win. Others use finesse. Some derive pure enjoyment from fencing their best game possible, win or lose. And others want to win at any cost."

Cal watched her closely. She was chattering nonstop, her face draining of color. He put his hand on her shoulder as she slowed to a halt. When she lifted her chin to meet his concerned gaze, confusion registered in her eyes.

"Cal . . ." The word slipped tremulously from her lips, her hand coming to rest on his chest. She heard him speak, but his voice seemed to be hovering in an echo chamber. Dev felt herself falling, her body turning to water, her knees buckling. She remembered no more.

HER LASHES FELT WEIGHTED, and Dev struggled to raise them.

"Take it easy, Dev." A low, masculine voice soothed her.

Dev was lying on a bed; someone was sitting next to her. The instant a cool cloth was placed on her brow, she opened her eyes. The light from the hallway spilled into the grayness of the room. She was on her bed, and Cal was watching her, his gray eyes dark. He pressed the cloth to her brow. Dev realized she was under a great many blankets, and she felt warm and safe.

"W-what happened? Why am I in bed?" she asked, her voice barely above a whisper.

Cal pushed several tendrils behind her delicate ear. "You fainted out in the hall."

Her eyes widened. "Me? Faint? Impossible. I've never fainted in my life—"

Cal removed the cloth and got to his feet, smiling slightly. "Just lie there. I'll be back in a minute, Dev."

She pulled her arms from beneath the covers, touching her damp hair. She desperately needed to shower. Cal came back and sat down, putting the cloth across her brow again. Just his touch brought sudden tears to her eyes, and emotions broke loose within her. "I—I feel so weird," she stammered. "As if—as if I'm shaking apart inside."

Cal ran his fingers down her bare arm in a motion meant to soothe her. "Posttrauma reaction, Dev. It's pretty common. I was waiting for you to come off that adrenaline high and crash." He caressed her shoulder, his voice low. "It isn't everyday you get someone who tries to injure you with a weapon. And before you open that beautiful mouth of yours to tell me it's a controlled sport, I know that. But Santullo was out to hurt you. Subconsciously, that makes a big difference, even if you don't want to admit it to yourself, Dev. And that's why you're having this reaction. It's as if Bianca had attacked in a dark alley with a knife with the intent of killing you. You're probably feeling pretty shaken up right now, wondering why anyone would want to harm you."

Dev swallowed against a sob that rose in her throat. "H-how do you know so much about the way I am feeling, Cal?"

He smiled tenderly, stroking her hair. "It comes from being a carrier pilot. If you've got a group of pilots from all the services standing at the same bar, you can always tell which ones are from a carrier."

She frowned, needing the continued reassurance of his touch, his fingers grazing her hair. "How?" she croaked, trying to fight the tears that wanted to come.

"Their hands always shake." He held his out in front of her to prove it. "Carrier duty wrings you dry of adrenaline every time you fly. When we land or take off, our blood levels are so high with the hormone that we shake."

Dev licked her chapped lips. "But adrenaline represents fear. And you don't faint."

"Dev, there have been times on landing my jet, when cables were breaking and snapping, that I wondered if I was ever going to make it down in one piece. I thought for sure it was all over. Afterward, I'd climb out of the cockpit on knees that felt like jelly and pray that I could make it down off the ladder and to the briefing room before I fell flat on my face in front of everyone." Amusement tinged his voice. "Once I damn near passed out in a passageway after a really rough landing. I was lightheaded, hands shaking, knees knocking." His gray eyes grew warm as he met hers. "That's how I knew what you were going to experience sooner or later after Santullo nailed you."

Dev blinked. "I never knew your job was so dangerous, Cal. My God..."

"Let's not worry about me. Let's just work you up and over this natural reaction, shall we?"

Her lips trembled, and she tried to suppress the huge fist of emotion that threatened to pummel her. "I—is it normal to want to cry?" she quavered. "I know you say you don't ever cry, but—"

Cal murmured her name reverently, sliding his hands around her body, drawing her up . . . up against him, so that Dev could lay her head on his shoulder. "Crying's good for you, didn't you know?" he asked huskily, placing his hand against her head. "It seems like someone I like one hell of a lot told me it was okay to cry. What do you think?"

Tears squeezed out from beneath her tightly shut eyes, and Dev's fingers dug into the fabric of his shirt. "Oh, Cal," she sobbed, "it was awful. Awful!"

"I know, I know, honey. That's my lady, just let it all go. Let out all that terror you're feeling. . . ."

Her sobs tore him apart, leaving him vulnerable to pain in a way he thought he would never want to be again. Cal rocked her, whispering unintelligible words of comfort in her ear, occasionally pressing small kisses along her hairline and temple. He tasted the salt of her tears, driven by an urge far greater than lust to follow their trail down her cheek. The instant his mouth touched the corner of her lips, he groaned. He felt Dev's hand curl around his neck, drawing him closer and tilting her head so that her tear-bathed lips could be covered by his questing mouth.

A wild, electrical jolt surged through Dev as Cal's mouth brushed across hers. She needed him, his physical closeness. She pressed against him, reveling in his maleness but also in the tenderness with which he took sips from her lips. His gentleness stunned her as he continued to explore, his kisses stabilizing her. Strangely tender, she thought, for a man who seemed born to the military, used to having to kill if necessary. Now he was in complete charge of his life, and now she lay in his arms, asking for that protectiveness that emanated so strongly from him.

His tongue slid across her lower lip; tiny prickles of pleasure shot down through her. She felt her nipples hardening against the quilted padding of her vest, and Dev mindlessly arched to him, wanting, asking for further contact.

"Sweet," he told her in a gritty rush of words, "you're so sweet, Dev. God..." And Cal pressed hungrily against her parted lips, wanting, needing all of her. Her breath was moist and sharp against his face, and he felt the wild beating of her heart beneath the vest. Her mouth opened like a flower blossoming beneath his onslaught, and Cal quivered as she allowed him total entrance to herself. Even as he tasted deeply of her natural sweetness, he knew he had to stop. He had to stop for their sake. And he laughed at himself. Since when had Cal Travis ever first considered what the woman he was bedding needed? As he moved his fingers up her rib cage, his palm barely brushing the curve of her beautifully formed breast, he was sorely tempted not to stop. He wanted Dev. More than he had wanted any woman in his life. The hardness of his body, the blood flowing like fiery lava through him, testified to that fact. He tore his mouth away from hers, his eyes charcoal, his desire barely in check. He gripped her arms, gently pulling her inches away from him.

"No, Dev, not this way. Not now." He swallowed hard, trying to catch his breath. He winced as her lashes moved upward to reveal eyes drugged with passion and dark with confusion. "Listen to me." He gave her a small shake. "I want it right between us, Dev. Not like this. You're coming off that high. Fear makes you want it. To want to be close and protected. I can't—won't take advantage of your vulnerability when you're like this."

His heart was thundering in his chest, and he ached to possess her. God, all of her! Cal could see his words weren't registering on Dev. "You're exhausted," he began, his voice a low growl, "and I want to love you, Dev. But not now." An unsure smile tipped the corners of his mouth. "Kiss me like that tomorrow morning and see what happens. Right now, you're not in full control of your emotions. What we have, what we share is special." His hands tightened on her arms, his voice fervent. "And when we love each other, I want that to be special, too, Dev. Not a spin-off of some trauma."

Dev blinked belatedly, prey to the feelings running rampantly through her. She only knew one thing: she needed Cal. In all ways. Embarrassed by her actions, she avoided his sharp gaze, her shoulders shaking with suppressed sobs.

"Come here," he said thickly, gathering her back into his arms.

Dev buried her head beneath his jaw, seeking his warmth, his strength.

His fingers brushed her damp cheek. "See how you feel tomorrow after you wake up, Dev. Then we'll talk about us, okay? Come on now, just lie here, let me hold you. Rest. Just rest...."

Her lids were so heavy.... Dev fell beneath the dark spell of his soothing voice, gradually relaxing in his arms. She hurt physically, but the ache in her heart was even more painful. Bewildered by her whirling emotions, Dev nestled deep into his arms, knowing she was falling in love with Cal Travis. It was all so crazy. So impossible. Yet she would not try to hide from her heart. She was afraid of the power of her feelings. But fear had never stopped her from embracing life's next experience. Dev wasn't going to shy away from Cal Travis or what he had come to mean to her in such a short period of time. She felt him shift, and her lashes barely raised. "Don't leave me...."

Cal gently laid her down, pulling the covers back over her. "Don't worry, I'll be right here," he reassured her, cradling her head. Dev's complexion was almost waxen, and that frightened him. She was in shock. Cal's heart wrenched in his chest when Dev barely turned, her cheek resting against his opened palm. The action was so unaffected and natural. Traits he had come to expect from Dev. "I'll be back in a minute," he promised her in a low voice.

By the time he had shut off all the lights and padded back into the room, Dev had sunk into a deep slumber. He stood there watching the soft rise and fall of her chest beneath the blankets. Her lips were slightly parted and still swollen from the strength of his kiss. How long he stood there simply absorbing Dev into his heart, his body, Cal didn't remember. Finally, he forced himself to move. Getting out of his shoes, he then shrugged out of his shirt and placed his watch on the bed table. Without waking her, he slid across the bed, remaining on top of the covers, and drew Dev gently back into his arms. He heard a small whimper as she snuggled close to him in her sleep, her hand sliding across his chest, coming to rest over his slowly thudding heart.

Cal lay there, staring up at the darkened ceiling, wide awake. Dev was in his arms, where he had wanted her to be since he'd first met her. A mirthless smile quirked his mouth as he absently ran his fingers across her bare arm. From the moment he had seen Dev, he had plotted and planned to get her into bed. She had been right: he was a hunter and he had been stalking her. He scowled. What had gone wrong, then? Why did he hate himself for using the moves he always put on a woman? They were both adults of consenting age, he told himself. Both had experience in relationships. So what in hell was it about Dev that made him feel like a first-class heel?

Frustrated, Cal placed his other arm across his eyes. There wasn't one second when he wasn't thinking about her or wanting to hear her voice or hungrily drinking in how she looked. A smile lingered. He liked the freckles that blanketed her nose and upper cheeks. They made her look like a little girl. But she wasn't a child. No, she was a provocative woman who was pulling emotions and quixotic feeling from inside him that he'd never experienced before. He removed his arm, staring darkly up at the ceiling again, as if looking at it long enough would give him the answers he sought.

Cal laughed at himself. If the guys back on the carrier could see him right now, they'd call him crazy. His reputation for getting any woman he wanted was almost legendary among his squadron mates. He had the lines, the confidence and the patience of a predator to get the prize he sought. He could have had Dev tonight. She was vulnerable to attack. He could have made love to her without even a whimper of protest. Now that seemed so distasteful to him. Why was he angry with himself when Dev had almost pushed him beyond his massive control to do just that? He hadn't backed down because he didn't want her. God, he ached to have her.

He snorted softly, still glaring at the ceiling. Dev felt so good lying next to him, her head tucked beneath his chin, her fingers softly curved on his chest. He was poignantly aware of her light, moist breath against his taut flesh and of her heady, feminine scent. Disgruntled and disgusted with himself, Cal shut his eyes. He had to get some sleep. There were a couple of things he wanted to do when he woke up. Dev's wrist needed further treatment. She was going to be a lot stiffer and sorer than she thought, and he had a few ideas on how to help her regain that fluidity she'd need for Friday's competition. *God, Travis! Since when have you put aside your own needs to help a woman?* And yet, as Cal felt sleep slowly encroaching on him, another part of him, a new part he'd never been aware of before Dev stepped into his life, made him feel good. It made him feel such a soaring sense of joy that, as he slid into sleep, a slight smile curved his lips, easing the hard planes of his face. It made him look hauntingly human.

DEV GROANED and opened her eyes. Sunlight spilled like a golden waterfall into the room. The moment she moved, pain flashed through her shoulder.

"How are you feeling?"

She raised her lashes to see Cal standing by the bed, his hands resting on his hips. She managed a grimace. "If I told you I felt like I'd been in a car accident last night, would you believe it?"

He met her grimace with a smile. "Yes. That's why we're going to use this morning to get you back on your feet."

Dev only stared at him, confused yet responding to the warmth in his gray eyes. He stood there, dressed in a pair of well-worn jeans, a dark-blue polo shirt that emphasized the magnificent breadth of his chest and a provocative smile on his ever-so-male mouth. Dev trembled inwardly. "You mean I may feel human again soon?" she croaked, slowly struggling to rise.

"Yep." Cal leaned over and pulled the blankets off her, holding his hand out to her. "It's almost 9:00 A.M. You slept for a good eight hours." Dev's ponytail had worked loose during the night so that a soft tangle of curls framed her pale face. Hair that he wanted to run his fingers through. . . . Cal gently set the idea aside.

"You look like a man with a plan," she grumbled good-naturedly, swinging her legs off the bed. Dev released his hand after she was standing, hotly aware of its firmness and strength. Looking down at herself, she muttered, "Not only do I feel like I've been in an accident, I look like it! I need a shower!"

"It's all ready for you. Come on."

Dev didn't quite trust that silver glimmer in Cal's eyes, but she didn't press the issue. The warmth that spun effortlessly between them was strong and good; she wouldn't question it. Her white knickers were terribly wrinkled and the vest she had worn all night was partly open, revealing the cleft between her breasts. Dev looked up at him.

"You slept with me. Didn't you?"

Cal nodded. "All night." He grasped her elbow and pointed her in the direction of the bathroom. "Why? Are you regretting it now?"

She touched her temple, a jumble of impressions from the night before hovering on the edge of her memory. Just Cal's nearness made her ache, and suddenly, the entire scene came back to her. Dev stopped, facing him in the hall.

"Cal," she whispered, "what's happening between us?"

He settled his hands on his hips, his smile tender. "I'd like to know the answer to that one myself, witch." He became more serious, his hand on her shoulder now. "Look, first things first. Get a shower, wash your hair and then wrap yourself in that fuzzy bathrobe I've laid out on the counter for you."

"But—"

He leaned down, silencing her protest as he kissed her longingly. Her lips were warm and soft and yielding, and Cal had to stop himself from crushing her in his arms and plundering her mouth as he wanted to. He drew away, a glimmer in his eyes. "No buts," he murmured. "You're what's most important right now. Remember, I've worked with injured horses. I'm going to treat you the same way as soon as you get out of the bathroom."

"What are you talking about?"

Cal guided her into the tiled expanse. "I visited a Chinese herb doctor this morning and got all the things we need. I've also got some herbal preparations for that épée injury and some for your wrist. The old doctor promised me these herbs will really draw out the soreness and drain the muscle tissue of the fluid surrounding that strain. Then I'll give you a good body massage. If you can't move and flex on Friday, you're going to be a sitting target—we both know that."

Dev's mouth dropped open, but she didn't have any time to protest. Her lips tingled hotly from his swift, branding kiss. A body massage? By him? Oh, God, she wouldn't be able to trust her responses to his long, tapered fingers sliding with knowing sureness over her. Could she trust him? "Cal, we need to talk about—"

"I'll see you in a bit." Then that irrepressible, little-boy grin surfaced. "Didn't you know? Never argue with a carrier pilot. You'll always lose."

Dev stood there stunned as he quietly closed the door behind him. To her amazement, a towel, shampoo, hair conditioner and the bathrobe had all been placed neatly in order before her. She shook her head and smiled grudgingly. "Cal Travis, what am I going to do with you?"

DEV CAME OUT a half hour later. Her hair was a soaking wet mass. Cal walked over to where she stood. Her cheeks had some color in them again, and her skin was beginning to look less waxen. He took a deep breath, grateful.

Dev gave him a miserable look.

"What's wrong?"

She held up her right wrist, which was swollen and bruised. "I managed to wash my hair, Cal, but it hurts to even lift a towel right now to dry it. Can you?"

"Sure. Go sit down on the bed."

She sat, slowly flexing the fingers of her right hand, feeling the pain lance up through her wrist. Her heart sank; it would take a miracle for her to make it to the finals on Friday. Dev raised her head when Cal came back. He knelt down on the bed beside her, placing a fluffy towel over her hair, gently gathering up the auburn curls within the folds.

"I've never dried a woman's hair before," he told her gruffly.

Dev was moved by how careful he was trying to be. "You're doing fine," she assured him, resting against him.

"How's your left shoulder?"

"It hurts to even raise my arm halfway up my chest. Between that and my wrist, I'm afraid I didn't wash my hair very well."

Cal leaned over her, inhaling the scent from her damp tresses as he put the towel around her shoulders. "Smells good. Like apricots."

Dev hesitated. "I have one more favor to ask."

"Name it."

She responded to the intimacy he always established with her. "C-could you comb it? It gets so snarly with all this curl if I don't."

"Dev, I'd probably rip your hair out." He held out his hand to her. "You want this to pull a comb through your hair?"

She stared at his beautifully sculpted fingers, thinking how much they resembled an artist's. Perhaps flying was like art. She saw his hand tremble almost imperceptibly, and the story he had told her last night about carrier pilots came back to her. Reaching out with her right hand, she barely touched the flesh of his palm.

"I trust you."

Cal dropped his hand. "Lady, you are really pushing the river. If any of the guys heard you say you trusted me, they'd be rolling in the aisles." Nevertheless, he retrieved her tortoiseshell comb. When he returned, he knelt beside Dev, taking the first strands in his hands, staring down at them. Her hair was like rich, heavy silk.

"Do all your friends think you're nothing more than a playboy?" she jibed gently, risking a glance up at him. He had the most stricken look on his face as he stared down at her hair. He really didn't know what to do with it! Dev gently leaned against him, relishing his closeness. "Go on, pull the comb through it. I promise my hair won't scream in protest."

He managed a nervous grin. "*You* might."

Dev laughed softly. "Big, tough carrier pilot who can fly in some of the most dangerous and deadly jets in the world, and you're afraid to comb my hair. Really, Cal. . . ."

That did it. His eyes narrowed. "Okay, just remember, I warned you. . . ."

Dev suppressed a smile, eyes dancing with devilry. "I'll remember."

The next fifteen minutes were pure pleasure for Cal. He had never realized how sensual the act of combing through her damp hair could be. The strands were clean and fragrant, sliding through his fingers as he gently worked out the snarls. He was aware of Dev's utter femininity in those precious golden minutes that spun around them. The robe parted just enough so that he could see the shadowed valley between her breasts. Her flesh had a golden glow, and he found himself wanting her all over again. Hell, he had never stopped wanting her, but now he was excruciatingly aware of how he longed to move his hand down her slender throat and touch the rounded flesh that peeked provocatively from beneath the terry cloth. By the time he had finished, Cal was quivering inwardly with desire for Dev.

"There," he said gruffly, getting up. If he stayed away from her, he could force himself not to touch her. His heart swelled unaccountably in his chest as she raised her head, a shy smile on her full, parted lips.

"Thank you. You'd put a hairdresser to shame—" The words faded away as she read the intent in Cal's eyes. She watched as he dropped the comb on the bed beside her, his fingers spanning her jaw, capturing her, tilting her chin upward. Upward to meet his descending mouth. She was completely unprepared for the hot, slanting kiss he branded on her lips. All her nerve endings seemed to explode as he hungrily molded his mouth to hers in a kiss that tore the breath from her body. He was powerful, strong and in command as his fingers slid past her jaw, moving up and caressing her scalp, bringing the damp mass of hair forward like a silken pillow against her face. Her heart pounded urgently as she felt the heat of his body, the moistness of his breath against her cheek and the onslaught of his tongue as it caressed the depths of her mouth. Her nipples hardened immediately against the nubby texture of the robe, the result of his over-whelming maleness and the drugging beauty of his kiss.

Cal slowly broke contact with her wet, glistening lips, now pouty in the aftermath of their kiss. Cal was immediately contrite, gently passing his thumb across her trembling lower lip. "I'm sorry. I didn't mean to get carried away." He inhaled unsteadily, closing his eyes, resting his brow against hers. She was as shaken as he was. He managed to draw away, then hunkered in front of her, his hands sliding down her arms, capturing her hands. She looked incredibly sensual, her mouth well kissed, her cheeks a flaming rose color and her wide, blue eyes gold flecked. He shook his head. "What am I going to do with you?"

Dev found her voice scratchy, her breathing sporadic. "I don't know. What do you want to do?" She was leaving herself vulnerable to him. Cal could destroy her emotionally, and she knew it. He would take her to bed. And yes, he would devote one hundred percent of his time to her while he was with her. But in four days, he was going to walk out of her life. Forever. He was a bachelor, a man of the world, a man used to having women on his own terms. "I remember last night, Cal. I remember how you held me and—kissed me. And when you did, all I wanted to do was melt in your arms and be loved by you." She lifted her lashes, seeing his troubled expression.

His fingers tightened on her hands. "You weren't in full charge of your emotions last night," he told her in a lowered voice.

"But I am now."

"Dev, listen to me." Cal paused and raised his eyes to the ceiling, glaring blackly at it for a moment before he returned to her wide, trusting gaze. "Damn it, I know what you're thinking. You think I'll take you to bed and make love to you one day and walk out of your life the next." His nostrils flared with the frustration. "I guess I deserve that because, frankly, I've treated every other woman that way." His tone softened, and Cal held her luminous gaze. "With you, it's different. Don't ask me why because I don't have any answers, Dev. All I know is that you're an extraordinary woman. And I find myself actually afraid of touching you. I want the expression of what we feel to be special. Damn it, I can't put it into words. I don't want to just take something from you for myself. I want to give something of myself to you in return." Cal released her hand and ran his fingers through his hair in an aggravated motion. "This isn't making any sense at all. My buddies would die laughing if they heard me right now. They wouldn't believe it was Cal Travis talking."

Dev whispered his name, resting her hand against his shaved cheek. Her eyes grew warm and misty as she held his unsettled gaze. "In the past, you made love *to* women. Now I think I'm hearing you tell me you want to make love *with* me. Making love to a woman is taking something for yourself. If you make love with a woman, there's a wonderful sharing, a giving and a taking of each other. Is that what you're trying to say?" She prayed that it was because she had never felt more strongly drawn or wanted any man more in her life than Cal, who sat before her, his lean fingers resting on her robed thighs.

He half smiled, digesting the statement. And then he reached up, caressing the velvet of her cheek. "Anyone ever tell you that you're pretty smart?"

Dev smiled shyly, basking in the warmth of his outpouring of caring. Affection lingered in his wide, gray eyes, touched the corners of his wonderful mouth and trembled in the richness of his voice as it fell over her like a cloak of love.

"Don't go putting me on any pedestals! I'll fall off them," she countered shakily. God, the want, the need for him was a throbbing, living bridge between them. Dev ached to reach out, open her arms and draw his head to her breast and complete their collision course to destiny.

"Dev?"

"Yes?"

"I want to love you. But not right now. You come first before what I might want." He held her startled gaze, his hands closing over hers. "We have all the time in the world to get to know one another. To explore each other. This is one time in my life I'm not in a hurry. I want to savor you like a fine, rare wine. I want to absorb you through every pore in my body and make you mine. The time's not right. You're here to fence. You're the very best, and we've got to get you prepared for Friday's meet." He gave her a tentative smile. "I can't believe I'm hearing myself say 'wait.'"

Dev was shaken and it showed. She sensed Cal had made some kind of decision. A very serious one about her and him. She picked up his hand, pressing a kiss to his palm. The words "I love you" were almost torn from her as she read his bemused expression laden with banked passion.

"All right," she whispered, "what's next on the agenda?"

He slowly rose to his feet, reluctantly releasing her hands. "You," he said.

6

"IF SOMEONE HAD TOLD ME a marine fighter pilot could be gentle like this, I'd never have believed them," Dev told him in a hushed voice as he completed dressing her wrist. Their heads were bowed and almost touching as they worked over her arm. A smile twitched the corner of his mouth as he wrapped her wrist in a hot, moist towel.

"Despite our image, we're sinfully human. Lie back."

Dev straightened out on the bed, laying her wrist across her stomach. She watched him with curiosity and tenderness. "I like your human side much better than the pilot side I saw of you the first night," she admitted, relaxing as he reached over on the bed table and picked up a jar that had Chinese characters written on it.

"You do?"

"Definitely."

"Watch it, witch, or I'm liable to abandon all my massive control and jump your bones here and now." Cal sat down beside her, easing back the robe from where it rested on her chest, being careful not to expose her breast. God knew he wanted to. He forced himself not to stare at the hint of curved firmness that lay there teasing him. He flicked a glance at Dev. She hadn't tensed when he had pulled the robe aside to expose her injury, which rested two inches below her left collarbone. She trusted him. It was that simple. And that complex. Normally, any woman would have flinched or protested over the intimacy of his act.

"Jump my bones—" She laughed indignantly. "Are marines always so crude? Never mind, don't answer that."

His smile disappeared as he got his first good look at Dev's injury. "No, you're right, I'd have to take the fifth on that. Damn, Dev, you've got to be feeling some pain." He gently placed his fingers well away from the laceration that the doctor had painted with a yellow tincture to halt any possible infection. An area around the wound half the size of his hand was an angry black and purple and badly swollen.

"Come on, it's no big deal, Travis. Quit looking at me like I got shot or something. I saw it this morning when I undressed. It looks worse than it is."

Anger stirred in him. Toward Bianca Santullo. "This is going to hurt, Dev. I'll try and be as gentle as I can." He smeared his fingers with the ointment, lightly applying it first to the outer edges of the bruised flesh. He looked up once or twice to gauge her reaction. Dev had her lower lip tucked between her teeth and lay staring up at the ceiling. He followed the curve of the swollen tissue to where it touched the upper part of her breast.

"It is a big deal," he told her quietly. "I don't like anyone marring your beautiful skin."

Dev sucked in a breath as his fingers glided over a particularly sore spot. "You're such a chauvinist, Travis. You think in terms of me as your woman and that you own me. Lord help the person who looks at me crossways or even *thinks* about touching me."

Cal looked up, a glitter in his eyes. "You are mine. You just don't know it yet."

A slight smile pulled at her mouth. "I thought your breed had died out with the advent of feminism."

He slathered more ointment closer to the laceration, feeling her tense. "Easy, I'll be done in a moment. Just bear with me a little longer. When I get the moist heat on this, it will take away the pain and reduce the swelling."

"I hope so," she muttered between thinned lips. That whole area was so tender! "What are you putting on me, anyway? How do I know this Chinese guy you went to isn't some sort of quack?"

He grinned, wiping his fingers on a nearby towel and putting the lid back on the jar. "This is Tiger Balm. Known throughout the world for taking good care of sprains, strains and arthritis. The trainer I worked with used it all the time on his racehorses. It almost produces miracles, bringing down swelling and taking out soreness in a day's time."

Her eyes grew round. "Now *you* sound like one of those medicine men from the Old West."

Cal laughed and got up. "Trust me?"

Dev shrugged good-naturedly. "Do I have a choice?"

"Do you want one?"

"No."

"Good. While I'm in there getting a towel soaked in warm water, I want you to strip out of that robe and lie on your stomach. Cover your pretty derriere with that towel, if you want. When I come back, we'll position the moist cloth on that wound, and then I'll massage you."

Her heart beat slightly faster, and Dev nodded. "Okay."

By the time he returned, Dev was comfortable. She had had a devil of a time getting the towel across her rear because her wrist was wrapped, making her attempts ungainly at best. When Cal ambled back, he repositioned the towel a little more carefully across her.

"Thanks." Her speech was muffled against the pillow.

Cal grimaced, thinking that if her derriere was one half as nice as the rest of what he saw, she was the stuff his dreams had been made of. "Just being an officer and a gentleman," he baited, placing his hand gently beneath her left shoulder, raising it carefully. He slid the moist towel across the injured area and allowed Dev to lie back down on it.

She turned her head to one side, watching him. He poured a good amount of almond-scented oil between his hands, and Dev found herself anticipating his touch. Massage, in her mind, was just another provocative form of making love.

Cal nudged off his shoes and then straddled her body. Her back had a golden tan. He became serious, his voice little more than a murmur as he splayed his hands across her lower back and added little initial pressure as his thumbs followed the indentation along her long spine. "I've never seen any woman in as good shape as you are, Dev."

Her only answer was a delicious groan as his fingers began to work magic, coaxing tense muscles to respond and spreading relaxation wherever he massaged. Dev closed her eyes, giving herself over totally to his very knowing and very experienced hands.

"That feels wonderful," she whispered. His fingers were strong and firm without hurting. "Where did you learn how to massage?"

"Working on the horses."

Dev barely opened her eyes, a smile on her lips. "I expected you to say on other women."

"Less romantic if I admit the truth, eh?"

She laughed with him, practically purring beneath his ministrations. "Well, if you hadn't remembered so much about horses, I'd probably be in a lot worse shape by Friday."

Cal shook his head, feeling himself growing hard, blood pounding urgently through him as he stroked and kneaded her firm flesh. "Don't worry, I intend to collect for all my services."

Dev barely heard his answer. All the stiffness in her upper left shoulder had disappeared beneath his cajoling touch. And as the pain eased, she slid into slumber without meaning to.

THE SOFTENED FM MUSIC gently pulled Dev from her doze. She blinked groggily, realizing she had fallen asleep. Blankets had been pulled over her, and she raised her head. Cal was sitting on the settee, immersed in the *South China Sea* newspaper.

"What time is it?" she asked.

Cal set down the paper, looking at his watch. "Close to 11:00 A.M." He smiled. "You needed the extra sleep."

Dev slowly turned over, remembering she was naked, and kept the covers over her. "I guess so. Actually, it was the wonderful massage you gave me." She struggled into a sitting position, pulling the sheet across her breasts and drawing up her knees. With a yawn, Dev buried her face in her hands, trying to force herself awake.

Cal got to his feet and came over to the bed. He removed her hands from her face and then studied the épée injury. "Looks better," he confided, lifting his chin and meeting her sleep-ridden eyes. God, she looked so beautiful. What would it be like to wake up every morning with Dev in his arms? The thought momentarily stunned Cal. That meant a commitment. Marriage. Love. Love? He tested the word carefully, watching as Dev gave him a slumberous smile, her lips pouty and begging to be kissed once again.

"I'm starved," she murmured.

He sat there enjoying her. Each moment with Dev was precious, blossoming into something deeper. He reached out and slid his fingers up the delicate line of her jaw.

"I am, too," he said thickly, leaning down, "for you...."

This time, Dev was ready. And eager. And wanting to kiss him in return for all that he had become to her. Automatically, her hands lifted to rest on his chest. Dev felt the hard thud of his heart beneath her palms as he relished her lips like a savored wine. Her lashes swept down across her cheeks, and Dev breathed in his scent, responding effortlessly to his coaxing mouth, which slanted hotly across her lips, sending liquid fire racing along all her nerves.

"I love the way you kiss me," she murmured throatily against his mouth.

Cal smiled, his charcoal eyes dark on her flushed features. "And I love the way you give me all of you. You don't hold back," he said huskily, kissing the tip of her nose, her lashes and then moving back to her eager parted lips.

As his fingers combed through her hair, Cal tipped her head back to drink more deeply of her. When he caressed the curve of her breast, Dev moaned. The sheet had fallen away when she had lifted her hands. She was lost in the heated plundering of his mouth. Her flesh tightened under his caress, the nipple button hard as his thumb lazily stroked it.

Cal gently broke their kiss, making her feel bereft. She trembled as he released her. He had used the word "love" where she was concerned, and in those shatteringly still seconds she drowned in the gray splendor of his wide eyes. He drew in a deep breath as if willing control over himself. She lifted her hand, caressing his cheek.

"Tell me why, Cal," she whispered.

"Why what?"

"Why I find myself needing you, wanting you...."

"It's no different for me." He cradled her face reverently between his hands. "But I'm finding that I like waiting for the right moment, the right time for us, Dev."

She licked her lips, her eyes turning cobalt as she searched his face. "I don't feel that," she went on in an anguished tone. "Why do I feel that you'll walk out of my life when I'm done with the fencing tournament?"

"Maybe you're reacting to my playboy past."

"It's still a part of you, Cal."

"Not where you're concerned, it isn't, Dev."

She wanted to believe him. Oh, how she ached to believe his words. "Cal, you just can't do an about-face in one day's time!"

"How about three days?" he teased.

Dev gave him a look of futility laced with pleading. "I know what you are, and I accept you as that. You aren't the kind of man to promise me everything when you intend to give none of it. You're honest, Cal. About yourself. Your life." Her voice became tremulous. "Ever since I saw you that first night, you've turned my world upside down. Normally, I'm wary of someone like you. Yet you're different. So different from anyone I've ever met, Cal. I'm old enough and honest enough to admit all that to myself." Dev lifted her eyes, pain shadowing them. "What I'm trying to say is that I want you to love me. Share this precious amount of time with me while we have it. I know you desire me. I feel it every time you look at me . . . or kiss me. . . ."

Cal gently ran his hands over her hair, realizing the courage it took for Dev to admit her innermost feelings. "I will love you, Dev, and before we have to leave Hong Kong. That's a promise. I can't go a month and a half before seeing you again without ever having known you." His tone grew rough. "There's no way I can convince you that my intentions are long-term. I know you don't trust me, Dev. I'm going to have to prove myself to you through my actions. Once I get settled in at Edwards, I'm coming to see you. Unless you don't want me to. . . ."

"See you? Of course I'd want to see you."

"All right, next item . . . loving you." He watched as a flush spread over her freckled cheeks. "After the tournament, honey. You're in no shape for a late night with me and early morning calls for fencing." Cal leaned over, brushing her full lips with a grazing kiss. "I think I know how important this meet is to you. I care enough for you to wait because I know that I'll be seeing you in Los Angeles, and we can pick up where we left off then."

Dev didn't know what to think. But then Cal's strong fingers were gently cradling her face, his mouth continuing to worship her lips, making thinking undesirable. Her emotions were held in thrall to Cal Travis; she accepted his decision. She had closed her eyes as he took small sips from her lips, lost in the warming texture of him. And when Dev felt him get off the bed and tuck the sheet around her, she smiled softly.

"Come on," Cal coaxed, watching her drowsy sapphire eyes open. "The coach said you had to make the 1:00 P.M. practice. Are you up to it?"

Dev gave him a nod. "With you rooting for me, of course I am."

"Good. I'm going to my room to make a phone call, and then I'll meet you back here."

THE BALLROOM WAS one huge exercise area for the fencers. Cal leaned against the wall, arms across his chest as Dev's coach Jack talked with her. The coach closely inspected her wrist, telling her she wouldn't have to fence today since he wanted to give the wrist a well-earned rest in preparation for the meet. Dev teamed up with the American épée champion, and they began rudimentary floor exercises to stretch and warm up. Jack Gordon ambled over to Cal.

"I think you've given Dev a shot at the finals on Friday," he said by way of greeting, standing near Cal as they both watched Dev work out.

"Tiger Balm works miracles."

Jack grinned. "So Dev tells me." The coach looked up and gave him a long, measuring stare. "You seem to be a man of many talents, Major Travis."

"Call me Cal."

"All right." Jack's blue eyes narrowed, and then he returned his attention to his fencer. He and Cal said nothing for almost five minutes. "Dev seems to have taken quite a fancy to you."

"I'm just as taken with her," Cal admitted.

"Dev said you'll be stationed out at Edwards. That's pretty close to where she lives."

"Yes."

Jack's sandy brows drew down. "How much do you know about Dev, Travis?"

Cal was suddenly on guard when he heard the coach use his last name. "In what way?"

"About her childhood."

"She was given up for adoption when she was born and has a set of foster parents whom she loves very much."

"Correction. Her father is a widower. Is that all you know?"

"Yes. Why?"

"Look, some of what I'm going to say is because I'm her coach. The rest of it relates to the two of you. Normally, I don't go sticking my nose in my fencers' personal lives."

Cal slowly placed his hands on his hips. "What do you want, Gordon?"

"You may not realize how much this meet means to Dev. It's a pivotal point in her life, the culmination of her work." He scratched his head thoughtfully. "Dev was given up by her real mother. She was in a foster home until another child in the family contracted polio. Naturally, they put Dev back in an orphanage. Well, she contracted the disease anyway, at age six. The shame of it was that the foster family she was living with hadn't immunized her or the other kids against the disease."

Cal's face froze, his gray eyes dark. "Go on."

"Nobody wanted a freckle-faced kid who couldn't walk, Travis. The people at the orphanage did the best they could.

But you know it couldn't be enough. Dev was bedridden for almost five years. And then her foster father, who eventually went on to adopt her, spotted her in the orphanage one day, hobbling around in leg braces. You see, Carl Hunter and his wife Susan always wanted a little girl. Susan died when Dev was twelve, and Carl raised her by himself. He never did remarry. I met Dev when she was eighteen. She came over to the university physical education department and begged me to teach her how to fence. If you had seen her then, she was a scrawny, underweight kid with shrunken calves. Her foster father had been a fencer many years before and had almost made the Olympic team. He missed that spot on the team because of an injury.

"Carl felt that Dev needed a challenge to get back into shape. He encouraged her to fence. I agreed to take her on, and I've got to tell you, that woman out there knows what pain is all about. Do you know what it takes to stretch muscles, tear them down and build them up again? I think you see my point. She's a walking miracle, Travis, and in more ways than you've had a chance to know yet. Dev is one of the two ladies in the U.S. that have been responsible for getting women the right to fence in épée and sabre. Carl Hunter wanted to be here for this meet."

"Why isn't he?" Cal asked grimly, watching Dev practice her retreat and advance footwork.

"Financial difficulties. Carl's dream was to see Dev win the international épée event for women."

Cal rubbed his mouth with the back of his hand. "She won't do it here, Gordon. You know how bad her wrist is. She'll be lucky to finish in the top three."

"You and I know that. Dev doesn't. But you're right, she'll be lucky not to get knocked out by Santullo."

Cal swore softly, glaring. "That Italian is nothing more than a damned tank waiting to run over her next opponent."

Jack nodded. "She's got the height and weight on her side," he agreed.

"So why are you telling me all this?"

"A couple of reasons. One is professional and important to me. The other is personal and vital to Dev."

Cal managed a sour grin, relaxing. "So?"

"First, you're good for Dev. I can see she's rallied with you around. The care you've given her shows. It will help her in the meet. Second, allow Dev to keep her mind on the fencing. On why she's here." Jack had the good grace to flush. "This is a backhanded compliment to you, Travis. I've never seen a man influence Dev like you have. She's a real down-to-earth woman who doesn't easily get the rug pulled out from under her." He paused. "Carl Hunter means the world to Dev. It's been her dream to carry the Hunter name to the Olympics. Carl's injury prevented him from making it. But maybe, if Dev can make third or fourth in the finals, carry home one of those medals, it will be enough for Carl. It would mean the world to both of them."

"I'm glad you told me, Gordon," Cal said softly.

"Dev says you have a lot of women. But I don't think so. I think you mean well by her. It's just that you've stepped into her life at a pretty important time. I'm asking you to give way to her dreams for her and her father."

Cal turned away from Jack. Warmth lingered in his eyes as he watched Dev laugh with her fencing partner. She was so much woman that she made his chest ache with some undefinable emotion that overwhelmed him. "Dev's the kind of woman who embraces the world," he murmured, more to himself than anyone.

Jack grinned. "Yeah, Dev just reaches out and touches you, and you're better off for it. You ought to see her with kids. She's terrific. Did she tell you she teaches a group of handicapped youngsters down at my *salle* once a week? She arranges a fencing meet for them once a month. Gives the kids a reason for pushing themselves and increasing their motor skills. It's such a popular program that the area hospitals have been sending referrals to us. If this keeps up, she could end up teaching every night of the week if she wants to. She's quite a lady."

Cal had so much to learn about Dev. "Yes, she is. . . ."

The coach clapped him on the shoulder. "Dev's not one to brag about herself or her accomplishments," he said good-naturedly. And then he smiled. "Thanks for understanding the situation, Travis. Kind of figured you would."

Cal nodded. By tomorrow afternoon, Dev could be on her way to the finals. And he was going to be there for her as she had been for him.

DEV GRATEFULLY TOOK the towel from Cal, wiping her sweaty face. She slid down to the floor and tried to steady her breathing. The épée was strapped to the palm of her hand so that now it rested on the floor next to her.

"You're doing fine." Cal gave her a quiet smile filled with pride. "You've made it into the finals. Not bad with a crippled wrist."

"Lost one and won three," Dev said, gasping, tipping her head back against the wall and closing her eyes.

Cal slid his fingers over her hot and sweaty left hand. He squeezed it gently. "Jack said you won't get less than third even if you lose to Santullo. That's one hell of an accomplishment."

Dev's lashes barely lifted, but she drank in Cal's handsome features. It was already 4:00 P.M., Friday evening. Where had the time gone? She cherished Cal's company. His stories. Their laughter. When had she ever laughed or smiled so much? Dev couldn't recall. "My wrist is holding up because of you," she murmured. "Jack was very interested in how you wrapped it this morning."

"I wrapped it like I would a horse's leg," he said, meeting her grin. Her face was lovely, flushed, glistening with perspiration, her large blue eyes luminous with life. Time was going too fast. Cal didn't want to be separated from Dev. He wanted to reach out, caress her cheek and tell her that she made life worth living again. What a brilliance his life had taken on. What would he do for a month and a half without Dev at his side? The prospect pulverized him. He hadn't slept well last night whereas Dev had looked refreshed this morning. He squeezed her fingers.

"You've gotten to the finals because you have a thoroughbred's heart, lady. You're a winner no matter what you do."

Dev blushed. "What am I going to do with you, Cal Travis? You make me feel on top of the world."

He was staring down at her long, slender hands. "Tell me you believe I'll see you when I make it to Edwards."

She swallowed, surprise flaring in her eyes. Dev had made a point of never saying "when you come to L.A." She desperately wanted to believe Cal, but her head, her logic screamed otherwise. Her heart was tearing apart inside her. Tomorrow morning, she would be boarding a Northwest Orient jumbo jet bound for the States. And Cal would walk out of her life. "All right," she said softly, "you come to L.A. when you get to Edwards."

"You still don't believe I'll come, do you?"

He spoke in such a low tone, and Dev saw the hurt in his eyes. "No."

Cal gave her a slight smile. "But you want to see me, and that's all I need to know. One of these days, Dev Hunter, I'll teach you to trust me."

She laughed gently and rose, readjusting her wet leather glove on her right hand. The scorekeeper called her name. Cal got to his feet and squeezed her left arm.

"Okay, this is for all the marbles. Go out there and give Bianca what she deserves."

Dev tucked the fencing mask beneath her left arm, a warm thrill coursing through her as Cal leaned over and pressed a kiss to her damp temple. "This bout's for you, Travis."

He grinned. "Want to carry my scarf into battle?"

"Is this chauvinism in reverse?"

"Just carry me in your heart, witch. That's all I ask."

Dev was stunned. The low timbre of his voice told her everything. Cal Travis did care for her. Her heart swelled with love. Yes, it was love. Dev didn't have time to examine those wonderful feelings exploding in her as she walked out to the copper strip to face Bianca. Dev raised her épée in salute to the director, scorekeeper and finally to her glowering opponent. This bout was for Cal. The meet was for her father. Men who believed in her without reservation. Her wrist was badly swollen and throbbing beneath the tight adhesive wrap Cal had applied. Thanks to him, her left shoulder was fine, the stiffness alleviated as a result of the hot packs and Tiger Balm ointment.

Bianca whipped her blade down in a sloppy salute. Dev smiled grimly, settling her mask over her face, resuming the fencing position, her toe touching the *en garde* line. Santullo had lost one bout. She had won the rest with a combination of her incredible strength and skill. A new energy invaded Dev that she recognized as a badly needed shot of adrenaline. It would give her the staying power she needed to fence Bianca. But more than anything, she had Cal's courage and belief backing her. She knew Jack didn't think she would finish in the top three. Calling on all her reserves, Dev pointed her épée at Bianca as the director ordered them to prepare to fence. All those years of constant pain to get her crippled muscles to stretch and move at her command had been worth it for this moment. After ten years of fencing, Dev was ready. More ready than she had ever been in her entire life. Her only regret was that Carl wasn't here to see her. "This meet is for you, Dad," she whispered between thinned lips.

Irresistible!

4 FREE NOVELS AND A SURPRISE GIFT

DELIVERED RIGHT TO YOUR HOME
WITH NO OBLIGATION TO BUY—EVER

**FIND OUT WHAT YOUR SURPRISE GIFT IS
SEE INSIDE**

YOURS FREE FOR KEEPS!

Your surprise gift ➡

DEAR READER:

We would like to send you 4 Harlequin Temptations just like the one you're reading plus a surprise gift – all **ABSOLUTELY FREE.**

If you like them, we'll send you 4 more books each month to preview. Always before they're available in stores. Always for less than the regular retail price. Always with the right to cancel and owe nothing.

In addition, you'll receive **FREE**...
- our monthly newsletter HEART TO HEART
- our magazine ROMANCE DIGEST
- fabulous bonus books and surprise gifts
- special-edition Harlequin Bestsellers to preview for ten days without obligation

So return the attached Card and start your Harlequin honeymoon today.

Sincerely

Pamela Powers

Pamela Powers
for Harlequin

P.S. Remember, your 4 free novels and your surprise gift are yours to keep whether you buy any books or not.

PRINTED IN U.S.A.

4 EXCITING ROMANCE NOVELS PLUS A SURPRISE GIFT

FREE BOOKS/ SURPRISE GIFT

YES, please send me my four **FREE** Harlequin Temptations™ and my **FREE** surprise gift. Then send me four brand-new Harlequin Temptations each month as soon as they come off the presses. Bill me at the low price of $1.99 each (for a total of $7.95 — a saving of $1.04 off the retail price). There are no shipping, handling or other hidden costs. There is no minimum number of books I must purchase. I can always return a shipment and cancel at any time. Even if I never buy a book from Harlequin, the four free novels and the surprise gift are mine to keep forever.

142 CIX MDKW

NAME_____

ADDRESS_____APT. NO._____

CITY_____

STATE_____ZIP_____

Offer limited to one per household and not valid for present subscribers. Prices subject to change.

Mail to:
Harlequin Reader Service
901 Fuhrmann Blvd.
P.O. Box 1394
Buffalo, NY 14240
U.S.A.

LIMITED TIME ONLY
Mail today and get a
SECOND MYSTERY GIFT

M AIL THIS CARD TODAY

You'll receive 4 Harlequin novels
plus a fabulous surprise gift
ABSOLUTELY FREE

BUSINESS REPLY CARD

First Class   Permit No. 717   Buffalo, NY

Postage will be paid by addressee

Harlequin Reader Service
901 Fuhrmann Blvd.,
P.O. Box 1394
Buffalo., NY 14240-9963

NO POSTAGE
NECESSARY
IF MAILED
IN THE
UNITED STATES

Jack came and joined Cal as the bout began. The coach's eyes narrowed. The Italian woman was put on the immediate defensive as Dev exploded from the *en garde* line in a flèche attack. The green light blinked, indicating Dev had scored! Jack risked a grin over at Cal.

"Dev's pulling out all the stops. She's going for broke on this one."

Cal's mouth was dry, his heart pounding heavily. He knew how much it meant to Dev. "She's one hell of a woman," he agreed, watching the two fencers. Santullo had turned a mottled red, breathing hard, a bull ready to charge. Dev flexed the blade of her épée, calmly preparing for the director to tell them to fence once again.

Bianca wanted to win at any cost. But Dev matched her point for point as the bout went to the five-minute limit. It was going into one minute of overtime with the score 4 to 4. Whoever scored the next touch would win the bout. He knew Dev couldn't place first because she had two losses. But if Bianca lost to her, first place would be decided on touches scored between the Italian woman and a Canadian, Priscilla Costello, who had one loss.

Either way, Dev was going to come in third place, with or without a loss to Santullo. Cal grinned at Dev's strategy: she was going to make the maximum amount of touches against Bianca so that in the end, even if the Italian won this bout, she could lose first place because Dev had scored more touches on her than had been scored against Costello. And Cal knew without a doubt that Dev could have taken first place if her wrist hadn't been injured. He loved her for her courage to be the very best she could under the circumstances.

At that moment, Cal saw Dev and Bianca lunge at each other; both lights went on. Dev threw up her hands, giving a cheer. They had scored a tie. Santullo muttered in Italian as she glared at the scoring lights. Cal walked out to the strip to unhook Dev, a big grin on his face. He was pleasantly surprised when she threw her arms around him, hugging him. Instantly, he wrapped his arms around her slender waist, stirred by her damp body against his own.

"I did it! I did it!" she said, laughing.

"You sure did. It was a great bout, Dev. Now come on, stand still long enough so I can get you out of this," he chided.

Dev shifted from one foot to the other. Once unhooked, she walked over to the sulking Bianca, offering her hand. The Italian woman glared at her and stalked off the strip. Dev turned back, fencing mask beneath her right arm, the widest smile on her face as she looked from her coach to Cal.

"Well, third place isn't bad, considering everything."

Jack came up and gave her a fierce hug. "It's great, Dev! Just great. That was the best round you've ever fenced."

Tears made her eyes bright as Cal began cutting away the tape holding the épée to the palm of her glove. "You think dad will like a bronze medal, Coach?" Dev asked.

"Dev, he'll cry when you give it to him, I'll bet. I'm going over to the scorekeeper. I want to see if your touches against Santullo have put her in second place."

Dev looked up at Cal as he gently removed the tape from her palm and placed the épée on the floor behind them. "There's more than one way to get even with someone like Bianca. If she gets second place, she'll probably explode."

Cal cradled her face between her hands. His gray eyes expressed both pride and warmth. "In my book, you're the real champion. You never gave up despite your handicaps. I'm proud as hell of you. We all are."

She beamed at him. "Oh, Cal, I'm so glad you're here. . . ."

He leaned down, his mouth gently touching her lips. Lips that tasted salty from perspiration and a mouth that was sweet as it opened to allow him entrance. Fire sang through Cal; he reveled in the depth of his feelings for Dev. Reluctantly, he broke the kiss, his face inches from hers as he stared down at her. "I'll always be there for you, Dev," he promised thickly. Cal had never told another woman that, but he no longer questioned the new emotions he held for Dev alone. She was so outgoing, so trusting. He saw surprise mirrored in her eyes. It didn't matter if Dev didn't believe him. Actions spoke louder than words. And all his life, he had been a man of action. . . .

IT WAS ALMOST 11:00 P.M. by the time the festivities were over. The awards were given after the meet, and Dev proudly accepted the bronze medal on a red grosgrain ribbon that was placed around her neck. She remained expressionless when Bianca Santullo accepted the silver medal. And she clapped wildly when Priscilla Costello accepted the gold as winner in the first women's international épée event.

After that, Dev took a quick shower and changed. Splashy jungle flowers bloomed in tangerine and white across her cotton dress. A wide sash of solid tangerine around Dev's narrow waist and a set of small pearl earrings completed the effect. Dev did her best to coax her hair into a topknot, but as usual it slipped. Tendrils framed her face, and Dev gave the topknot one last annoyed glance before slipping into her white sandals and grabbing her small white purse. Cal was meeting her in the lobby. Then they would join everyone else for the dance to be held in another of the sumptuous ballrooms of Shangri-La.

Cal was doubly handsome in his tan slacks, pale-pink, long-sleeved shirt and sport jacket that matched the color of his hair. Her heart pounded when his gray gaze roved approvingly over her as she approached. Breathless, Dev found herself floating on a cloud of euphoria. Never had she felt more of a woman, responding to the maleness that Cal exuded. No matter what the future held for her, she wanted to complete her destiny with him. She knew in her heart it was much more than passion that simmered between them. Much more. And she refused to think about tomorrow morning. This one night, they would be like meteors flashing across the dark heavens, fleeting but brilliantly beautiful. Special moments were rare; Dev recognized what they shared was all that and more. She had never felt this way about a relationship before, always having believed that it took a good amount of time for one to blossom. But Cal had walked into her life and turned it upside down, showing her that time meant nothing. Nothing at all.

"LET'S TAKE CARE of that wrist," Cal said once they were in her room after the dance.

Dev licked her lips, her heart pounding in her breast. That wasn't a playboy's line. When she gazed up into his shadowed face, Dev saw he was serious. "Okay," she murmured.

Cal stopped at the bathroom and flipped on the light. "Better change first. I don't want to get any ointment on that pretty dress."

She halted, giving him a strange look.

"What's wrong, Dev?"

"Me," she admitted finally. And then went on in a hushed voice. "I know what's going to happen, and I'm so nervous and scared. I expected you to seduce me the instant we came into the room. . . ." Dev stole a painfully shy look up at him. "You really aren't the playboy you seemed the first night we met, are you?"

Cal rested his shoulder against the doorjamb; she was standing just inside the bathroom. He slipped his hands into the pockets of his slacks, studying her. "I kept telling you I wasn't, Dev. I get nervous and scared just like you," he admitted softly. "I find myself wanting to please you, to make you as happy as you've made me, so much so that I get sweaty feet."

Dev blinked. "Sweaty feet?"

"Yeah. You know, nerves. My hands don't get clammy, my feet do."

She relaxed, leaning against the other doorjamb, her eyes sparkling. "Cal Travis, you are so wonderfully human. Now I'm not afraid anymore."

"No sweaty feet, eh?"

She held up her hand. "Just a cranky wrist."

Cal nodded. "Hurry up and get changed, and we'll hot pack it and wrap it for the night."

Later, Dev sat obediently on the edge of the bed as Cal doctored her wrist. He had taken off the jacket, gotten rid of his tie and slipped out of the shoes. Dev was wearing her cool, cotton, floor-length granny gown sprigged with rosebuds. Her hair was still up in the loose topknot that refused to stay centered. And her body was tingling beneath Cal's hawklike perusal. What was he thinking? Dev wished she had brought something more sensuous along. But she had never expected to be going to bed with a man, either.

"Heat is bringing down the swelling," Cal murmured, interrupting her wandering thoughts.

"What? Oh, good. . . ." And Dev raised her chin, drowning in his dove-gray eyes that worshiped her. She saw his hint of a smile and wanted to lean over and kiss him.

"Did I tell you how beautiful you look? That nightgown makes you look old-fashioned."

She wrinkled her nose. "Not very exciting, I'm afraid," she said, her heart in her throat. "And I guess I'm like this nightgown in many ways. Not that my present situation proves that."

"I like you this way, my redheaded witch. You're like a breath of fresh air, did you know that? You don't wear any makeup, you're happy with who and what you've become. I like a woman who's confident of herself and her abilities. And my idea of sensual isn't a slinky black nightgown," he told her in a roughened voice, reaching up and gently loosening the bobby pins from her hair. In a few moments, the heavy silken strands fell in an auburn avalanche into his hands. A look of satisfaction crossed Cal's face as they settled gracefully around her shoulders and covered her breasts.

Her mouth became dry, a pulse leaping at the base of her throat as he caressed her slender neck.

"You affect me as strongly as I do you, Dev," he went on in a low, vibrating tone as his thumbs gently pulled her nightgown aside, exposing her collarbone.

Dev closed her eyes, lifting her chin. Cal leaned forward, placing moist kisses along the nape of her neck, then around to the base of her throat. Her flesh heated beneath his touch. "W-what do you mean?" she whispered.

He inhaled her sweet, feminine fragrance with the hint of jasmine, his tongue weaving wet patterns down toward the valley between her taut breasts. "You're in my blood. I can't think two single thoughts in a row without thinking of you, too. No woman has ever affected me like you do.... " Cal raised his head, his eyes turbulent as he carefully pulled the thin cotton gown downward, exposing her shoulders and beautifully formed breasts. Her lashes were auburn fans against her rose-flushed cheeks, her lips parted, her breathing rapid as the gown fell around her hips. "God," he breathed, spanning her delicate jaw with his hand, "you are perfect. Perfect for me.... "

Heat bolted through Dev as Cal's mouth caressed her lips; she was captured by him. The instant he drew her against him she lifted her arms, sliding them around his shoulders. Hungrily, he nipped and coaxed at her lips, sending pleasure prickling through her. Dev responded to the pressure of his worshipful kiss, giving him as much in return. A soft moan escaped her as his hands brushed the curves of her breasts, the nipples hardening beneath his skilled onslaught.

Dizzy with rapture, she felt him shift, urging her back on the bed. She raised her lashes, feeling delicious joy as Cal brought her beside him. With trembling fingers, she unbuttoned his shirt, exposing his chest taut with muscles. The dark hair was soft beneath her exploring hand, and she felt Cal tense as she brushed his flesh. Cal was primal. She felt the quiver of his tightly leashed body as his hand skimmed the flat of her belly, pushing the nightgown away from her and finally nudging it off her feet. Cal lay propped above her on one arm, studying her in the silence. He made her feel beautiful. And perfect. Even though she wasn't. The adoration and pride in his eyes made her want to cry. Finally, she understood just how much she had come to mean to him.

Cal dragged in a breath. "You're mine, Dev. You always have been," he whispered thickly, capturing her wet, pouty lips. She was as sweet as clover honey, her responses giving and unselfish. As he drank deeply of her lips and hardened nipples, Cal knew he had waited a lifetime for Dev. This was his woman. His. All of her. He shuddered as her hand slid inside his unbelted pants, then he froze. God, he wanted what they shared to be good for her. Cal clenched his teeth, crushing her possessively against him. He buried his face in the silken curls of her hair, gasping.

"Easy, honey. When you touch me like that, Dev... You know how much I want you, but don't push me over the edge. I want to please you first...." He was actually trembling. But giving her a reassuring kiss, he quickly got undressed and came to lie beside her. The instant the pliant softness of her flesh met the hard plane of his hips, Cal groaned. His blood boiled, his body throbbed in agony as her lips scalded his face, neck and chest. Slowly, she began a campaign to shatter the controls he had insisted on. He gripped her upper arms and gently forced her to lie down once more, positioning her beneath him. The love that Cal saw shining in her eyes almost reduced him to tears. She wanted to please him as much as he was pleasing her. It didn't matter to Dev who satisfied the other first.

Capturing her hands and placing them above her head, he held them gently beneath his fingers. "You are a witch," he groaned suggestively, running his hand down her firm, slender body. "You drug a man with your touch, your kisses."

Dev moaned as his hand grazed her leg, stroking the velvety inner thigh. Her lips parted when his weight settled upon her. She waited, screaming silently, wanting to complete their union on all levels. "Love me, Cal," she begged softly. "Just love me...."

Cal released her hands, lifting her hips slightly, and moved slowly into her dark, moist depths, another groan tearing from him. She felt so good...so alive. She was life, he thought dazedly as he froze with pleasure. He savored the tightness of her embracing him, and then he felt Dev tremble and grew concerned.

"Is something wrong?" he rasped.

Dev's lashes lifted. "I'm trembling because I've wanted you for so long, Cal. So long...." She reached up, her fingers caressing his sandpapery cheek. "As much as you want me, I want you—" He moved his hips and her words were strangled. Fire flared to life within her, and she arched, filling herself with all of him, all of his raw power that consumed her, devastated her with a joy she had never known existed.

He felt her shudder; her lashes dropped closed, her lips parted, and Cal knew he was giving her pleasure. She had offered herself to him in trust, finally, and now he was going to soar with her. Two unchained eagles reaching the very limits of the stratosphere where oxygen was sparse, where midnight fused with the azure of the sky. Each thrust of his hips took them higher and higher; Cal knew joy and completion as never before within Dev's loving vessel of a body. Each rhythmic thrust shattered another level of pleasure, and they soared ever upward, their bodies fused by indescribable heat....

7

CAL DREW DEV TO HIM, pulling up the covers to keep her from getting chilled. The soft smile on her well-kissed lips told him everything as she moved into his arms. Hair spilled across his glistening chest when she placed her head on his shoulder, her hand moving languidly across his torso.

"Is there such a thing as dying from happiness?" Dev whispered, nuzzling upward, placing a kiss on his strong jaw.

Cal closed his eyes, contentment washing over him. He ran his hand idly down her back. "If there is, we both came close to committing suicide."

"What a way to go," she agreed and sighed languorously. "You make me happy, Cal Travis."

"I know," he said thickly. "It's mutual, honey. You and I. We're good together." He caressed her shoulder, feeling its velvety pliancy. "But I knew we would be."

Dev laughed. "The voice of experience."

"Partly." Cal glanced down at her, his eyes a liquid gray. "But a feeling more than anything else," he admitted, kissing her damp cheek. "And that's what has me buffaloed about you."

She rose up on one arm, her hair framing her glowing face. She traced patterns across his dark-haired chest, delighting in the taut play of muscle beneath her fingertips. He was so male. So exciting. "What do you mean?"

He combed his fingers through her silken auburn mass. "You make me feel. I find myself responding to you more than to any other woman I've ever known."

"Oh, sounds bad, Travis," she teased throatily.

Cal grinned, gently pulling her down so that he could kiss her lips. She tasted salty and sweet, and she was warm and willing all over again. "Watch it," he warned darkly, releasing her.

"What's the matter, hasn't a woman ever given you sweaty feet before?"

"Plenty of carrier landings have, but never a woman."

Her look was one of exaggerated horror. "That means you're scared to death of me, Travis."

His gaze moved appreciatively from her slender throat to her breasts. "Scared? Yeah, I guess I am in a sense, or I wouldn't have gotten sweaty feet." And then he raised up and captured one budding pink nipple, pulling it into the moistness of his mouth. He heard Dev gasp with pleasure, melting within his embrace, her fingers curving against his flesh in response. God, she was so sensitive and easily pleased! Watchful of her left shoulder, Cal drew her down so that she fitted next to his body. He raised his head, a glitter in his gray eyes. "But not so scared as to let you walk away from me."

Dazed by the rekindled fire throbbing through her all over again, Dev murmured huskily, "There's nothing to fear about me. I'm a harmless rabbit, remember? You're the predator. The stalker."

"I am frightened, Dev," he said softly, running his hand down her responsive body in a worshipful gesture. "Frightened of how you make me feel. I keep asking myself how in the hell I'm going to live two months without you. Without your laughter or—" he touched her lips "—that wonderful smile."

Dev caught his hand. And that was simultaneously powerful and gentle. "If I told you I was scared, too, would it make you feel any better, Cal?"

One eyebrow rose slightly. "What are you afraid of?"

"You," she whispered. "And I've wondered how I'll survive two months without you, too."

"So I've finally convinced you that I'll see you after I get settled in at Edwards?" he teased.

"My heart believes you. My head doesn't."

Cal gathered her to him, kissing her lips, cheeks and eyes. "Don't listen to your head, Dev. If the past few days haven't proved I'll be there for you, nothing will."

"I know," she said in a small voice, holding him tightly. "But you know so little about me, Cal."

"Tell me about you," he urged huskily, the conversation with Jack Gordon coming back to him.

Dev felt the scalding tears beneath her lids. "You really want to know?"

"Everything about you interests me, Dev," Cal assured her. "What we've shared in bed has been good. But what we share outside the bedroom is equally important to me."

Dev tucked her head beneath his chin and began to talk. She told him something of what Jack Gordon had but avoided her own feelings about the past. The luminous dial on the clock read almost 4:00 A.M. when they finally fell into an exhausted sleep in each other's arms. One day, he prayed, she would have enough faith in him to tell the rest.

CAL AWOKE FIRST. He scowled as he read the dial on the clock: it was 8:00 A.M. Dev had to be at Kai Tak Airport by eleven. He shifted his awareness to her. She lay sprawled beside him, one arm and leg across him, her hair tickling his jaw. He lay very still, absorbing her gentle breathing, the moistness of her shallow breath on his upper chest and the slow, steady beat of her heart. Dev stirred, nuzzling like a kitten beneath his chin. Automatically, Cal caressed her arm in a motion meant to lull her back to sleep. "Cal?"

"Right here, honey. Try to go back to sleep," he urged softly.

"Mmmph."

A grin pulled at his mouth. "Did you say something?"

"I don't want to sleep," she mumbled, pulling her hand from across his chest and rubbing her puffy eyes.

Cal rose up on one elbow, studying her in the morning light. Her auburn hair curled in abandon around her face, bringing out the peach tone of her flesh and the rosy hue of her cheeks. He smiled tenderly and traced her brow, nose and lips. "Why don't you want to sleep?" he asked in a low, vibrating voice.

Her lashes rose. "Because I'm with you. I can't believe it. You're here. And you're real." She slid her hand up his arm. "I suppose it would go to your head if I told you you're the man I've always seen in my dreams." She sighed, content to revel in the caress of Cal's fingers brushing her cheek and neck.

"You have to be careful what you tell a jet jockey. They're pretty arrogant." He lowered his head, tasting the budding hardness of her pink-tipped nipples, feeling Dev respond by pressing her length against him. He sucked on each one, burying his head against her, aware of the wild fluttering of her heart.

Dev moaned, heat stealing quickly through her, creating an ache in her lower body. She ran her fingers through the thick silk of his hair, down his corded neck to his shoulders. There wasn't an inch of fat anywhere on him. She trembled as his tongue wove patterns across her belly. He made her feel wild and free, as if she could share all of herself with Cal. Another delicious shudder coursed through her when he skimmed the soft triangle of auburn hair with his tongue. His hand eased between her thighs, reaching the very center of her swollen femininity, and Dev gasped, a flurry of shocks licking through her. Her fingers stilled, her body arching suddenly as his tongue moved with molten impact on her. She called his name, once, twice, and then a hot lava flowed through her body.

Dazed by her own explosive pleasure, Dev was barely aware that Cal had knelt between her thighs, settling his hands on her hips, drawing her upward. Upward to couple hotly with him. She released a cry of utter pleasure, throwing back her head, the slender expanse of her throat exposed. She absorbed Cal's thrust, his body utterly male within her moist female confines, and heard him growl like the sensual animal he was to her. Each movement was deep, engulfing and branding. She was his!

Euphoria vibrated through Dev as she opened her arms to welcome him down on her glistening body, as his hips drove forward, propelling her to the rim of a tottering universe of pleasure. And when she stiffened against him, Cal gripped her hard, increasing the ache of pleasure until she thought she would faint . . . when the second climax shattered her into a million pieces in his arms. Only moments later, she heard Cal groan and held him, prolonging his pleasure as he had done unselfishly for her. And then Dev was falling, blissfully relaxed, into the safety of his arms. Close to his heavily thudding heart pressing against her breasts.

"You're . . . one hell of a lover." He breathed quickly. His arm rested wearily against her hip, and he nuzzled her hair. They lay in each other's arms, their bodies slick with sweat, weak with pleasure, their hearts pounding in unison. He caressed her cheek, his hand coming to rest on the curve of her neck. "I don't think I can wait two months to see you again. You're in my blood, Dev. In my soul."

"Not to mention your very loving body," she whispered, raising her chin to meet his lambent gray eyes. Dev drowned within the love she saw shining in them. The words "I love you" were there on her tongue. Begging to be said. But this was too soon. Their relationship hadn't stood the test of time.

"You're the one with the loving, giving body," Cal murmured, kissing the tip of her nose. Then he sobered, glancing at the clock whether he wanted to or not. "Listen to me," he said. "I want your address and phone number, Dev."

She nodded, licking her lower lip and not realizing how sensual the action appeared to Cal. "It's been my experience that men are lousy letter writers."

He grinned. "Ask my sister Storm if I write."

"And if I did, what would she say?"

He shrugged. "That I have two broken hands and haven't written to her in over a year."

"Cal! Your own sister. How could you?"

He grinned sheepishly, enjoying her vehemence. "My parents have come to expect phone calls from me when the carrier comes into port."

"And how often is that?"

"Depends. Every three, maybe six months."

Dev struggled into a sitting position. "That's inexcusable."

"Yeah, that's what Storm keeps telling me."

"Your sister's right." She gave him a dirty look. "And you're telling me you're going to write? Or are you warning me you have good intentions but will fall back into your evil ways, Travis?"

He ran his fingers down her slim arm. "I'll write," he promised, losing his teasing smile. "So that when you start getting my letters, you'll begin to understand that I'm serious where you're concerned."

Dev was silent, absorbing every nuance of Cal into her memory. Into her heart. In less than two hours, she would be leaving.

"Hey, what's this? Tears?"

She swallowed against them, avoiding his sharp gaze by turning her head away. "One thing you'll find out about me sooner or later is that I'm a sentimental slob. I cry at birthdays, weddings—you name it." Blinking away the tears, Dev lifted her head and looked at him. Cal's face expressed pain, and her heart lurched.

He cupped her face, his voice soft. "Just as long as you share your feelings with me, I don't mind if you cry."

"Really?"

"Really. Now come here, let me hold you for a little while longer. This has to last us two months...."

DEV STOOD WITH CAL'S ARM draped around her shoulder. They were in the lounge waiting for the boarding call. Cal was casually dressed in a pair of body-hugging jeans and a blue plaid shirt with the sleeves rolled up to his elbows. Her body tingled hotly from their recent lovemaking, yet Dev cast an anxious look up at him. Cal's expression was closed, just as it had been when they first met. Dev knew this was a mask to hide behind his real feelings whereas the pain of their imminent separation showed plainly on her face.

Jack Gordon had said hello to Cal once they had caught up with the main group of fencers waiting in the gate area. Blond-haired Sarah ogled him and gave Dev a brilliant smile. Now she felt Cal's fingers tracing patterns on her bare shoulder. She had worn a simple heather-colored sundress with spaghetti straps that tied at the nape of her neck. Cal turned and met her inquiring look.

"I'll be getting to Edwards by late December, Dev. The first thing I'll do is call and let you know I've arrived. The next thing I've got to do is drive down to Arizona and visit Chief's sister." His voice faltered, and pain shadowed his gray eyes. "I promised him I'd see her when I got to Edwards, and I want to tell her in person what happened to him."

Dev rested her head against his shoulder, sliding her arm around his waist. "I understand," she said softly.

"All Kaya got was a couple of officers going out to the reservation to notify her of her brother's death. They never gave her details. I want to do that."

She nodded, feeling his anguish. "I know she'll appreciate seeing you, Cal." Dev wet her lips. "W-would you like some company on that trip?" she asked shyly, thinking that Cal had been there for her throughout the week, tending her injuries. She could do no less for him. Only Chief's death was an injury to his heart and to the very core of his soul.

"It won't be pleasant, Dev. I'm not going to be in a good frame of mind. I don't know what the hell I'm going to say to her. Say something like, 'Well, I'm alive and Chief's dead. I'm sorry it wasn't me.'"

"No!" Dev whispered urgently, putting her arms around him. "Never say that, Cal. You're feeling guilty about something that was out of your control."

He shut his eyes, taking a deep breath, and rested his head against her brow. "I just needed a few more seconds, Dev. I had that damn lap belt almost sawed through. If the jet hadn't turned over, if—"

She pressed her fingers to the line of his tortured mouth. "Don't say that, Cal. My God, you could have been killed, too."

He raised his head, his eyes dark with memory. "I feel guilty about being alive, Dev."

With a low moan of despair, Dev gripped his shoulders, giving him a small shake. "If you hadn't survived, Cal, we'd never have met. I'd never have fallen in love with you—" Dev froze, the words out of her mouth, never to be taken back. Her heart plummeted as his eyes grew almost colorless. He stared uncomprehendingly down at her. His fingers dug almost painfully into her arms, and she bit back a cry, her blue eyes luminous.

"Northwest Orient Flight 254 now boarding," the announcer called, shattering the silence between them.

Dev uttered a little cry, trying to escape his grasp.

"No," Cal breathed softly, forcing her to look at him. "Dev . . ."

"I'm sorry, Cal. I didn't mean to say it. I—"

"But you did mean it? Dev?"

She looked at him through a blur of tears. "Yes." Oh, God, she had sealed her fate. By admitting her innermost feelings, she was scaring Cal off. Time. They needed time! Not her blathering! When would she *ever* think before she spoke? Misery flooded her. She couldn't stand the intense look in Cal's eyes.

"Hey, Dev! Come on!" Sarah called cheerfully from the boarding ramp.

Dev started to pull free to avoid Cal's shocked expression. "I'm sorry," she blurted out, moving to pick up her luggage. Before she could get to it, Cal neatly lifted her off her feet. Air rushed from Dev's lungs as he crushed her against him.

"I'm not," he whispered fiercely, his arms pinning her hard against his body. "Come here, Dev, I'm not letting you get away without a kiss," he growled.

Dev felt his hand capture her chin, tilting her head upward. Up to meet the molding strength of his mouth as it took hers in a kiss that left her knees jellied, her heart pounding and her hands damp. His mouth pressed insistently, fire igniting between them as she returned the plundering kiss. Her arms moved of their own accord, sliding across his broad, capable shoulders. Dev moaned as molten heat throbbed through her. When he released her, she blinked unsurely up at him while he kept his hands on her arms to steady her. He was smiling. A predatorlike smile that reminded her he was stalking once again. Stalking her. She touched her throbbing lips.

"Here," he said, digging out a gift-wrapped article from the pocket of his jeans. He pressed the gold-wrapped gift into her hand and then picked up her hand luggage, walking her to the ramp. "Open it when you get on board," he told her thickly. "Something to remember me, witch, because I'm coming back into your life."

She was barely coherent. Cal had kissed her with all the desire she knew he possessed. Dev looked down at the gift and then up at him.

"Thank you, Cal," she whispered tremulously. She closed her eyes as he tenderly caressed her cheek with his lips one last time.

"My address is in there along with the gift. Write to me. I promise I'll write to you." His gray eyes were unnaturally bright as he stared hard down at her, as if imprinting her face in his memory.

"Cal—I—"

"Don't be sorry," he said huskily, putting the strap over her shoulder. "Never apologize for being yourself, Dev. I don't ever want you any other way. I'll see you in two months. Count on it."

Those were his parting words. Somehow, Dev made it on watery knees to the airliner and found her assigned seat. Luckily, no one was sitting next to her because she needed to be alone. She needed time to think. And to feel. She sat with the gift held in her hands until the jet had taken off and was heading toward Japan. Slowly, she unwrapped the carefully folded foil. Had Cal wrapped it? Probably. He had told her at one time that the mark of a good test pilot was his attention to detail. The package had been wrapped to perfection.

Dev pried the small latch off the black velvet case. Her eyes widened. There in the center was a teardrop sapphire on a delicate gold chain. With trembling fingers, she picked up the necklace, staring at it. It was a small gem, flawlessly cut and beautifully set. Dev knew enough about gemstones to know that clear sapphires were worth a fortune. There was a neatly folded piece of paper in the bottom of the box that she thought was Cal's address at first. She put the necklace on and unfolded the hand-printed letter, penned on a piece of notebook paper torn from a binder.

Dear Dev: When I met you, I didn't want to live any-more. I had lost my best friend, and I felt as if a huge piece of me had just died with him. I no longer cared if I ever made it to test pilot school. I was ready to walk away from the greatest challenge. You see, all my life I've lived to achieve goals I've set for myself. What counted the most to me was getting rank, flying the hottest jets, getting top-slotted squadron assignments and finally, a chance at test pilot school.

Chief's death changed how I saw the world. Once I'd seen him drowning before my eyes, I never knew how much he meant to me until he slipped away.

If you were to ask which one of us was the injured one at the moment, I'd have to say it was me. I'm crippled emotionally, Dev. This week, you've taught me by sim-ply being yourself that it doesn't hurt to allow yourself to feel. You taught me that eloquent lesson the night I wept openly in your arms and you held me. It was the first time I've ever cried since I was eight years old.

There's so much I want to talk to you about. To ex-plore with you, Dev. I'm changing. I can feel it. I'm not too sure about the changes taking place in me, but I'm going to allow them to happen because you taught me that it's safe to feel. I noticed that none of the fencers ever wore any jewelry, but I wanted to give you something special. I chose the sapphire because it reminded me of your clear, smiling eyes. And the gold of the necklace represents the purity of your love that you give so ef-fortlessly from your heart. Wear it for us.

Your arrogant jet jockey,
Cal

"OKAY, THAT'S IT for this week," Dev told her panting troupe of little fencers. She smiled and set down her mask and foil. The ten eager youngsters made their way off the polished wood floor toward their parents waiting on the sidelines. Some of the children wore braces on their legs; others had cerebral palsy or were mentally handicapped. Pride shone in Dev's eyes as she covertly watched her charges, who were all wearing white fencing jackets. She knelt down to slip her foil back into the green canvas fencing bag.

"What do you think, Dad?" she asked, looking up at her father, who sat nearby. Darkly tanned with thinning brown hair, he was still healthy and fit.

Carl Hunter broke into a gratifying smile, his brown eyes twinkling. "I'd say they're coming along real well, Punkin. Terry's got more motion in his wrist. The parry exercise has loosened up his arm."

Dev put her mask and glove into the bag and zipped it up. "And did you notice how well Claire is coming along on her footwork? Last week, she was having trouble just keeping her balance. Now she's more confident."

Carl nodded, pleased. "One of these days, they'll have fencing events in the Olympics for the handicapped. And when they do, it will be your kids who'll win."

Standing, Dev smiled. Salle de L'Aigle was busy for a Tuesday night with fencers practicing in all three weapons. She heard Jack's voice punctuate the noise as he gave a lesson to Sarah on the finer points of *remise*. "It's not the winning, Dad, it's the getting there that's fun," she murmured. "Want to go home now, or do you feel like staying a bit longer?"

"I'll stay," he said with a wave of his hand. He came down once a week to the *salle* because he had never lost his love of the sport. And this was a special time he shared with Dev.

"Okay. I'm going to grab a quick shower and get back into street clothes."

"Great, Punkin. Then we'll go to our favorite café."

Dev nodded and smiled. "Sounds wonderful. I'll be back in about twenty minutes." She walked the perimeter of the well-lit *salle* that boasted one of the finest fencing floors in the United States. Her thoughts were balanced equally between her father and Cal. When a thrill arched through Dev, she acknowledged the source of that euphoric happiness. Automatically, she touched the hollow of her throat where the sapphire rested beneath the thick padding of her uniform.

Two months had seemed like two lifetimes. And yet Dev had been sustained by Cal's letters. All twenty of them. She smiled as she went to the women's locker room. Stripping out of her damp fencing jacket, knickers and socks, Dev allowed herself to center on Cal as she always did in quiet moments. The first letter she had received had been some twelve pages long, painstakingly printed neatly and legibly. Dev had sat in her apartment absorbing each word and each feeling behind what he had written. Typical of Cal, he had given a great deal of thought to his series of letters, telling her of his growing up years, his struggle to become a marine corps fighter pilot and the many incidents in between. Sometimes Dev howled with laughter over his letter. Other times, she found tears trickling down her cheeks. She received two letters close to Christmas, and she couldn't have wanted any other gift from him.

Turning on the shower, Dev stepped under the hot stream of water. Her letters to Cal were no less revealing. She wrote to him every night before she went to bed and felt as if she were still a part of his life even though he was on a carrier floating around the South China Sea. It would pull into the port of San Diego, and soon Cal would be released from his duty to begin the next phase of his career at Edwards.

Dev hurriedly washed her hair and stepped out of the shower. He hadn't been able to give her an exact date for when the ship would arrive except that it would be in a day or two. As the time drew near, she was barely able to cope with Tucker's quixotic moods at the television station or to focus on her work.

Slipping into her jeans and a midnight-blue sweater, Dev grabbed her canvas bag and left the locker room. She and her father would have their weekly pie and coffee at Mable's Café around the corner from the *salle*. This was a routine they had started when Jack had invited her to join the prestigious *salle*. Her father hadn't missed a Tuesday night's fencing in the past five years. Dev could always look over to see him there, watching her fence, pride glowing on his face. He'd root for her and call out encouragement. Between bouts, Dev would sit with him to discuss her style and what she was doing right or wrong. Yes, Tuesday nights were always special.

Dev bounded up the stairs two at a time, her damp hair curling around her shoulders. The blinding light made her squint momentarily, and Dev halted, looking for her father. She found him standing with Jack and—her heart slammed into her throat, beating wildly. Cal! It was Cal standing with the other two men, talking and smiling with them. She nearly dropped her canvas bag. He looked so good. And so tanned. A hundred impressions cartwheeled through Dev, along with overwhelming happiness. Cal wore a pair of charcoal-gray slacks the color of his eyes and a white, long-sleeved shirt with a light-blue sweater over it. He looked collegiate. He looked wonderful. As if sensing her presence, Cal lifted his head.

With a small cry, Dev dropped her bag and ran across the room. Cal's smile was warm with welcome as he met her halfway, arms open wide to receive her.

"Cal!" she cried, throwing her arms around him.

He whispered Dev's name, closing his eyes, feeling the soft yielding length of her body against him. He crushed her hard to him, inhaling her feminine scent, nuzzling into the silk of her damp hair. "I've missed the hell out of you, Dev."

She laughed, unable to keep her hands off him. "Oh, Cal. How? I thought you were going to call! I never expected to see you..." And Dev caressed his cheek, drinking in his smiling face. "You look wonderful," she quavered, tears brimming her wide eyes.

He laughed and leaned over, capturing her lips. She was like honey to his hungry mouth. Dev returned the fervor of his welcoming kiss, pressing the length of her body to him. Cal groaned and gently broke inches away from her wet, full lips. "And you look like my dream come true," he told her in a low growl. His eyes passed over her flushed face, down the length of her neck. There in the delicious hollow of her throat rested the sapphire necklace he'd given her. His hands caressed her strong back, coming to rest at her waist. "The carrier got in this morning. I cut some red tape and got my orders for Edwards early. Since I had to drive up through L.A. anyway, I figured I'd drop by and see you." He gave her a studiously careless smile. "You did want to see me, didn't you?"

Dev laughed and hugged him tightly. "You're such an arrogant jet jockey, Travis. When did you get to the *salle?*"

Cal reluctantly released her, still holding her hand. "You had just gone for your shower when I arrived. Coach Gordon recognized me and introduced me to your father. I like Carl Hunter. Almost as much as his daughter."

Tears of happiness came into her eyes. "He's been waiting to meet you."

"Come on." Cal put his arm around her shoulders. "This is a happy occasion. Carl invited me to come along with you for pie and ice cream. And frankly, I'm starved. I haven't eaten all day."

"You're right, this is a happy day." She hugged him again as they walked back to her father and Jack. "When do you have to leave for Edwards?" She hoped against hope that Cal could stay for a little while.

"I managed to wrangle a day of leave out of them. I don't have to report to Edwards until Thursday morning." His gray eyes glinted as he caught her surprised look. "And you'll call in to work tomorrow morning and tell them you're sick. You and I are going to have that day together," Cal promised softly.

Dev nodded. "The way Tucker's been acting, he deserves it."

Cal frowned as they stopped. "Has that idiot been putting you into dangerous situations?"

"He's just been a first-class boob lately. I can tell you more about it later." She looked up to see her father studying her intently. Then he awarded her one of the biggest smiles she had ever seen.

"Well, come on!" Carl urged. "Shall we get that pie and ice cream? Cal, you'll join us?"

Cal gave Dev a warming glance. "I was planning on it, Mr. Hunter."

"Carl. Call me Carl. Come on, you two young ones. We've got a lot to catch up on!"

IT WAS almost 10:00 P.M. when they arrived at Dev's apartment. With the advent of cloud cover in late December, the California night was damp, and she was chilled. Dev led Cal up the steps to the Spanish-style stucco apartments. Palm trees were silhouetted against the brilliance of Los Angeles to the southwest. That was the only thing Dev regretted: she could barely see the cape of stars overhead because of the profusion of light from the monstrous city.

"I'll bet you're tired," Dev said over her shoulder as they made their way down to the fourth apartment.

Cal came up behind her as she stopped and dug for the key. He moved her hair aside and kissed the nape of her neck. "A little," he admitted, watching her hand tremble as she placed the key in the lock. He smiled to himself. He liked to know he had affected Dev. "Actually, I'm starved."

Dev gave him a puzzled look and opened the door, stepping in and flipping on the lights. "You ate a huge meal at Mable's!"

Cal quietly closed the door behind him and pulled her into his arms. He nuzzled her delicate ear with his tongue and then placed several moist kisses down her neck, feeling her shiver against him. "Starved for you, Dev Hunter."

She dodged away from him, laughing. "You're impossible, Travis. Make yourself at home. The bedroom is on the left. You can put your bag in there or the bathroom. Take your pick."

The apartment reflected Dev and her tranquility, Cal thought as he ambled through the quiet confines. The white rattan furniture and hanging ferns represented a peacefulness he craved. Cal smiled as he halted at the door to her bedroom.

The other rooms indicated one facet of Dev, he decided. The bedroom shouted another: she was decidedly old-fashioned in private. The brass headboard and footboard were set off by the quaint flowered print on the double-ruffled bedspread. Cal set down his bag, strongly feeling Dev's presence in the room and wanting to share that romanticism with her alone. He quietly left and found her busy in the kitchen.

"How about a nightcap?" She turned, smiling up at him. "I usually make myself some tea and lace it with a tad of orange liqueur."

Cal walked over, sliding his arms around her waist and drawing her back against him. "Sounds good," he sighed.

"I can feel your heart," she whispered, closing her eyes and resting her head against his.

Cal rocked her gently. "Know what it's saying?" he asked, rubbing his cheek against her hair.

"What?"

"That it's been lonely. Missing you terribly."

Dev slid her fingers along his steel-corded forearms. "If you could feel my heart, it would be saying the same thing," she admitted softly, wrapped in the blanket of love that Cal folded so effortlessly around her.

"On the way up here, all I could think about was how you would feel in bed next to me. And now I'm content just to hold you. To have you near me. It's enough. It's everything."

Dev was touched by his admission. "That's a nice compliment to me. To us."

"I'm not going to keep my hands off you, however," Cal warned her in a low tone, pressing small kisses along her temple, which was feathered with auburn tendrils. "But for now, all I want to do is talk with you, hold you and hear your honey-rich voice pour over me."

She murmured something unintelligible as Cal's mouth traced a wet pattern around her earlobe. "That's all I want, too," Dev said a little breathlessly, "for now."

Cal grinned and reluctantly released her. He leaned against the drainboard and watched as Dev put the teakettle on the stove. Each movement was so graceful that he found it hard not to ask why she hadn't been a dancer. But then he recalled her episode with polio and knew the answer to that.

"Jack was saying that the international fencing meet in Hong Kong was so successful that there's going to be another one here in mid-April. Looks like you get to go up against Bianca again."

Dev flashed him a look, pouring the orange liqueur into china cups. "Hmph! This time it will be different." She held up her right wrist. "Look at it, Cal. Completely healed. Coach is amazed at what the Tiger Balm did."

Cal cradled her wrist in his hand, sliding the sleeve of her sweater up to get a better look at the injured area. His thumbs moved with expertise as he gently pushed and probed. "Just like new," he agreed and pulled the sleeve back down. "And just in time to beat Bianca."

Coming to rest her head on Cal's shoulder, she felt his arm go around her. "The coach has high hopes that I'll take first. But we're getting women épée fencers from Hungary, and in case you didn't know, Hungarian fencers are known to be some of the best in the world."

He squeezed her. "You'll do it because you're championship material, Dev. Besides, I'll be there to cheer you on."

She gazed up at him. "You mean that?"

Cal uttered an expletive. "Do I mean that? Of course I do. Did you think that just because I'm an hour and a half away, I'd only drive down to see you once a month or something?"

Drowning in the gruff warmth of his voice, Dev shrugged. "Well, I didn't know, Cal. I know we've shared letters, but..."

He gripped her shoulders, giving her a small shake. "But what?"

"Well, I never want to take what we share for granted, Cal. I don't want to assume anything. Sure, I'd love to see you every chance we get." Dev licked her lower lip. "There's a difference between my wishes for us and reality. It's not fair to you to demand so much of you."

"It's not fair to us that we'll have so little time," he countered. "I can't promise that I'll see you every weekend, Dev. School is going to be a royal bitch. Twenty-five applicants from around the world were chosen to compete against each other for forty-two weeks. My grades determine whether or not I'll get a shot at that new jet they'll be testing for the navy at Edwards late next year." His arms tightened around her. "I'm going to have to live at the bachelor officer's quarters at the base. And when I'm not pulling test flights, I'll be studying until my eyes cross."

"Well," she murmured, "your schooling comes first."

Cal released her as the teakettle began to whistle shrilly. "Maybe."

Dev prepared the tea, then took the tray into the living room where they sat down next to each other on the rattan couch. "Your letters have told me a lot," she said, tucking her coltish legs beneath her. Dev sipped the fragrant tea with relish as she watched him through her thick lashes. Cal nudged off his shoes and placed an arm behind her, balancing his tea on his crossed leg. "And I think I'm beginning to understand how much becoming a test pilot means to you."

"You never did say anything about that note I enclosed with the necklace, Dev." Cal's expression was thoughtful.

"I—I know."

"I bared my soul to you," he admitted ruefully. "As a matter of fact, I've never been so honest with another person in my entire life. Not with Chief. Not even with Storm or my brother Matt."

Dev slid her hand down the hard length of his thigh. "I know you did," she said, "and I sat there crying because you had. That letter touched me like no other, Cal, because I know you were being brutally honest with me. About yourself, how you saw your life changing before your eyes." Dev shrugged helplessly. "I couldn't answer that letter because I wanted to see you in person to discuss it. You deserved nothing less than that."

He nodded, staring darkly down at the rug. "I thought it might scare you off. I didn't know." And then he smiled slightly as he risked a look at Dev. "I guess I've always been a test pilot in some ways, trying new things and pushing back some borders that might not want to be pushed back. But I've never taken chances with people. It's an entirely new experience for me."

"I see," she murmured. "Test pilots risk physically. You took an emotional risk by being honest with me, Cal. Is that another one of your new traits surfacing?"

He shook his head, his brow wrinkling as he sought her compassionate blue eyes. Eyes that he could drown in for the rest of his life. "If you want the truth, Dev, that was the first time in my life that I've put myself on the line with a woman." His voice lowered. "Last year, my brother Matt was shot in an undercover FBI case. I got called from the carrier to fly to Houston: he was in critical condition in the hospital. When I arrived, Dev, I've never felt so damn helpless. If it hadn't been for Kai Eastman, the woman who had been kidnapped and protected by Matt, I don't know what I would have done."

"Why, Cal?"

Just the husky richness of Dev's voice made it easier for him to hold her unwavering gaze. "Matt had sustained a bullet wound to his skull. When I got there, the doctor said he didn't know if he would live or die. I was the only family member present. Our parents were out of the country in a remote area of Australia on vacation, and they couldn't be reached. Storm and her husband Bram made it up the next morning from Florida." Cal's shoulders sagged. "After the doctors said that Matt might remain in a coma for the rest of his life, everyone was looking at me to make a decision. The doctors wanted to know what they should do." He placed the cup on the coffee table, his face twisted in pain. "I was ready to abandon him to some empty hospital room, to be kept alive with an array of tubes and needles stuck in him. Kai, who had suffered through the trauma of the kidnapping, came forward and volunteered to take Matt to her father's ranch and try to help him. She was a physiotherapist in the U.S. Navy and had had quite a bit of experience with military men with similar injuries."

Cal clasped his hands between his thighs. "Kai had to beg me to release Matt to her care. I had already given up on him. I had told her the day before that I felt some battles in life were just too big to fight. I felt it was acceptable to back away from them. And I was backing away from my responsibility as the oldest family member." He shook his head. "My own brother, for God's sake."

"You haven't told me a lot about your brother, Cal," Dev said softly, encouraging him to go on.

"Matt was the complete opposite of me, Dev, all the time we were growing up. I was high school football captain and an all-American in college. Matt was quiet, sensitive. He collected silly weeds that he called herbs. Kai taught me a real lesson. She took Matt to the ranch, cared for him and eventually he regained consciousness. She nursed him back to health. After he'd fully recovered, they got married. Now they're expecting their first child." His tone turned bitter. "If Kai hadn't been there, Matt would have rotted like a vegetable and died. I was a coward, Dev. I sidestepped an obligation to someone I love very much because I was frightened of what demands might be made on me. I'll never forgive myself for that, even though I know Matt has." Cal's eyes were tortured as he held her shimmering gaze. "That's why I'm not backing down where you're concerned." He reached out, his fingers entwining with hers. "I'm in love with you, Dev. And I'm scared to death."

Dev stood up, placing her cup and saucer on the table. She held out her hand to Cal.

"Come to bed with me," she coaxed softly.

8

WITHOUT A WORD, Cal followed Dev down the dimly lit hall to her bedroom. She shut the door and slowly turned to him, placing her hands on his chest, searching his ravaged face. Cal was so vulnerable and hurting. And she felt like crying. But right now he didn't need her tears; he needed her strength and love. Moonlight spilled like molten silver between the priscilla curtains, giving the room a translucent glow. Dev unbuttoned his shirt, gently pushing the fabric off his broad shoulders, allowing it to drop to the wooden floor. She tilted her head, meeting his dark, stormy eyes.

"I love you, Cal," she said huskily. "And I'm frightened, too. But not of taking the emotional responsibility like you are. I'm afraid because I do love you, and you can hurt me more than I've ever been hurt by anyone in my entire life...."

Cal gently cupped her face and leaned down, seeking her lips. A groan started low and deep inside him as her lips softened beneath his hungry assault, opened to allow him entrance into her moist depths. She trusted him, was giving herself to him. When she swayed unsteadily, he felt such an incredible ache in his chest as if he loved Dev too much and would die from the joy he felt at being with her once again. "God," Cal breathed raggedly, "I've missed you, Dev. Missed your voice... your sweet kisses...."

Dev felt herself being lifted, and she placed her arms around his naked shoulders, content to be carried to the bed. Their bed. After he had gently deposited her on the bed and undressed her and then himself, Dev welcomed him into her arms. They lay quietly beside each other, sharing what was more than just physical intimacy. Cal's heart beat like a hammer against her breasts as he tenderly kissed her brow, her eyelids and her cheeks, his breath moist on her flesh. She skimmed her fingers across his back, taking pleasure in his lean, hard physique. Lifting her lashes, she stared up into his eyes. Cal's feelings were no longer masked, hidden from her. His mouth was turned softly upward at the corners, the naked hunger in his eyes for her alone, his facial muscles relaxed. Dev caressed his face as if he were a priceless work of art.

"Chief's death brought you new life, Cal," she began quietly. "He has made you aware that experiencing your human and emotional side is equally as important as rising to all the challenges." Pressing a kiss to his mouth, she felt his heated response. "If Matt were injured now, you wouldn't run away like you did before."

Cal stared off into the shadows of the room for a long minute, digesting her comment. "I don't know. I'd be damned uncomfortable, and I'd try to do what was right...."

Her lips parted in a tender smile. "I love you for what you are and for what you're trying to become, Cal."

He buried his face in her neck, inhaling the jasmine scent of her. "What I've become is very shaky about everything." He muffled a laugh, kissing the hollow of her throat where the sapphire lay. "Test pilot school looks like a piece of cake compared to everything else I'm experiencing. Hell, testing is black and white. People, well, they aren't black and white, are they?"

Dev gently pressed him back on the bed, propped herself up on one elbow and ran her fingers over his magnificent chest. "We people whom you've managed to sidestep for so long aren't like Gordian knots, either, Cal."

He stared at her. "But women are complex."

She chortled softly. "As if men aren't. Cal," Dev breathed, pressing herself to him, her voice low and urgent, "men and women both have hearts that feel and heads that think. One sex is no less complicated than the other."

He grinned carelessly, combing his fingers through that unruly mass of auburn hair that delighted him so. "Well, let's just say some of the plumbing is different. Other than a few blueprint changes in anatomy, I agree with your premise."

"You're incorrigible, Travis!"

He reached up and pulled her on top of him. A shudder of need boiled through him as her hip rested against his hardness. "But not impossible." He drew her forward. "Am I?" His mouth teasingly met Dev's parted, glistening lips.

Dev moaned, lost in the moment. His hands freed her face and moved downward to caress her breasts, making desire explode through her. Lost in his seduction, Dev barely realized that he was lifting her. Hot pleasure shafted through her . . . gently he slid into her moist, welcoming depths. She arched upward, her back a taut bow, a soft gleam to her flesh as he gripped her hips. A whimper broke from her throat as he moved his hips upward, slipping deeply into her.

Dev had missed Cal terribly, had missed the utter maleness he exuded. She gave herself to him, allowing him to orchestrate and choreograph each heightened, melting movement.

"Yes," he said hoarsely, watching as pleasure flowed across her face, her eyes softly shut. "Feel me, Dev. Feel my love for you. . . ."

Her arms stretched outward, fingertips barely raking his chest as he increased the pressure, moving his hips to give her the ultimate in mindless pleasure. A cry tore from her; she stiffened against his supporting hands. And then Cal relinquished control over his own burning body and released fire deep within her.

Minutes later, Dev groaned softly, falling weakly against Cal's body, her hair a silken carpet against the darker hair of his chest. Her breath came in small gasps as she lay there. Cal smiled into the darkness, running his splayed fingers up and down her damp back, willing her to relax totally in the aftermath. Her heart was beating wildly, and he turned his head, kissing her brow.

"Oh, Cal," she whispered, "I've missed you so much."

"I can tell," he assured her thickly. "But I'm here now. From now on, you'll see me in person, or I'll be talking to you on the phone."

"Do you know something?" she asked in a wisp of a voice.

"What, honey?"

"I'm so glad you're here, Cal. My dad—" And she couldn't finish.

Cal gently dislodged Dev, fitting her beside him, his eyes dark with concern.

"Is something wrong with him?"

"No. It's just that he's so high on this international fencing meet. I want to win the gold for him. I know how much it would mean to him."

"I know it would, Dev," he soothed quietly, pressing small kisses to her cheek. "But don't let him pressure you too much. All you can do is your best. No matter what happens, I'll be here to help you. Do you hear me?"

A strangled sob tore from her. "Dad and Mom were the first ones to ever care about me, Cal. They saw this freckle-faced kid in pigtails and leg braces and decided to make her a part of the family. I had never allowed myself to love as a child because everything was taken away from me. They taught me that love is giving and asks no return. Dad got me started in fencing. He gave me a reason to live, Cal. He gave me back my dignity."

Dev lay back, her cheeks wet with tears, eyes dark with memories as she looked up into Cal's shadowed face. "Mom died when I was twelve, and I saw a part of Dad die with her. I tried to make up for the loss, to make him happy again. I love him so much and—and I won't ever be able to love him enough in return for all he's given me. He wants to see me win so badly, and I'm afraid I'll disappoint him. He's the most wonderful man I've ever known besides you."

Cal felt a very real pain in his chest. He felt so damn helpless as he gathered her back into his arms. As helpless as when Matt had lain in a coma. What words could he give Dev to help comfort her? Why hadn't he ever paid attention to how people cared for each other in crises? Because, Cal thought rawly, he had ignored or turned away from those who were experiencing pain. Well, now it was different. He loved Dev. And he wanted to give her support for the forthcoming meet.

"Listen to me, honey. I know your father realizes how much you love him. When I walked into the *salle* tonight and saw him sitting there, he looked so damned happy. And after Jack introduced us, he got the biggest smile on his face. Carl gripped my arm and told me how courageous you were, how you had fought to overcome polio and had ended up blazing new trails for all women in fencing." Cal kissed her cheek, his voice barely audible. "When you walked out of the locker room, it was your dad who saw you first. You should have heard the tone in his voice, Dev, when he told me you were standing there across the fencing floor. He's proud of you, honey." Cal held Dev in a tight embrace, his lips near her ear. "You're his legacy, Dev. Don't you realize that? You're a continuation of Carl Hunter's dreams that he couldn't fulfill himself. You've helped him realize them by being all that you can be. Don't worry, honey, he knows how much you love him."

Dev sniffed, all the anxiety she had held in so long washed away with her tears. Cal's chest and shoulders were wet, but he didn't seem to mind as he continued to stroke her shoulders and back. Slowly, she pulled out of his embrace and sat up, wiping her cheeks dry. Dev reached out, her hand on Cal's chest. "You have a beautiful way with words, Cal," she whispered, her eyes dark sapphires. "Thank you. . . ."

He frowned, capturing her fingers against her chest. "The words come hard, Dev. We'll take that hurdle together. I'll try to be there for you. I promise." He kissed each of her fingers, wanting to absorb her pain and remove it.

Dev managed a smile, her fingers tingling pleasantly. "You've already given me more than I'd hoped for, Cal."

"Come on," he told her huskily, "let's get up and take a shower together. Then we'll call it a night."

THE INSISTENT RINGING OF THE PHONE woke them the next morning. Cal groaned, flinging his arms across his eyes, the sunlight blindingly bright through the windows. Dev mumbled something, rolling away from the warmth of Cal's body and groping for the phone.

"Mmmph?"

Cal raised his arm, a slow grin spreading across his mouth as he watched Dev grapple with waking up. She looked glorious with the golden sunshine bathing her tanned body and auburn hair. This was what he wanted, he thought drowsily. To wake up every morning with Dev in his arms. In his bed. Sharing the love that burned brightly between them. Sharing all their fears and laughter.

"Who? Oh . . . hi, Dad. Uh, no . . . that's okay, I'm waking up," Dev mumbled, her voice husky with sleep. "Dinner? Just a minute, I'll ask him." She turned over on her back, looking at Cal. "Want to have dinner at my dad's home tonight?"

"Sounds good." Then he grinned boyishly. "Your father a good cook?"

Dev gave him an arch look and ignored his baiting, turning back to talk with her father.

Cal reached out, running his hand over her hip, thinking how beautifully she was built. Dev hung up the phone and rolled back over, her eyes still puffy with sleep.

"'Your father a good cook?'" she mimicked. "I could strangle you, Travis."

His grin broadened, and he pulled Dev back into his arms, liking the way her soft curves fitted against the hard planes of his body. "Is he?"

Dev gave him a playful jab in the arm. "Of all the . . . of course he is!"

"Never could turn down a home-cooked meal."

"I ought to cook your goose, Travis, for all these smart-mouthed cracks so early in the morning." She pouted playfully, leaning down and running her tongue tantalizingly across his lower lip.

"Watch it, witch, or I'll jump your bones," Cal growled, his fingers splayed across her back, pressing her against him.

"Jump my bones," she taunted softly, giggling. "Am I going to have to get used to all your perverted marine corps slang?"

Cal tried to look properly wounded, but it didn't quite come off. Dev slid out of his grasp and got up, slipping on a silky lavender robe that lovingly caressed every curve of her body. Fire burned in Cal's eyes as he watched her sit down at the vanity and struggle to tame her hair.

"I'm not perverted," he insisted, sitting up and placing a pillow behind him. She looked beautiful. He simply soaked up each of Dev's graceful movements as she coaxed her hair into a Gibson girl.

Dev laughed throatily, staring at his reflection in the mirror. She wanted to tell Cal how masculine and sensually appealing he was to her, the light-blue sheet draped low around his waist, his bronzed chest darker still with its covering of hair. In her eyes, he was dangerous and exciting. The shadow of a beard only emphasized his lean, hawklike features, and Dev's heart swelled in her breast. "I suppose you're going to tell me you were an innocent babe until the marine corps got hold of you."

Cal grinned slowly, placing his hands behind his head. "The corps doesn't exactly take an innocent approach while molding men into soldiers, you know."

Dev added two more bobby pins to the mass of hair. "I keep seeing magazine ads. They're always looking for good men, it seems."

"Not to mention some good-looking women."

"You're still a chauvinist of the worst sort, Travis," she muttered, standing up.

"But you love me that way."

Dev turned, putting her hands on her hips. "I'll have to admit it was nice to feel protected by you. I thought you were going to throw a punch at Bianca when she broke that blade against me."

Cal scowled. "I gave it serious thought."

"Good thing you didn't. It would have caused an international incident. Can you see the worldwide headlines now: Marine Nails Italian Fencer." She went to sit on the edge of the bed. Cal was a feast to her eyes, and the way his gray gaze roved hotly over her body made her feel deliciously female.

Cal chuckled. "The scandal would have been the end of my career."

Dev chuckled with him, then asked, "Feel like some breakfast? It's nine o'clock. I was supposed to be at the station at ten. I'll give them a call and tell them how sick I am."

He captured her hand. "I'm starved."

"No secret how a woman gets to you, Travis—through that stomach of yours that has a hole in it."

"I'm still a growing boy," he protested.

"I'll agree to the boy part." Dev laughed, rising. "Come on out when you want. I'll fix us some coffee first and then put on some eggs and bacon."

Cal reluctantly released her hand, thinking he wanted to pull her back onto the bed and love her all over again. "See you in a few minutes, witch."

THE INTIMACY REMAINED strong between them after breakfast as they enjoyed a second cup of coffee. Dev was nestled between Cal's legs; she was a floor sitter by nature. She leaned back against his strong thighs, content as never before.

"I think I'm in heaven, Cal Travis," she murmured, opening her eyes and tilting her head back to look up at him.

He grazed her flushed cheek with his knuckles. "We both are. I just wish someone had told me that falling in love was going to feel this good. I'd have done it a long time ago."

Dev curbed a smile and paid attention to her coffee. She had pulled open the pale-green drapes earlier, and they could see that the last day of the year was going to be sunny with an azure sky. The palms waved gently in the inconstant morning breeze, mirroring Dev's lazy contentment. She slid her hand across Cal's knee.

"When are you planning to go see Chief's sister?" she asked softly.

"I called her as soon as I got off the ship. She said it wasn't necessary that I come visit her."

Dev twisted to look up at him. "Is she bitter?"

He shook his head. "No. Chief discussed some of his ideas with me. They don't share our Western belief in heaven and hell. Kaya thanked me for the offer, but she said that as far as she was concerned, Chief was still living, just in a different state."

Dev saw the bewilderment on Cal's face. She set her coffee aside. "What is it?" she probed.

"It was the damnedest thing, Dev. Everything got reversed. Instead of me consoling her, she was consoling me. I must have spent close to an hour on the phone with Kaya. I told her everything about the crash. How I missed Chief." He gave her a wry glance. "I got off the phone feeling better, but don't ask me how it happened."

Kneeling in front of Cal, Dev placed her hands around his neck and embraced him. "I think it was a beautiful gesture on Kaya's part."

Cal nuzzled her hair, kissing her neck. "She told me to go on living, to hold the memory of Chief in my heart and to work through my grief."

"She's right, darling. Tomorrow you start a whole new chapter in your life."

Cal wrapped his arms around her slender waist, drawing Dev solidly against him. "I started that new chapter in my life when I met you," he whispered, seeking and finding her welcoming lips.

THE LATE JANUARY WEATHER at Edwards had turned ugly. First sleet and ice swept across the Mojave Desert, nearly paralyzing activity. Two feet of snow followed, causing chaos. Cal found out later that it never snowed at Edwards as a rule. Just his luck, he decided. With flights canceled and only so much homework that could be assigned along with his ground duties, Cal managed to slip free the third weekend, negotiating the tortuous drive out of the desert in his silver Corvette. It was close to noon before he arrived at Dev's apartment. A one-and-a-half-hour trip had taken four hours. Hours stolen from them. Cal wasn't in a very good mood when he knocked at her apartment door.

The door flew open, and she gave a little cry, throwing her arms around him like an exuberant child. All grouchiness and tension flowed out of him as she smothered him with kisses. Cal found himself laughing, holding her tightly to him, starved for the warm, curved softness of her body against his. He managed to shut the door before Dev attacked him again.

"Oh, Cal!" she said with a gasp, holding him at arm's length, her eyes dancing with happiness. But some of her joy dissipated as she studied him closely. "You've lost weight! You look terrible."

"Thanks one hell of a lot," he said, grinning. He recaptured her, pulling her to him. "All I need is you. Now come here and quit telling me how bad I look. You look damn good."

Dev buried herself in Cal's arms, pressing the length of her body against him, wildly aware of his arousal. "But look at you! Haven't you been eating? I know you said it was a rough school, but I never realized..." she said lamely, placing warm, moist kisses the length of his jawline, then meeting his hungry mouth as it seared hers. Further exclamations of anxiety were smothered by his mouth drinking deeply of her. Dev moaned, allowing him to take her full weight.

Gradually, Cal released Dev, absorbing her beauty, her vulnerable upturned face and moist lips. "How have you grown more beautiful?" he asked huskily, combing his fingers through her hair.

Dev smiled, unable to keep her hands off him. "I think you've been on the military reservation too long, Travis. What's the matter, aren't there any women up there?"

"Sure there are. We've even got two women flight engineers in our class. But—" he pressed his mouth to hers, taking small sips from her lower lip "—they aren't as beautiful as you."

"You're underweight," she murmured, running her hands knowingly down his torso.

Cal straightened and gave her an aggravated look. "It's been three weeks since I last held you, and all you worry about is the few pounds I've lost. Why don't you tell me how much you've missed me, witch? How lonely you are in bed at night without me being there? That you're glad to see me?" he teased.

"Oh, I do. I mean, I am." Dev pulled out of his embrace, grabbing his hand. "Come into the kitchen. I just finished making a pot of vegetable beef soup. I'll fix you some biscuits and stuff you."

"I'm not a turkey, Dev." Cal's gray eyes warmed as Dev practically dragged him into the sunny kitchen. She was wearing a pale-pink sweater that brought out the natural rose color of her cheeks and cranberry slacks that fit her tall, loving body to perfection. Dev fussed over him like a mother hen, but Cal was grateful for her care and attention. After consuming two bowls of the meaty soup and six biscuits, Cal thought he might live. Then Dev shooed him into the living room, bringing him a thick slice of homemade cherry pie topped with ice cream and a cup of freshly brewed coffee.

Cal groaned and rolled his eyes as she set the dessert down on the coffee table in front of him. Dev made herself comfortable on the floor, facing him.

"God, Dev, I am stuffed. Like a turkey."

She smiled happily, attacking her pie and ice cream with relish. "So eat. You've lost at least ten pounds, Cal Travis, and I'm not letting you go back to Edwards until you gain some of it back."

Cal picked up the plate and began to nibble at the pie. "It's good."

Dev snorted. "Why do you look so surprised? Do I appear to be the kind of woman who can't be good at home as well as at work?"

He winked. "You're good all right."

"Pervert."

"With you I am."

Dev's eyes were flecked with gold as she held his warming gaze. "How have you gotten more handsome since I saw you last?"

He shrugged. "I shouldn't be. If I don't have dark circles under my eyes, I ought to. I knew TPS was going to be rough, but it's damn near brutal."

She sobered and stopped eating. "In what way, Cal?"

"I fly every morning. At least we did until that storm hit. Right now, Edwards is shut down for all intents and purposes."

"Fly for how long?"

"It's not the amount of time, Dev. Each flight is a test flight, with an instructor sitting behind you or beside you, grading you. By noon each day, we're on the ground, and all afternoon is spent with heavy aerodynamics, math that's a bitch and computer programming." He shook his head. "TPS reminds me of going for a doctorate—it's sheer hell. The tension never eases. Someone is constantly monitoring you, if not your flight skills, your grades on the daily tests. The cutting edge is the competition among all the students. How good your grades are determine whether you're going to get a test pilot assignment after graduating."

"How are you doing, then?" Dev toyed with her coffee cup, watching him closely. Cal had wanted test pilot status so badly. It was such a rarefied vocation; only the best were selected.

"So far, I'm fifth in the standings."

"Well, that's wonderful!" Dev cried. "I'm so proud of you!"

Cal had the good grace to flush at her bubbling enthusiasm. "You're such a child. What am I going to do with you?"

Dev gave him a mischievous grin. "Take me to bed later and make love with me?"

"That's the real dessert," he baited her, meeting her heart-stealing smile.

"So don't you think that some of this stress will ease as you get used to the way TPS runs?"

"More than likely," he agreed. He lifted his head. "How's Carl?" In their phone calls to each other, he had to pull information from Dev as to whether her father was still pressuring her about the meet.

"He's fine," she said, putting aside the pie.

Stepping around the coffee table, Cal took Dev in his arms, gently holding her.

"Come on," he murmured. "I want to be near you."

She leaned into his strong, seemingly inexhaustible body. "Hold me, Cal. Just hold me. . . ."

"Forever," he whispered huskily, closing his eyes. They stood in each other's arms for long minutes before Dev raised her head from his chest.

"You know something?" he asked, kissing her temple.

"What?"

"I love you. Every day that goes by, Dev, you own a larger piece of my heart. Every split second that I don't have to focus on flying or on studies, I'm thinking of you. Of us. And when I get back to quarters in the late afternoon, I find myself dreaming that you'll be there, waiting for me."

"You're a glutton for punishment, then," she said, the words muffled against his chest, "when we can't be together nearly enough. As for me, I'm so jumpy about this upcoming meet. My moods are continually up and down."

"I love every one of your moods, Dev."

"But I'm rotten to be around. Just ask Tucker. At work, I snarl back at him. He says I've turned into a bitch. When I get home, Lord knows what hour sometimes, I'm depressed. It's a good thing I don't own an animal, or I'd probably drop-kick it off the balcony."

Cal laughed softly, gently lifting Dev's chin with his hand. "You wouldn't hurt any animal. It isn't in your nature."

"No, I guess you're right," Dev muttered. "I'm so glad you're here. . . ."

He nodded, the smile fading from his lips. "I'll come down more often, Dev," he promised.

"Don't, Cal. That school is murdering you. You can't afford to take any more weekends off than—"

"Hush," he ordered sternly, silencing her with a kiss. When he gently broke contact, he said, "I learned one of the most important lessons of my life three months ago, Dev. I discovered people were more important than a goal." He ran his fingers down her back. "You're important. But don't worry, I'll hang in there with TPS."

Her expression was anguished. "But you can't let your grades drop, Cal. Not if you want a chance to stay at Edwards after graduating and test that new navy plane."

He swore under his breath and swept Dev off her feet into his arms. "Are all witches as stubborn and single-minded as you?" he demanded, walking toward the bedroom.

Dev gave up, relaxing in his arms, content just to be near him. "I don't know," she said wearily. And then, "Cal?"

"If this is another protest, shut your pretty mouth," he growled, pushing open the bedroom door.

"It's not."

"What is it, then?"

"I love you."

"I know you do. . . ."

9

"HEY, HUNTER!" Tucker craned his neck, looking first right, then left as he stood in the doorway to the studio. His blond brows fell in aggravation. "Damn it," he muttered. "She's never around when I need her." Grumbling for probably the hundredth time that camera*men* were more reliable, he shoved through the door of the television studio, watching his step as he walked over the snakelike cables strewn across the concrete floor. "Probably powdering her nose...."

"What'dja say, Tuck?"

Tucker shoved his hands in the pocket of his neatly pressed tan slacks, glaring at Brent Carney. "Oh, nothing. Just talking to myself. You seen Hunter?"

Brent gently moved the huge camera around on its wheels. "I think she's with Jeff, over in editing."

Looking at his watch, Tucker took off in that direction. He jerked open the door opposite the one he had come in.

"There you are."

Dev lifted her head. She and Jeff were looking at some recently shot film. Automatically, Dev tensed at the thundercloud look on Tucker's round, moonlike face. The phrase "pretty boy" should have been coined for him. "What's up?"

"Damn it, Hunter, I wish you'd hang around. We've got the chopper warming up out back. Grab your gear and let's get going."

Jeff gave Dev an apologetic look. A look that spoke volumes. Dev patted Jeff's shoulder. "Okay, Tucker. I'll be right there. Jeff, thanks. I'll see you later."

"Sure thing, Dev."

She ignored Tucker's narrowed brown gaze, walking past him. The morning wasn't starting off right. As usual. Dev tried to release her dislike of Tucker, concentrating instead on the assignment. Taking out the helicopter meant it was something big. Of course Tucker would rant, rave and plead with the editorial director to get the lead spot on the five o'clock news. Competitive was Tucker's middle name. She glanced at her watch: 11:00 A.M.

"Come on!" Tucker barked over the slow wash of the helicopter blades.

Dev glared at him. For all of his hurry, Tucker didn't lift a finger to help her with the minicamera or shoulder case. No, Tucker was *the* reporter. He considered her little more than necessary baggage. With emphasis on the word "baggage." Dev carefully stowed her gear and climbed aboard, sliding the helicopter door shut and locking it. Grabbing a pair of earphones, she plugged them into a jack as the chopper lifted into the brilliant blue California sky.

"Where are we going, Tucker?"

Tucker sat in the copilot's seat. Without so much as looking around, he adjusted the lip mike. "Edwards Air Force Base. Got a big story up there."

Edwards! Dev's heart beat faster. Cal's base. "What's going on?"

"Got seven busloads of protestors lined up at the main gate in a Mexican standoff with the base's military police. They're trying to take a coffin onto the base to protest MX missiles." He rubbed his hands together. "And guess who's heading up that group?"

"Who?"

"Dave Barstow. He's the most aggressive of all the peace demonstrators. If we get lucky, maybe we'll catch him going after the air police. Damn, this could turn out to be one hell of a story!"

Dev sat back, compressing her lips. She would never understand Tucker's excitement over potential violence. The more danger and action there was, the more Tucker turned into an aggressive, elbowing reporter. His attitude left a sick feeling in the pit of her stomach.

Would Cal hear of the demonstration? She frowned. His school sat only four miles from the main gate. He wasn't very happy about her job anyway, so this particular assignment would hardly thrill him. Her palms grew damp, and she rubbed them along her thighs, praying that the demonstration would be peaceful and that Cal would never know what had gone on.

"HEY, WORD HAS IT we've got a confrontation going on at the main gate," Kyrsiak said, poking his head into the locker room.

While Cal removed his G suit, he glanced over at the air force major. He had just finished his flight and was getting ready to break for lunch. "What's going on?"

Tim settled his blue cap on his head. "I'm going down there and take a look. I guess it's a protest against the MX. Supposedly, every major television station has a chopper up here with Minicam crews."

Immediately, Cal thought of Dev. Would she be here covering the event? Grimly, he headed for the door. "Let's go." He wrestled with his burgeoning feelings, anger tinged with fear. The day was too bright, blue and awash with sunshine to augur anything as dangerous as a demonstration.

As soon as they crested the last hill in the silver Corvette, Cal's hopes were dashed. He saw four helicopters sitting off to the left on the dry alkaline desert as well as three hundred demonstrators and a thin line of air police confronting them at the main gate. Placards, signs, chanting and shouts filled the air as they pulled to a stop.

The hair on Cal's neck bristled; he walked slowly toward the line. The air was electric with tension; a bullhorn wielded by the demonstrators was blaring across the invisible line drawn between the two factions. Cal worriedly searched the sea of faces pressing closer and closer to the air police, who stood tensely. His heart began to beat heavily when he spotted Dev carrying the Minicam on her shoulder, following a man who elbowed his way toward the leader of the demonstration. Tucker, he'd bet. Cal started forward, but Kyrsiak's hand shot out, gripping his arm.

"Don't do it, Cal. Stay back. This isn't our business."

Frustration roared through him. Tim was right. The demonstrators had a right to protest. But damn it, Dev was right in the middle of it! His gray eyes narrowed dangerously on Tucker, who was thrusting a microphone in the face of the leader of the protestors. Cal remained on guard, his legs slightly apart, fists curled. What if the leader decided to rush the line of air police? Dev was standing in that mass of people, who looked as if they wanted more than a peaceful confrontation. She would be hurt. She could be killed.

"I think we'd better go, buddy," Kyrsiak said, glancing at him. "Come on, Cal, there's nothing we can do here. I recognize Dev from your description, but our hands are tied. If you step across that line in your flight suit, all hell could break loose. Let's get back to the school...."

It took every last shred of Cal's discipline to turn away. He clenched his teeth, taking one last look over his shoulder before they got into the car. Didn't Dev realize how much danger she was placing herself in? He swore softly. *Tonight*, he promised her silently, *tonight we're going to have a talk, Dev. Face to face. You and I.*

THE KNOCK on her apartment door was heavy and angry. Dev frowned as she came from the kitchen, drying her hands on a towel. It was almost eight o'clock, and she wasn't expecting any visitors.

"Cal." She stood in the doorway, staring up into his almost colorless eyes and implacable face, instantly aware of his throttled anger.

"May I come in?"

Dev stepped aside, stunned by his icy composure. She had never seen him like this. Shutting the door, she turned to him, the towel gripped between her hands. He looked devastatingly handsome in a pair of jeans and a plaid shirt with the sleeves rolled up to his elbows.

"What's wrong?" she asked quietly, the air crackling between them.

Cal settled his hands on his hips. "What's wrong? Don't you know what's wrong?"

"No, I don't know what's wrong! Why are you acting like this? You nearly pound down my door, and then you come charging in here like I've committed a crime or something." Dev lowered her voice. "Look, it's been a long day. Why don't you sit down. Have you had dinner yet?"

"I'm not hungry."

Dev set her lips, anger in her azure eyes. "All right, out with it, Cal. I guess if we're going to have our first fight, we might as well fully address whatever it is that's bothering you."

He raked his fingers through his hair, stalking to the living room. He was too upset to sit down. Hell, he hadn't been able to concentrate the rest of the day at school, an entire afternoon lost. A part of him felt guilty about bulldozing his way in here. When Dev had opened the door, he had simply wanted to sweep her into his arms and hold her. God, just hold her. Instead his anger had gotten the better of him. He turned slowly, leveling an icy look at Dev.

"Just what the hell did you think you were doing up there today?" he ground out.

She tilted her head, confusion evident. "At Edwards? Covering a peace demonstration."

"I saw the whole damn thing, Dev. You were right up front between the protestors and the air police." His voice lowered. "Haven't you got a brain in your head? What if someone had thrown a rock or something? The air police would have retaliated. Did it ever occur to you that you were in a hell of a lot of danger?"

Dev's eyes narrowed. "Now just a minute, Cal. You have no right—no right to come busting in here like this, trying to call the shots on *my* job!"

"Like hell I don't!" he snarled, advancing on her. He gripped her by the shoulders, his face contorted. "When it concerns you, it concerns me, lady. I love you. I remember the last time that idiot Tucker dragged you into a confrontation. That time you damaged your wrist. Didn't it cross your mind that you were in just as much danger today?"

She wrenched free of him, placing some distance between them. Her breasts rose and fell rapidly as she stared at him. "I don't understand all your anger, Cal. Damn it, you act like I've—"

"I won't have you hurt, Dev. That job's too dangerous. Tucker's a first-class idiot. The more chance of violence, the more he gets turned on by it. I saw him out there today. I saw the look on his face. The man lives for something to happen. He cared about the story. Not about the danger he places you or himself in. Why can't you see that?"

Dev tried to steady herself. This was a side of Cal she had never seen. He was acting like a total chauvinistic male straight out of the cave age. She wanted to fling that fact at him but had the good sense not to. He was reacting out of love for her, not to prove a point. She swallowed against a forming lump, her voice suddenly growing softer. "I would hope," she began tremulously, "that you would support me as I've supported you, Cal."

He stared at her for seconds, digesting her sudden change of tone. "What do you mean?" he rasped.

"When we met and you were going through the trauma of Chief's death, I supported you completely. I didn't yell at you because you were in a dangerous situation when it occurred. I didn't pass judgment on you one way or another. It wasn't my place. It wasn't anyone's place to do that. Why can't you give me your understanding and support in my job, too? Why do you pass judgment on me?"

He gave her a bitter look and began to pace the length of the living room. The silence became explosive. Finally, he spun on his heel, pinning her with his gaze. "I've told you before, Dev, that job is too damn dangerous for you!"

"Address my question, Cal. Don't sidestep it. And don't ignore what I have to say as if it's irrelevant."

He glared at her. He wanted to throttle Dev in that second. In all his life, he had never had to confront a woman this way. He had never allowed anyone to reach this far inside him or to touch him to this degree. Dev had. And he loved her. "You're not irrelevant," he muttered, staring down at his shoes for a moment. Then he lifted his head. "Look," he said, spreading his hands out in a gesture of peace, "I was worried about you, Dev. That protest could have turned ugly."

She smiled tentatively. "I know it could have. I was scared, too."

"Then why do you do this job? You're an intelligent woman. You could have a safer job in any area you wanted, Dev. Why place yourself in danger?"

Tears glittered in her eyes as she stared at him. "Support me, Cal. Don't tear me down. Or apart. I love my job, or I wouldn't have been in it as long as I have. Please, back me on this. Love me for what I am and am not, Cal. Part of love is believing in the other. You may not agree with all that I think I am or want to be, but give me the freedom of that choice. Believe in me as I believe in you."

Her plea tore him apart. When he saw the tears silently trickling down her cheeks, he felt like a first-class bastard. Muttering an oath, Cal crossed the room, taking Dev in his arms. The instant she melted against the hard planes of his body, overwhelming protectiveness surged though him. "Dev," he whispered thickly, "I love you so much."

She pressed herself close, sliding her arms around his neck, holding him as tightly as she could. "I—I know you do," she said brokenly.

He buried his face in the silk of her hair, inhaling her wonderfully feminine scent. "When I stood out there today and saw you in the middle of that protest, I almost came unglued. I wanted to walk past the police, reach out and grab you. I wanted you out of there, Dev."

"I was fine, Cal. I love you for wanting to protect me, but you've got to trust me to gauge a situation like that."

He combed his fingers through her hair, never wanting to let her go. "I could kill Tucker."

Dev leaned back, looking up at him, laughing a little. Her cheeks were damp with spent tears that he awkwardly tried to brush away. "There have been times in the past when I've refused to obey Tucker's orders, did you know that?"

Cal shook his head, his eyes reflecting his anxiety. "No."

"If I thought the mood of the crowd was ugly, I wouldn't have followed Tucker up to the protest leader. I would have angled a view and used a long-range lens." She placed a kiss on his compressed mouth. "The crowd was in control today, Cal. They really didn't want trouble." She gave him a small shake, her expression tender. "Trust me, darling."

He grimaced, enfolding her in his arms. "I've never done this before. I've never gotten close enough to anyone before to have to trust or support them, Dev."

"Well," she murmured, kissing his jaw and finally moving to his mouth, "you will have to with me."

Liquid fire raced through him as her soft lips caressed his mouth. Cal shuddered, pressing his hips demandingly against hers, letting her know just how much he loved her. "I just don't want you hurt," he murmured thickly. "I won't lose you, Dev. I won't." And he closed his mouth over her parting lips.

A sigh of pleasure rose in her throat. After a long moment, they stood looking at each other. Merriment glinted in Dev's eyes. "It's more dangerous out on the fencing strip than behind a Minicam, Cal."

He shook his head morosely. "I don't know which is worse."

"Take all your accumulated frustration out on Bianca Santullo next week."

TULIPS, DAFFODILS and late-blooming hyacinths graced the carefully kept lawns in front of the Salle de L'Aigle. Little impinged on Dev that second week in April except that she had to be in top form, not only physically but mentally and emotionally. The din was constant as fencers from around the world, both men and women, used the early Saturday morning time to warm up, do stretching exercises and prepare themselves for the final round of bouts that would determine the winners in foil, épée and sabre.

Dev rocked back and forth on her legs, knees bent, feeling the pull of her firm thigh muscles as she continued her warm-up. The international meet had begun on Monday with hundreds of qualified fencers registering. The meet was held in the U.S., and it brought fencing enthusiasts from around the nation to San Bernardino, California, to vie for the coveted gold, silver or bronze medal in each class. Through five grueling days of constant fencing to whittle down the competitors to the best six for the final on Saturday morning, Carl Hunter had been sitting in the audience, cheering Dev on.

She assumed the fencing position, advancing and retreating. Blood was pulsing through her. She had never felt more

alive. Cal had come down from Edwards on Friday evening
to be part of her cheering section. He sat with her father, who
watched with bated breath while she fenced each bout that
would eventually place her in the prestigious finals. At the
end of the bout, the audience would break into polite applause. Fencing had been a nobleman's sport up until quite
recently. That image was intact. Crowds were always sparse
and boringly polite. Dev grinned. Of course when Cal arrived, he whipped them up into enthusiastic applause.

A buzzer sounded, alerting the fencers to go to their assigned strip and prepare for the final round of bouts. Dev's
body still tingled from the tender love Cal had made with her
earlier that morning. Dev had been tossing and turning all
night, mentally preparing herself for this morning's final.
Until Cal had finally trapped her in his arms and taken her
mind off the meet. Completely. Dev smiled tenderly as she
saw Cal standing with Jack Gordon near the scoring machine. Good, Cal would be down on the floor with her. She
needed his strength, his belief that she could take the gold for
her father, who watched from the viewing stands. Tension
had drawn up her shoulders, and Dev made a conscious effort to relax. If only she could win. If only she could hand her
father that gold medal . . .

"Ready, Dev?" Jack asked when she joined the two men at
the scoring machine.

"Ready, ready now," she replied, smiling over at Cal. He
had taught her the military phrase that the SAC bomber pilots
used all the time. Cal's face was closed, his gray eyes measuring as he returned her smile. Dev put on her green headband and struggled into her épée glove. Jack then taped it
tightly to her forearm so that no loose fabric or a section of
the glove could be caught in the deadly accuracy of another
fencer's épée point.

"Okay," Jack told her in a low voice as he checked her
weapon over with a knowing eye. "Here's your fencing or-

der: Hulbert from Germany first, Costello from Canada, Sandor from Hungary, Gambroni from Italy and finally, our mutual favorite, Bianca Santullo."

Dev groaned, taking the épée by the pistol-grip handle. "Great. I've got my tough bouts last."

"Not good, but there's nothing we can do, Dev. Just try and save your physical strength for Gambroni and Santullo. If I know the Italian coach, he'll order Gambroni to try and tire you out, to drag out the bout for the full six-minute limit if possible so that by the time you have to meet Santullo, you'll damn near be dead on your feet."

"So Gambroni is the sacrificial lamb in all of this?" Dev muttered.

Jack smiled grimly. "Let's face it, Santullo hasn't lost a bout, and Gambroni has. The Italians want the gold. They don't care *who* takes it. If they've got to throw one fencer away so that the other can win, that's a good tactical move."

"Well," Dev said, "I went 4-5 with Santullo last bout. This time it will be the other way around, or one of us is going to be dead trying."

Cal rested his hands on his hips. "That's not funny, Dev."

Dev checked to make sure her ponytail was tight before picking up her mask. "Well," Dev murmured, "this time she's going to walk away with the bruises, not me."

"Dev," Jack pleaded, "now come on. You know better. You let revenge mess up your focus and concentration, and you'll blow the bout. You know that."

Nervously, Dev ran her hand down the triangular steel blade, gently flexing it. "I know, I know. It's just talk," she reassured him. "I'll keep my cool."

"Hunter and Hulbert!" the announcer called.

Dev's heart began a slow pound and she recognized the familiar adrenaline pumping into her bloodstream. She felt Cal's hand on her shoulder, and she turned, tilting her face upward. He placed a swift, heart-wrenching kiss on her lips.

"You're the champ," he told her quietly, his eyes dark on her.

A knot formed in her throat so that Dev couldn't speak. She nodded her head and walked toward the strip to be hooked up for the first of five grueling bouts. She had to win each one or she would place second or third because Bianca Santullo had beaten everyone handily with scores of 5-1 or 5-2. Dev had been the only one to make Santullo work hard to win. As Dev stepped onto the copper strip, she flexed the blade of the trustworthy épée that had seen her through so many years of competition. The blade felt good in her hand as Dev saluted the director, scorekeeper and finally her opponent. Above all, this was for her father. Dev assumed the *en garde* position, calmly waiting for the order to be given.

Cal divided his time between Dev and keeping Carl Hunter company. Carl had been sitting in those same bleachers for five days in a row, cheering Dev on, giving her advice when she would come over between bouts to sit with her proud father. Cal had thought long and hard all week about his fight with Dev. Looking back on it, he felt guilty for charging in on her as he had. But damn it, he loved her. And his natural instinct was to protect and care for her. How could his love be seen through her eyes as a lack of support or trust on his part? He'd lost many hours of sleep pondering their heated conversation.

Cal followed Dev with his eyes as she came over to where they were sitting. Her face was beaded with sweat, a towel thrown over her head to keep her from getting chilled between bouts. Her eyes were a large dark lapis lazuli. Cal felt an undeniable rush of love for her as she gave both men a wide smile. She was so damned courageous under the circumstances. Her father's expectations were almost impossibly high.

Cal wanted to reach out and simply hold her, augment her own strength. All Cal could do now was remain in the background, allowing Carl and his daughter to spend every moment with each other. Dev gave him an intimate, private look, and Cal returned that silent gaze charged with so much meaning.

"Well," Dev said with a gasp, sitting down next to her father. "Three down and two to go."

"You're doing well, Punkin. What's the coach say on how to handle Gambroni?"

Dev rubbed the sweat from her face, her uniform damp. She grinned. "Pray a lot."

The laughter broke the tension between them, and Carl nodded.

"Gambroni fences with absence of blade. Which is okay by me," Dev said to her father. "I'm keeping my épée up and pointed at that big chest of hers."

"Watch for her to roll that épée blade over and sting you on your chest or right thigh," Carl warned Dev. "A lot of fencers who don't keep their blades up or in line do that."

Dev had already realized that, but she listened attentively to her father. Each time she met his eyes, she felt a knot forming and rising in her throat. Tears threatened to cut off her breathing, and she didn't dare cry! She desperately wanted to win the gold for her father. After all his years of belief in her, he deserved that from her as thanks for his support. Cal's lean, strong fingers closed over her own, giving her a silent message meant to buoy her. Cal knew how much she was suffering under the load. He also knew how to help her carry it. "Right, Dad," she murmured.

"Santullo's really chewing up her opponents."

"Running over them is more like it," Cal added.

"That's all right, Cal. Dev knows how to stop tanks, don't you?"

Dev saw the glitter in her dad's eyes. "You bet I do."

"Well, if you have to use that particular action, Punkin, you use it against *her*," Carl counseled her gravely, patting her knee.

Cal had no idea what they were referring to, but he could see the seriousness in each of their faces.

"Gambroni and Hunter!" the announcer called.

"Go get 'em, Punkin."

Dev leaned over, giving her father a kiss on the cheek. "For you, Dad."

Cal walked down the strip with Dev and hooked her up to the reel as she slipped on her fencing glove and then picked up her épée.

"How're you doing?" he asked in a quiet voice.

Dev barely turned her head. "Shaking inside. I don't know whether to throw up or cry. Or do both."

"You're doing fine, witch. I'm proud of you, you know that? You're giving your dad the greatest day of his life, no matter whether you win or lose." He gave her a pat on the shoulder. "After this bout, meet me in the side hall, okay?"

She nodded, her eyes revealing her tension. "Okay. The side hall."

"I love you. Just remember that."

"I know...."

A slow grin pulled at his mouth as he stepped away. "Take Gambroni out in a hurry. You can do it."

JACK GORDON STOOD THERE with an open mouth. But then so did the Italian coach, who was glaring at Dev when the bout swiftly ended with a final score of 5-1 in the American's favor. The bleachers exploded into cheers. As Dev shook hands with the Italian and unhooked, she was breathing hard. She had taken Gambroni out in two and a half minutes' fencing time. Not bad. She allowed herself a smile while gulping in some air. Dev waited patiently as Jack prepped her for the final bout against Bianca Santullo. Armed with his advice on how best to fence the unbeaten Italian, Dev went over and took similar instructions from her father. Carl Hunter's face was positively glowing with pride as she left to find Cal.

Cal stood down at the end of the hall near the water fountain, hands thrust deeply into the pockets of his dark-blue slacks. She had draped a towel over her head and one around her shoulders. At this stage, she couldn't afford to allow her body to lose heat, which meant loss of muscle flexibility. Not with the critical bout coming up. She'd need every trick, every wile she had ever learned in fencing to turn the tables on the Italian.

"That was an impressive bout, witch," Cal told her, sliding his arm around her and giving her a well-deserved hug.

"I was motivated by pure fear." Dev laughed tremulously, pressing her body against him. She closed her eyes, content simply to be held by Cal. His heart was so strong and steady sounding at her ear. Hers was flipping and jumping like a rabbit's.

"Pure skill and courage are closer to the truth," he whispered, nuzzling her ear, his breath moist and warm. "How are you feeling?"

Dev opened her eyes, staring unseeingly down the empty hall. "More scared than I've ever been in my whole life, Cal." A quaver came through. "I want this win so badly."

"I know."

She shut her eyes tightly. "I feel like I'm falling apart inside." She clutched at his shirt. "Hold me, Cal. Please...."

"It's all right, witch, you're doing fine," he crooned. "I'm here. I'll help you through it. We're a team, you and I. A damn good one. Alone, we're okay. But together, we have a combined strength that can deal with anything, Dev." He leaned down, kissing her eyes, sealing his mouth against her trembling lips. She clung to him, all firmness and curves in his hard embrace. Her face was flushed.

"Listen to me, Dev. It doesn't matter if you win this last bout. You've been the very best you can be for your dad. You're made of the right stuff. You've got the mettle, the heart and the fire to be more woman than anyone I've ever known or am likely to know. I love the hell out of you, lady."

Her vision blurred, and Dev blinked back the tears. She didn't doubt Cal's fervently spoken words. His voice washed over her, a balm to her frayed nerves. His eyes were penetrating, touching her heart. Dev nodded jerkily, hearing her name being announced for the last bout. She touched Cal's cheek, her eyes fraught with tenderness.

"I love you," she whispered and then turned, jogging down the hall and back to the meet. Back to face her nemesis: Bianca Santullo. The woman who stood between her and the gold medal she wanted so desperately.

Jack gave Dev a worried look when she walked quickly to the strip. He came over to hook her up.

"You're going to have to attack Santullo. If you allow her the offensive, she'll bully you off the strip."

An incredible sense of calm flowed through Dev's quivering insides just then. Her eyes widened as that steadiness embraced her. "I know that, Coach." Even her voice had changed. She checked the pistol-grip handle, making sure it hadn't come loose in the interim. What was happening? She'd never experienced this odd sensation. Jack placed his hand on her shoulder.

"You're the best, Dev. Never forget that."

Bianca was standing opposite her, six feet tall, her thick shoulders proudly thrown back, her square chin lifted and a haughty glitter in her eyes as she glared at Dev. The Italian stood at perfect fencing attention, mask under her left arm, épée down with the point barely resting on the copper strip in front of her.

Dev saw Cal. He leaned with languid grace against the wall. Their eyes met and locked; a silent message passed between them.

The entire *salle* stilled as the director walked up. Everyone knew that the épée championship would be determined by this last bout. There wasn't a fencer, spectator or judge who hadn't turned out to watch the ensuing match.

The director cleared his throat. *"Etes-vous prêts?"* he demanded crisply.

Simultaneously, both fencers saluted. Bianca whipped the bell of her épée up to her face and then made a slicing downward motion, an arrogant and incorrect salute, especially for such a prestigious occasion. Dev's face remained impassive, her mouth compressed as she snapped to attention, bringing her épée bell up to her face, saluting first the director, scorekeeper and then . . . she executed a flawless about-face, raising her épée, and with a flourish saluted her father. Finally, she acknowledged Bianca. Not a breath was taken, not a movement made as both women settled their masks over their faces and took the familiar fencing position.

"Oui!" Dev called.

"Oui!" Bianca snapped, shoulders hunched in preparation.

"Allez!"

Dev struck with a fury honed by precision, flèching, her glinting blade an extension of her straight arm as she aimed herself like a human projectile at Bianca. The red light flashed.

"Touche gauche!" the director called. Touch left.

A roar went up from the stands.

Santullo cursed as Dev calmly walked past her to once again take her place behind the on guard line.

Dev flexed her blade, eyeing her opponent, her heart beating slowly and steadily. One hundred percent of her attention was on the Italian. Dev had long ago recognized the killer instinct that some fencers possessed, and now it was in charge of her. Her senses were screamingly alive. Her eyes cataloged and computerized even the slightest hint of movement from Bianca. As they got ready, that same cool composure kept Dev steady.

"*Allez!*"

Bianca shrieked, launching herself at Dev in a flèche, her blade aimed murderously high at Dev's vulnerable throat.

In a snaking motion of lightning reflexes, Dev flicked her parry to the left, then twisted aside as the Italian's blade slid centimeters past her throat. Executing a follow-through, Dev jabbed once, her point sinking deeply into Santullo's shoulder blade. The red light went on.

A tumult broke the silence; the applause went on for almost fifteen seconds.

Bianca stalked by Dev, glaring at her. Dev's eyes narrowed, her nostrils flared, sweat running down her face.

"You're dead," Santullo hissed so that no one else could hear above the frantic roar of the spectators.

"Try it," Dev gritted back, giving her a mirthless smile.

Santullo made the mistake of trying the same attack again, and Dev capitalized on the situation, to the delight of the crowd.

"Score 3-0, Hunter."

"*Etes-vous prêts?*"

"*Oui!*"

"*Oui!*"

"*Allez!*"

Bianca's arm suddenly dropped, the blade point aimed upward as she lunged. Dev parried the unusual attack, retreating. The Italian remised, thrusting her arm and shoulder forward in a savage continuation. The green light flashed, indicating Bianca had scored.

"*Halte!*" the director cried. "*Touche droite.*"

Cal had never witnessed the coolness Dev was exhibiting as she walked up to the on guard line. She reminded him of a lioness that had been challenged and was now defending her cubs. He saw Carl leaning forward with rapt attention.

"*Etes-vous prêts?*" the director called.

"*Oui!*"

"*Oui!*"

"*Allez!*"

Come on, come on, Dev chanted silently as she stalked Bianca. She flicked her épée outward, snapping it against the Italian's blade. *Come on. Come and get me.* Dev advanced rapidly, knowing Bianca would not tolerate her attack for long. The instant the Italian lunged, Dev clenched her teeth, locked her elbow and thrust forward from the shoulder, putting all her weight behind the charge. The tip of her épée was aimed squarely for the center of Bianca's mask.

There was a simultaneous collision, both lights going off. Dev felt the jolt all the way up her arm as her épée point connected solidly with Bianca's mask. The force of their collision knocked the Italian woman backward from the fury of her attack. Bianca fell flat, stunned by Dev's perfectly legal blow.

"*Halte! Touches droites et gauches!*" the director shouted. Touches on both sides.

The *salle* rolled with wave after wave of cheering and clapping. Dev stood a few feet from her opponent, breathing hard. Her wrist hurt. Her shoulder felt as if she had just been in a wrenching car accident. But the hit had been solid. Dev grinned a little, watching Bianca being helped to her feet by her coach and Gambroni. For a moment, Santullo seemed dazed.

Dev waited as the Italian coaches screamed and gesticulated to the officials, vociferously protesting Dev's attack. *Tough,* she thought. Bianca seemed shaken up. Good. It would make her all the easier to finish off.

"Etes-vous prêts?"

"Oui!"

"Oui!"

"Allez!"

Bianca had expected another furious attack from Dev and had prepared herself accordingly. But when Dev smoothly lunged forward, dropped the point of her épée at the last second and executed a beautiful toe touch, the Italian went into shock, standing there openmouthed after the red light went on and the director called an end to the bout, giving Dev the win.

The crowd roared and applauded. Dev slowly took off her mask, her face pale and serious as she studied her opponent in the aftermath. Dev went forward after Bianca had taken off her mask and extended her hand.

The Italian looked at Dev's fingers and then at her face. Bianca's brown eyes were as unblinking as a snake's, but she smiled grudgingly, thrusting her hand out to meet and clasp Dev's. It was over between them. At least for this meet.

"We will meet again," Bianca promised throatily.

"I suppose we will," Dev agreed, breaking the handshake. As she turned away, her face suddenly blossomed into the biggest victory smile anyone had ever seen. Dev thrust her mask and épée above her head, acknowledging the wildly cheering crowd. She had won! She had won for her father! Tears streamed down her face as she met Cal's eyes; he was walking toward her. Without his loving encouragement, his quiet strength backing her, Dev knew she never would have held herself together to win the gold for her father.

10

"DEV! GET AN ANGLED SHOT of that burning refinery," Tucker ordered, pointing down at the black oily mass of smoke that was boiling skyward.

Wind tore through the cabin of the helicopter as she placed the lens of her camera out the small window. Two thousand feet below them one of the huge holding tanks for oil was burning out of control. The sun was near its noon point, and Dev squinted, angling for the best shot under the circumstances.

"Man, will you look at that!" Tucker hooted excitedly from his copilot seat. "That baby is burning."

"You sound like a closet arsonist," Dev commented dryly into the microphone near her lips.

"Feature story material. You sure you got a good angle?"

Dev pressed her lips together. It was Friday. Why did this oil fire have to occur just as she was supposed to be leaving work early to meet Cal? They had planned a picnic at the beach. As he glanced at her watch, Dev's heart sank: Cal would be in San Bernardino right now. He had a key to her apartment so that wasn't a problem. At least this oil fire had happened right outside the city limits. Once they wrapped up the shoot, it would be a quick flight back to the television station and a short drive to her apartment.

"Looks like we've got company," Tucker said unhappily, pointing out two other helicopters with huge fuselage markings identifying them as rival television stations.

Dev shook her head. Tucker was so competitive. Did he think they'd be the only ones to cover a spectacular blaze like this?

"Hey!" Tucker called to the pilot, Sam Sharp, "get closer! If those buzzards are going to take long shots, we'll get some real good close-ups!"

"Heat's too hard on the chopper engine, Tuck," Sharp countered, shaking his head.

"Damn it, I want close-ups! Come on, Sam, do me this one favor. This one time."

"I won't go any closer than a thousand feet, Tucker," Sharp growled. "The updraft from that fire is hell to fly in. You have any idea how hot that fire is? At least three to five thousand degrees Fahrenheit. It would stall this bird's engine if I got too close—"

"Okay, okay. A thousand feet. Dev? You ready?"

"Yes," she answered, giving Tucker a dirty look. Tucker would march his mother straight into that blaze if he thought he could get better pictures than the rival news choppers at the scene. Dev noticed the other helicopters were staying a healthy distance away from the fire. So should they be. As she changed lenses, Cal came to mind.

Ever since the incident at Edwards with the protestors, he had exhibited a more protective attitude toward her. Did all aggressive fighter jocks have the cave man reflex to defend and fight for the women they loved? She cringed inwardly. Cal was having a tough time respecting her career choice— only because he didn't want her to get hurt in the line of duty. A part of her understood his feelings. But she couldn't stop living her life for him, and he had to come to grips with that idea.

"This is it, Tucker!" Sharp growled, coaxing the helicopter around the gigantic black mushrooming clouds of smoke shot through with livid welts of orange flame.

Dev could feel the heat of the fire as she placed the len
outside the window, readying herself. Just as she prepared to
shoot, a warning screech ripped through the cabin.

"What the hell—" Tucker yelped.

Sam gripped the collective and cyclic hard as the helicop
ter suddenly lagged. He drew in a swift breath; the engine wa
silent.

As the chopper plunged earthward, Dev was thrown
backward, tumbling end over end, her feet slamming into the
bulkhead.

"We're in trouble!" Sam yelled. "Brace yourselves. We're
going down!"

CAL HEARD of the helicopter crash on the radio. He was in
Dev's kitchen putting the finishing touches on the picnic
lunch when the AM radio station interrupted the music for
an announcement.

A WSAN helicopter has just crashed near an oil refinery fire on the outskirts of San Bernardino. Reports are
sketchy, but firefighters on the scene say survivors are
being taken to the St. Jude Hospital. Stay tuned for more
details.

Cal froze where he stood, taking several seconds to digest
the announcement. Dev wasn't home. That meant she could
have been on that helicopter, finishing a last-minute assignment. Icy terror hit him as he ran through the kitchen, grabbing the keys to his car and racing outside. He had never used
his Corvette for its speed and maneuverability. Now he did.
His superior reflexes and skill as a pilot helped him weave
through the early afternoon traffic toward the hospital. Dev
had left him a greeting card on the kitchen table. She often
sent warm or humorous cards to the base. And on many Fridays she was late getting home from work. As if to assuage

his disappointment if she wasn't there to meet him, she would leave a greeting card on the table to let him know she loved him.

Cal tried to ignore the pain as the cover of the card wavered in his mind's eye. It had a dark-blue background that reminded him of Dev's eyes and of the sky he flew in. The stark beauty of two sea gulls wafting on an invisible column of air completed the composition. Inside was penned the words, "I ask no more of life than to love and be loved by you...."

Cal blinked away the scalding tears that blurred his vision. Was Dev dead? Badly injured? His gut told him she had been on board that helicopter. *Oh, God, please let her be alive. Let her be all right.* Cal swallowed hard, cornering the Corvette hard, the wheels screeching in protest. Up ahead, he could see the hospital. He had never prayed to God before. But now he did. He braked the car in the parking lot nearest the emergency exit. Taking long strides, Cal covered the last few hundred yards to the hospital. *Let her live. Let her live... I'll do anything...anything you ask of me. Just let her be alive....*

Dev heard the commotion at the entrance to the emergency room, sharp commands and ... Cal's snarling voice. *Oh, my God.* She swallowed, sliding off the gurney, and quickly walked out of her cubicle to the center of the room. Cal must have heard the news of the helicopter going down. Dev stared at him as he broke free of the orderlies who were trying to restrain him. His face was drawn and white as he strode across the linoleum floor toward her. She had never seen him so upset, gray eyes colorless and narrowed, lips compressed into a single, hard line. The instant he saw her, his expression changed. In that split second, she realized just how fiercely Cal loved her.

"Dev?" His voice was like a whip as he covered the last few feet between them. He missed nothing in his inspection of her.

Dev's hair was in disarray, there was a bruise on her brow and she looked generally disheveled. Other than that, she appeared unharmed. With a groan, he swept her uncompromisingly into his arms, nearly crushing her.

"God." He pressed kisses to her hair, her cheeks and then her lips. "I thought—" He looked at her, his eyes full of tears, his voice quavering. "I thought you were dead. The radio report—"

Dev sobbed, throwing her arms around his neck, holding him tightly. "I'm fine . . . fine . . . ."

He couldn't trust himself to say anything else, afraid that he might burst into tears as Dev had. Cal swallowed the tidal wave of emotion and just held her. Held her and rocked her in his arms. She felt so good. So warm and alive, her body soft and molding to the more angular planes of his.

Dev tried without success to dry her cheeks. She lifted her chin, her lashes beaded with tears, meeting Cal's dangerously bright eyes. It shook her to her soul to realize how close he was to crying. Memories of that morning when she had held him in her arms, when he had cried for the loss of Chief, sheared through her. "Oh, Cal," she whispered tremulously, cupping his face. "I'm all right. Really. Just a few bruises . . ."

Cal was looking at her as if he didn't believe her. He worked his mouth awkwardly, fighting for control. "But the radio— it said 'survivors.'"

Dev reached up, kissing his cheek, aware of the sandpapery warmth of his flesh. "Our pilot sustained a few cracked ribs. And Tucker has a fractured wrist. I wasn't strapped in when Sam began to autorotate the helicopter so we wouldn't crash, so I got bounced around a lot." She tried to muster up a smile for his benefit, the adrenaline making her shaky. "I must have been flying through the air when we hit the ground. That's probably why I didn't get any broken bones."

Cal's mouth thinned as he held her. "This is Tucker's fault, isn't it?" he asked softly, looking around, trying to find the reporter.

Dev hedged. "He wanted to get a close-up of the refinery blaze. We were at a thousand feet when the engine suddenly quit."

His nostrils flared. "That bastard had you fly that close to an inferno like that?"

"The pilot told him he wouldn't go any closer than a thousand feet, Cal."

He'd kill Tucker. His hands tightened on Dev's shoulders; he'd ferret out which cubicle Tucker was hiding in. "Damn it, Dev, you had no business being that close! The temperature probably stalled the engine. Your pilot should have known better."

Dev gave him a pleading look, gripping his upper arms. "Cal, please. It's all over. We're safe. I'm unhurt."

Rage boiled over in Cal. "Knowing Tucker, he browbeat that pilot into flying at a lower altitude, didn't he, Dev? He wanted more dramatic pictures. Where the hell are they keeping him?" he growled, releasing Dev.

"Cal!" she cried, trying to stop him. It was no use. Cal strode to the opposite side filled with cubicles. Although he wore a pair of casual, faded jeans and a polo shirt, Cal exuded a chilling sense of power that left Dev stunned in its wake. Was this how he appeared in combat?

Tucker's shriek jolted her into motion.

"Hey! What do you think you're doing?" Tucker's eyes bulged as he saw an officer push aside the sheet to his cubicle. Tucker was sitting on a gurney, legs dangling over the side, holding his broken wrist when Cal entered. He had guessed the man's identity and had no wish to tangle with him. But before he could utter another word, the officer lifted him up and off the gurney as if he weighed nothing. Tucker opened his mouth to scream, but Cal pinned him against the wall. The breath was knocked out of Tucker for a moment, and the officer's fists were white knuckled as he gripped his shirt front.

"You son of a bitch," Cal snarled. "You damn near killed her." He tightened his grip on Tucker's collar, pressing him hard against the wall. "Now you listen to me. You *ever* pull a stunt like that again with Dev along, and I'll make sure someone gets a story on *you*. You understand me, Tucker? Risk your life if you like, but leave Dev out of your glory seeking. Understand?"

"Yeah—" Tucker croaked, keeping perfectly still, afraid to even breathe.

Cal's eyes were glacial with rage, his face devoid of emotion. He slowly released Tucker. Tucker was shaking, breathing hard. Without another word, Cal turned to find four nurses and two doctors standing there, staring open-mouthed at him. No one challenged him as he eased between them and took Dev by the arm, propelling her out the doors of the emergency room.

"Do you need to pick up a prescription or something?" he asked tightly, waiting while she got her purse.

Dev shook her head. "No. The doctor said I was to take some aspirin for my headache and get some rest, that's all."

"All right, let's get you home."

Dev said little on the way to her apartment. Cal's clipped words and take-charge attitude left her feeling wary. Or maybe she was just experiencing a letdown after the adrenaline high. Dev wasn't sure. She could feel the explosiveness in Cal, and she was afraid to say anything that might set him off. Right now, she couldn't handle another confrontation.

CAL SILENTLY PACED the length of the living room, ignoring the beauty of the sun hanging low on the horizon. Dev had been sleeping for almost four hours and that worried him. What if that idiot of a doctor had misdiagnosed that bruise on her head? What if she had a concussion? Sleeping was dangerous in that case. More than once, Cal headed in the direction of her room to wake her and see if she was all right. But every time he stood in the open doorway of her bedroom gazing at her sleeping form, he knew better.

Wearily, he rubbed his face, halting at the window. Never before had he acted as he had today. Cal felt no guilt about threatening Tucker. The arrogant little bastard was long overdue for a lesson in thinking about someone other than himself. No, it had been the look on Dev's face that had bothered him. He had bulldozed his way into the situation, not even letting her get a word in edgewise. He was angry with her. Far angrier than he had a right to be. But he couldn't help himself. He loved her. And he had almost lost her to that job she insisted on keeping. Cal had found himself snipping and snarling at her when they had gotten back to the apartment. He had wanted to hold her, comfort her, but he was just too damned angry and so punished her by not touching her.

"Cal?" Dev's sleepy voice broke through his turmoil. He turned. She looked like a harmless kitten that had just awakened, the thin, floor-length, cotton gown making her appear that much more vulnerable. In that instant, all his anger dissipated. Without a word, Cal went to her, gently taking her into his arms, kissing her hair.

"How are you feeling?"

Dev hungrily soaked up his tenderness, needing it. Cal had been so brutal and cold earlier that it had left her on the verge of tears. She hadn't been able to fathom his anger toward her. "Okay." She nuzzled her head beneath his chin, closing her eyes. He was so strong and capable. "I feel so safe when you hold me," she whispered.

His arms tightened momentarily. "I'll always keep you safe, my redheaded witch." Cal pressed a kiss to her rosy cheek, aware of the velvety quality of her skin. "Headache gone?"

"Uh-huh...."

He grinned, splaying his fingers down the curve of her back.

"You're not very awake yet, are you?"

"No . . . I kept dreaming that the helicopter was going to crash, and we were all going to die. I woke up just as we hit . . ."

"You'll have dreams like that for a while," he said soothingly. "It's normal after a traumatic accident."

Her arms slid around his waist, and she rested contentedly against him. "Like you had when your plane crashed?"

"The same. Come on, let's get you sitting down. How about some tea laced with your favorite orange brandy?"

Dev smiled, lifting her face, waiting for him to drop a kiss on her lips. She wasn't disappointed. Cal's mouth brushed hers with aching tenderness, and she drank deeply of his offered love. She had come so close to death . . . so close to losing him. There was so much she wanted to tell him about what she had discovered in those last twenty seconds before they had crashed. Suddenly, life was more precious than ever before. Cal had been depressed and guilty after his plane had dropped like a wounded bird into the ocean. Was he finally glad to be alive?

Cal guided her to the couch, and she sat down. Later, Dev was still lingering over her second cup of spiked tea, comfortably wedged between Cal's outstretched legs. They were both silent, and his hand rarely left her shoulder. How did he know she needed his touch just now? She set her cup on the coffee table and leaned back, resting her head on his thigh.

"Feel better?"

"Much. The tea is nice, but having you here is better."

Cal gently caressed her unruly hair, his gray eyes burning with tenderness. "I never want to have something like this happen again," he admitted softly.

"Me, either. Now I'm beginning to understand how you felt at the time of your plane crash."

"Not a very pleasant feeling, is it?"

"Awful. One second I'm so high and thanking God I survived. The next I'm flung into a pit of terror I felt, believing I'm going to die."

"It's a hell of a way to make you appreciate living, isn't it?"

"A hell of a way," she agreed mutely, closing her eyes as he stroked her shoulder.

Cal dragged in a breath, his hand growing still. "I want you to quit your job, Dev."

Her eyes opened, dark and unseeing. She felt his fingers grip her shoulder more firmly as if he sensed her immediate negative reaction to his request.

"First you were knocked around by a bunch of union strikers, then you were in the middle of a protest and now this."

She sat up and turned to face him. "Cal, I didn't get hurt at that protest. I've been a Minicam operator for five years now, and I've never been injured except for these last two incidents in the past seven months."

"Listen to me, honey. I know you love your job—"

"Then don't ask me to quit, Cal."

"Damn it, Dev!" He got to his feet, shoving his hands in his jean pockets, resuming his pacing. "I love you. And I don't want to live in terror of either getting a phone call up at the base or finding out on some damn radio news flash that you're dead or dying." He turned, his face hard and uncompromising. "I can't take that. Don't you see?"

Dev slowly got to her feet, holding his anguished gaze. "Oh, Cal, don't you realize it's the same for me?"

"What are you talking about?"

"Your job. You're a test pilot. Hasn't it ever occurred to you that I worry about you? A million things could go wrong with one of those planes you fly. I worry about you because I love you. Don't you think I live in dread of someone calling me from Edwards to tell me you're dead or in the hospital because of an accident?"

Cal raked his fingers through his hair. "That's different! Testing is safe."

"It is not!"

"It's a hell of a lot safer than what you're doing."

Her cobalt eyes blazed. "Then why are they always needing so many new test pilots? They can't all be replacements for men who have already done their tour. God, Cal, your profession is dangerous from the instant you step into that cockpit. At least in my job, every day isn't potentially my last."

He continued to pace like a caged panther, throwing a glare in her direction every once in a while. "You don't know what it was like for me when I heard that radio broadcast, Dev. I died in that kitchen. I *knew* you were on board that chopper. I was lucky I didn't get in an accident on the way to the hospital. All I could think of—pray for—was that you were alive." His voice grew hoarse. "I prayed, Dev. Do you know that's the first time in my life I've ever done that?"

Tears glimmered in her eyes. She took a step toward him and then stopped. Her voice was tight. "Cal, we love each other. I know your job is dangerous, and I accept that because I know how much you love flying. You've shared your dream to become a test pilot with me. Now you have your chance. I wouldn't ask you to leave your job because I was scared to death of losing you." She opened her hands in supplication. "I support you in whatever you want to do, Cal. If you love someone, you don't put them in whatever gilded cage you think is best for them. You have to let me be as free as I allow you to be...."

He stood there, shoulders broken, hands in his pockets, simply staring at her across the living room. His face reflected his churning emotions, his eyes were hurt. "Do I hear you saying that I don't love you enough?" he asked in a low voice.

Dev shrugged her shoulders. "There's no question of my love for you, Cal. But no one has a right to put another human being in a cage. That's what I feel you're trying to do with me. Love should free us to achieve whatever we set out to do. You're strangling me with this ultimatum to quit my job—quit or else what? What do you want?"

His mouth tightened, and his tone was harsh. "I want you safe, damn it! That's all. Maybe you're right, Dev. Maybe I don't love you enough. Maybe I love you too much. I know what I feel. Is it a crime to want you to work at something safer because I love you?"

"Cal," she cried softly. "I could be killed just driving down the street! There are no guarantees for any of us. Love me enough to understand my position."

He was breathing hard, his chest rising and falling sharply. He felt the sting of tears and angrily forced away the reaction. Cal felt as if some huge, invisible hand had slammed him in the chest and was trying to rip out his heart. The pain was so real, so agonizing that he rubbed his chest. Frustration curled through him. Why couldn't Dev see how much he loved her! He wanted to shake some sense into her but realized that wasn't the way to go about this.

"All right," he muttered, giving her a sharp look, "have it your way." He walked toward the door.

"Where are you going?"

Cal jerked open the door, and the sun spilled brightly into the room. He steeled his heart against the agony he saw on Dev's face. God help him, she looked so damned vulnerable and beautiful standing there, stirring up every known protective defense within him. But his anger and inability to cope with her stubbornness pushed all that aside. "Back to Edwards," he ground out.

Dev stood frozen, shocked. "Cal, we can talk this out. Like we have before. Please...."

He gripped the knob until his knuckles whitened. "We're at an impasse, Dev. Frankly, I'm madder than hell at you. I don't understand you. I guess I don't understand all the demands of love. I guess I never will." With that, he stalked out of the apartment and out of her life, quietly shutting the door behind him.

"WHERE'S THAT BOYFRIEND of yours been lately?" Tucker asked as he wandered into the film-editing room. His lower right arm was still in a cast and sling. Tucker was now the local hero at the television station, brandishing his cast as if it were a medal of honor, recounting to anyone who would stand still long enough the story of his harrowing escape from the helicopter crash.

Dev concentrated on watching the film she had just shot of children at a local grade school. She flinched inwardly. Tucker always asked about Cal ever since Cal had nailed him in the emergency room.

"Up at Edwards. Like he always is," she muttered, hoping her brusqueness would get rid of him. To her dismay, Tucker sat down next to her.

"He used to pick you up here on Fridays. What happened? He staying away because he's afraid of me?"

Dev snorted. "Give me a break, Tucker. If Cal showed up here, you'd go hide in the women's rest room, and you know it."

Tucker grinned. "Touché, Hunter. It's Friday. You going home early?"

What for? Dev wondered in anguish. Two weeks . . . two of the most miserable ones in her entire life and not a word from Cal. She had hurt him deeply with her stand on her job. But it couldn't be helped. If he couldn't realize that she was allowing him the same freedom, despite his dangerous career, then they had little ground on which to build. She felt tears coming to her eyes and wished Tucker would go away.

"No, I'm staying late."

"What's the matter—you break up with him?"

Dev lifted her head, her eyes dark with hurt. "Tucker, you've got the manners of a bull in a china shop. Haven't you got anything better to do than bug me about my personal life?"

"Just teasing you, Hunter. No need to get sore." He gave her a cheery smile and rose. "Even I could have told you to stay away from those fighter-jock types. They're all the same: filled with themselves."

"You should have been a fighter jock, Tucker."

Dev watched him go, grateful to be alone once again. She quickly wiped her eyes and got back to work in the darkened room. *Oh, Cal, I love you. I miss you. Why won't you call?* She had tried to reach him by phone on four different occasions, to no avail. He wasn't returning her calls. He should have gotten her letter today. What if he wouldn't open it? What if he sent it back marked Return To Sender? Dev rested her forehead in her hand, exhausted. Time . . . perhaps time would be on their side. That thought was all she had left to cling to.

CAL STARED GRIMLY at Dev's letter. A five-page letter carefully penned on pale-pink stationery. He refolded the letter once again, placing it in a pocket of his flight suit. He needed to fly, simply fly. That would clear his head and help him think. Going to the locker room, he climbed into his G suit, put his helmet and flight gloves in his duffel bag and walked out to the ramp. It was Friday. Ordinarily, he'd be straining at his nylon harness to leave Edwards and drive down to see Dev for the weekend.

Cal climbed into the cockpit of the sleek, needle-nosed T-38 Falcon jet. No one flew on Friday afternoon. No, they all had somewhere to go. A girlfriend to visit. A wife or children to go home to. *Stop it, Travis! Stop torturing yourself.*

He settled the helmet on his head, snapping the oxygen mask across his face so that only his gray eyes, shadowed with pain, were visible. Within fifteen minutes, he was no longer earthbound. As he launched the swift T-38 skyward across the barren Mojave Desert, Cal felt more suppressed emotions break loose. He was a lone eagle again, sailing through the sky, free. Free and unhappy. An eagle had a mate. One mate for life. Had he lost his? And Dev was like an eagle to him, proud, free and so incredibly beautiful from the heart outward. His fingers tightened on the stick between his legs as he eased the jet into a wingover, sliding down in a graceful arc for fifteen thousand feet before leveling off and screaming across the desert five thousand feet beneath him.

He thought better when he flew. He had to try to see her point of view. It had never occurred to him that she worried about his flying. He had taken for granted that she approved of his career. How could anyone be afraid of flying or testing? Didn't they know that computers, flight engineers and designers all made testing so safe that they'd only lost a handful of pilots since the early sixties? Cal's eyes narrowed under the dark visor across his face. He pulled back on the stick and gently moved the throttles forward, knotching them into the afterburner range. The T-38 quivered, shoving him hard against the ejection seat as the afterburners engaged, hurling the aircraft up . . . up into the dark-blue sky that reminded him of Dev's eyes.

When he landed more than an hour later, Cal felt a little closer to what Dev was trying to explain to him. Her reasoning was still out of his reach, but he sensed that if he kept on mulling over her words, reading her letter again and again, something would click in his brain, and he'd understand. And with that understanding, they might overcome the hurdle he had placed between them. If she still loved him. He frowned. Could he have destroyed Dev's love for him by his actions? Cold dread wound through his stomach, leaving it in a hard knot. For the thousandth time, Cal cursed the fact that he had no experience to rely on. He had always sidestepped getting involved, he couldn't fathom why now. And right now, he felt so alone and scared. Scared that he had made another blundering mistake most men wouldn't have made. And because of it, Cal could lose Dev.

THE PHONE RANG, pulling Dev out of her deep, exhausted sleep. What time was it? She groped for the phone in the darkness.

"Mmmph?"

"Dev?"

Dev's eyes flew open, and she sat up in bed, gripping the receiver. "Cal?" Her heart took a terrifying leap, then steadied at a galloping beat. He sounded exhausted.

"Yeah, it's me."

What time was it? She fumbled for the clock on the bed table, turning it toward her. It was two in the morning. "What's wrong? You sound terrible. Are you all right?"

His laughter was slight and awkward. "Yeah, I'm okay. I guess. How about you? I didn't mean to wake you...."

Her voice dropped to a husky whisper. "I'm glad you called, Cal. Call anytime. I don't care." She shut her eyes tightly, fighting back a deluge of tears. "You sound tired. Are they working you too hard up there again?"

"No . . . I guess I haven't been sleeping very well lately."

A tremulous smile touched her lips. "Me, either. I've missed you, Cal."

"You have?" There was relief in his tone.

"Yes."

"I got your letter today. I mean yesterday."

She held her breath. Dev had put her heart and soul into that letter. "And?"

There was a wistful quality to his voice now. "You remember that note I slipped into that jewelry case I gave you at Kai Tak?"

"I'll never forget it as long as I live, Cal. Why?"

There were a few seconds of hesitation. When Cal answered, his voice was strained. "Uh, your letter affected me like that one I wrote to you. As if you were baring your soul to me, Dev. Like I had to you."

"I was. I mean, I did." Her hand went to her pounding heart; she hung on each of his words. How she had ached to hear from him. She put her hand over the receiver, afraid he would hear her sob of relief.

"Dev?"

She cleared her throat. "I'm right here, Cal."

"What's wrong? You sound funny."

"Just a cough."

"You aren't sick, are you?"

The alarm in his voice made her smile. "I'm sick. Sick of the loneliness. I do miss you, Cal."

"I miss you, too," he said slowly. "I'm still thinking about our impasse, Dev. I haven't completely figured out the solution yet."

"We have time, Cal. All the time in the world. All we need to do is talk. And write. We've done that before. We can do it again."

"I guess communication is a big part of any serious relationship," he said diffidently.

"One of the most important ingredients," Dev agreed.

"I'd better let you get back to sleep."

"That's okay, I'm wide awake now."

His voice held a hopeful note. "Sure?"

"Positive...."

"How are things going at work? Is Tucker leaving you alone?"

She smiled, inwardly relieved. Cal didn't want their phone call to end, either. His voice gave her indefinable sustenance. "Tucker is walking on eggs around me."

"He'd better."

"He goes around holding up his cast, lying through his teeth about his heroic helicopter crash to any poor soul who stands still for two seconds." She laughed softly. Her heart wrenched when she heard his own laughter. For those precious few seconds, Cal's tone was free of strain.

"Well . . . it's getting late. . . ."

She closed her eyes, gently holding the receiver as if it were an extension of him. "I guess it is."

"You are all right? You sound kind of funny. Sure you don't have a cold or a flu bug?"

The only bug I've got, Travis, is you in my blood, she thought wryly. "My voice is always husky when I wake up."

There was yearning in his voice. "Yeah, I remember that. . . ." And then he sighed as if recalling those times when they had awakened in each other's arms. Sometimes they would lie there, kissing and stroking. Other times, desire ignited into hot passion that consumed them completely. "Sleep well, Dev. . . ."

Dev wanted to say, "No, let's just talk, Cal!" But she didn't. Cal had to grapple with this in his own way. The very fact that he had called her gave them both hope. She loved him fiercely for this concession. "Are you going to become the midnight caller?" she teased him gently.

Cal's laugh was lighter. "It's better than not hearing your voice, Dev. Get some sleep, witch. I intend to write to you."

She closed her eyes, relief washing through her once again. He hadn't said he loved her. He was hurt too badly to say it. Or perhaps she had destroyed his love. Dev was grateful for whatever was left between them. "I'll be waiting for it," she promised huskily. "Good night."

"Good night. . . ."

11

"CAL, WHERE ARE YOU taking me?"

"Back to Shangri-La," he replied enigmatically, hauling the suitcases they had packed out of the small Cessna aircraft and putting them into a waiting car.

"Look, I know the last month's been a strain on both of us," Dev began softly. She felt a keen rush of guilt, turning away with a sigh. The past few weeks had consisted of tentative phone calls from Cal. Dev always felt wary every time he called. His letters tackled the core of their problem, and Dev agonized with him. Would he ever acknowledge or understand his job was just as frightening to her as hers was to him?

"Yes, the time apart has been a strain." He shut the trunk and smiled grimly at her. He caressed her cheek, lowering his voice. "I haven't been easy on you, Dev."

"I'm not angry with you," she whispered.

"I know that."

"Cal, I'm—"

His eyes asked her to hear him out. "I've felt like I've had two left feet with you. I wanted to be there for you, and I've screwed up in so many ways—"

"No," Dev said, throwing her arms around him. "You haven't, Cal. I know you're trying. That's what really counts."

He smiled tiredly and held her for a long time. "Even if I have two left feet?"

Dev nodded, pressing her cheek against the cotton of his shirt. She was content to be held by him as they stood on the tarmac of the quiet airport in Crescent City, California. Cal had come unannounced to her apartment at 6:00 A.M. Saturday, hauled her out of bed, cajoled her into packing enough clothes for ten days and then driven her to the airport in San Bernardino. A small rental plane had been prepared and was waiting for them. Throughout the seven-hour flight up the coast of northern California, Cal refused to say anything about his behavior. The late May sun was warm, and the tang of salt air cleared away her depression. A slight, inconstant breeze lifted strands of her hair from where it lay on her shoulders. She felt his unsureness and saw it in his eyes from time to time throughout the trip.

"Come on," Cal coaxed, opening the door to the black compact, "hop in."

Dev nodded. Cal gave her a reassuring smile as he started the car and drove slowly away from the airport.

"Now what was that look for, witch?"

"Are you going to tell me why you're abducting me?"

His hand settled over hers, and Cal lost his teasing demeanor. "Because, my beautiful redheaded lady, you needed to get away from your job, your fencing, your father, your apartment—"

"But not from you."

"Nope."

"Why are you doing this, Cal? I mean, you've told my boss at the television station I'm suddenly on vacation for ten days. I find out you called dad on Friday and told him I'd be gone."

God knew he had blundered through the last month. And Cal had felt as inadequate as hell at times with Dev. More times than not, he added to her pain rather than alleviating it. He hated himself for doing that, but somehow he had to find an answer to help both of them. He had done so much wrong. Had he done the right thing by bringing Dev here? Cal only wanted to understand her demands on him, to realize how love could bind no matter what problems had to be dealt with. And he knew, without a doubt, that he loved Dev. What he wasn't sure of was if she loved him any longer.

"It's time for us to heal, Dev," he told her quietly. "Just like you helped to heal me after Chief died." Even if Dev no longer loved him, he wanted to remain a friend to her. Cal's fingers were warm and dry against her clammy ones. "Where am I taking you? To a small, rented beach house in a deserted cove five miles south of here. I've got a ten-day school break before we have to start the second half of the curriculum. I thought this might be good for both of us." Mentally, he added, *I wanted to spend the time with you, Dev.*

She rubbed her forehead, willing the tears away. She had cried for weeks after Cal had walked out of her life. The last month without him had cast a pall over her days. Would she ever feel good again? Dev stole a look at Cal's strong features, and her heart flooded with love. "I'm glad you abducted me," she admitted in a hoarse voice. Maybe this was his way of saying goodbye to her. To tell her that their relationship couldn't stand the stress of her chosen career.

A flicker of surprise appeared for a split second in his eyes. Then he smiled tenderly. "Sure? You were acting like a prickly pear about it all the way up here."

Dev wanted to throw her arms around Cal's broad shoulders and hug him. "Well, you wouldn't tell me anything, Travis! How would you feel?"

It felt good to have Dev teasing him again. Maybe there was hope for them. Maybe. . . . "How would I feel?" he asked with a boyish grin. "Excited. Curious. . . . This is our adventure, Dev." His voice expressed hope. For both of them. "I made friends with an air force colonel by the name of Ty Phillips. He's testing a jet at Edwards and over at Nellis in Nevada. We had a couple of beers at the O Club one night, and he told me about his cabin up in Brookings, Oregon, that sits overlooking the Pacific. I got to thinking that that's what we needed, time away. Time for us to talk and heal. And—" he turned his head, meeting her grave blue eyes "—I need you."

"It sounds wonderful, Cal," she said, meaning every word of it. "How soon will we be there?"

"About ten more minutes. We can fish for our dinner every night off the beach, walk in the sand holding hands and lie in front of the fire every evening and watch the sun go down."

Her heart lifted; emotions warred with logic. If Cal wanted to say goodbye, why would he take ten days to do it? Did this mean he was finally going to support her? Dev took a deep, unsteady breath, too frightened to hope for such a change in him. Her eyes widened in appreciation as they negotiated a ribbon of a road clogged with late spring flowers and coarse sea grass. Below them was a perfectly shaped crescent cove. To the left was a beach house built from cedar that had long ago turned silver, weathered by the wind and the blue-green Pacific. New life flowed into Dev, and she actually felt the first stirrings of a happiness that seemed to have been destroyed the day of that oil fire. She grasped Cal's hand excitedly.

"It looks beautiful, Cal!"

"Our Shangri-La, Dev. Just you, me, and Mother Nature for a neighbor."

Cal watched Dev covertly as they carried the suitcases into the beach house. Before, Dev's face had been pale, her eyes lifeless. Now there was a faint flush to her cheeks, and her glorious eyes contained that childlike spark he had grown to love so much but that had been extinguished when he had issued his ultimatum at the apartment. The cry of seabirds melded with the waves that spilled on the golden sands of the gently sloped beach. Various types of driftwood dotted the cove, as did long, tangled lengths of kelp, washed up by high tide. A smile lingered on Cal's lips as he followed Dev into the single-story cabin.

Dev clapped her hands delightedly after inspecting the fully furnished rooms. Cal joined her in the living room, and they stood staring through the floor-to-ceiling glass windows at a complete view of the cove and the ocean. He put his arms around her, drawing her next to him. Cal sensed her subdued vibrancy, silently thankful that his idea wasn't a dismal failure—yet. He had made so many mistakes. When they fought, he ended up frustrated because he didn't know how to support Dev. The past four weekends had strained him to the breaking point.

Cal gathered all his shaky courage and pressed a kiss to Dev's hair, inhaling her special feminine fragrance combined with the lingering scent of jasmine. He ached to simply hold her, to whisper to her how much he loved her. Everything was so tenuous between them right now. He saw it in the shadowed look she gave him, felt the tension in her every time he came near or touched her. He might well have destroyed that bridge of trust they had built between them in Hong Kong.

THE SUN WAS LOW on the horizon, with crimson and gold bathing the cove, when Dev walked barefoot out to where Cal was fishing. She had put on a pair of old jeans and rolled them up to her knees. Although June was just around the corner, northern beaches could become cool at night. Dev had put on a pale-pink fisherman knit sweater to keep warm.

"Well, have you caught us anything yet?" she asked.

Cal grinned. "Look in the bucket behind me." He cast again with a hefty fiberglass rod, the line singing beyond the breakers, live bait on the treble hook. Cal glanced over his shoulder as Dev squatted down by the huge yellow plastic bucket at his feet. She looked so natural, he thought, with her hair piled into that topknot that never quite stayed centered. He wanted to set the rod down and pick her up in his arms. There was more color in her face now so that he began to breathe easier. Once in a while, a ghost of a smile would touch her full lips. "Well?"

Dev wrinkled her nose. "Ugh, what are they?"

He looked wounded. "They're rock bass. Three of them. That's a pretty good catch considering I haven't fished since I was a kid."

Dev poked at one of the mottled fish as it swam leisurely around in the bottom of the bucket. "They're ugly."

"Ugly is only skin-deep. They'll taste great after we pan-fry them in butter tonight."

Dev rose, giving the fish an unconvinced look, then wandered over to Cal. "You're going to clean them, aren't you?"

Cal divided his attention between her and reeling in the line. "Well, I wasn't going to be a chauvinist about it, Ms Hunter. I thought since I spent the past two hours catching our meal, you could clean it. Fair's fair and all that. Right?"

"You can't be serious!"

He enjoyed watching the gold in Dev's eyes flare to life. "You've never pulled the double standard on me before. Is our relationship taking a U-turn?"

She dug her toe into the grainy sand at his feet, trying not to show how his question terrified her. She wasn't thinking about fish now. Had they changed so much that their relationship had to end? "*You're* the one who abducted me," she shot back in a deliberately cheerful tone. "I think it's your responsibility to take care of me on this trip."

Setting the rod aside, Cal took her into his arms, watching as she pouted and refused to meet his gaze. "Sort of like being taken care of, do you?" he prodded softly, leaning down and nibbling on her earlobe. Dev dodged away, lifting her head, a warm smile on her mouth. There was hope burning in the depths of her eyes.

"Yes, I'm finding I sort of like it on occasion, jet jockey. Now wipe that cat-eating grin off your face. You'll get a swelled head."

His laughter was full and free for the first time in over a month. "All right, witch, you've put me under your spell. But

I wonder if I might be able to beg your help in choosing a wine and making a salad to go with this great dinner I've just caught."

Dev nodded, sliding her hands down his darkly tanned, corded arms. He was so lean and masculine, she ached to possess him. "I think I can do that much."

Cal reluctantly released her, giving her a pat on the rear. "I'll be in after I clean these critters, in about fifteen minutes," he promised.

Dev nodded and jogged back to the house, enjoying the sand beneath her bare feet, the cry of the gulls overhead and the heavenly scent of the ocean. Her heart sang. Cal had taken her in his arms! Was there still hope for them? *God, please let there be*, Dev prayed. *I love him so much....*

"Well, what do you think?" Cal asked later as they sat eating their dinner on a bamboo table covered with glass. "Do you like fresh rock bass?"

The flesh was flaky and tender. Dev hadn't realized just how hungry she was. "Wonderful!" she murmured between mouthfuls.

Cal gave her a lopsided smile, pouring more white wine into their glasses. Dev was finally eating. She had lost a few pounds since they'd been apart, as he had. After lingering over a dessert of butterscotch pudding and coffee, Cal pulled Dev to her feet.

"Come on, let's gather some driftwood and have a fire for the evening."

Dev shyly took his proffered hand, following him into the deepening dusk. They stood arm in arm near the house, listening to the sounds around them. Dev sighed and rested her head against Cal's shoulder.

"It's lovely here, Cal."

"Good. Just for you, Dev."

Dev walked slowly at his side, held close as they headed down the beach. "How did you know?" she asked softly.

"What?"

"That I needed this?"

"I wish I could take credit for brilliant human insight and experience, but I can't." Cal glanced at her, clearly worried. "I was racking my brain for some way to get us back together, Dev."

Her heart took a painful leap. Together again. "I've been bitchy and out of sorts, too," Dev admitted, trying to meet him halfway.

"My attitude and the pressure at school were putting us in a hurt locker."

Dev grinned. "Hurt locker? Is that more marine lingo?"

"No, that's a navy phrase. Like it? Good. I'll let you use it from now on."

"That's big of you, Travis. I can hardly wait to use it on Tucker when I get back. He'll probably give me one of his nonplussed looks and wonder if I'm speaking in a foreign language," she said dryly.

He kissed her cheek. "Let's get back to what we were talking about before."

"Okay." They stopped, and Cal found several good pieces of driftwood, stacking them in his arms. "We weren't fighting, at least."

"Want to call them creative arguments, then?"

Dev walked ahead and found two more pieces of wood. "We never hit below the belt in our arguments, Cal. I know you never meant to hurt me. God knows, I didn't want to yell at you, either." She shrugged helplessly. "I warned you, I'm emotional about some topics."

He set the wood aside and placed his hands on her shoulders. "We need to talk." His mouth worked into a line of grim tension. "I know I'm not good at saying things sometimes, but . . . in the past month, I've been a first-class bastard."

Her eyes grew luminous, and Dev reached up, caressing his jaw. "Never that. Sinfully human, but I like you that way."

"I shouldn't have walked out on you like that, honey."

"I've had more practice at discussing emotional issues than maybe you have, Cal. I know you meant well. Neither of us wanted to hurt each other. But we did."

"That's what I'm scared about, Dev. Us."

"W-what do you mean?"

He hung his head, trying to frame the words. "Us. I love you. That will never change, Dev. But—" He dragged in a deep breath and pushed on. "I wasn't sure that after that last night and the strain we were both under you hadn't fallen out of love with me. I guess I can understand why you would—"

"No!" The word was torn from her, and Dev threw her arms around his stooped shoulders. "God, no," she whispered fiercely against his ear. Tears squeezed from her tightly shut eyes as his arms went around her in a crushing embrace. "I love you, Cal. I love you—"

He kissed her hungrily, roughly and then tenderly, starved for the taste and texture of her eager mouth beneath his own. She loved him! She hadn't given up on him. *Oh, God!* He managed a laugh.

"You didn't give up on me?"

Dev lifted her head. "Give up on you?"

"I've been such a screwup with you since the helicopter crash."

She didn't know whether to laugh or cry as she stared up at Cal in the waning light. "And all this time, you thought I didn't love you because of our disagreement?" Of course Cal would have interpreted their stormy episodes differently, Dev realized now, stunned. He had never allowed himself to get close enough to anyone in his life to have a serious disagreement. Dev framed his face with her hands. "Cal, you and I have negotiated so much together. Don't you see? If we hadn't loved each other, these incidents would have torn us apart." The look she gave Cal was charged with love. "I never stopped loving you, you crazy jet jockey. If anything, everything you tried to do, although frustrating, only made me love you more."

"It did?"

"Yes."

"Why?"

Dev gravely met his gaze. "Because I knew all your actions, right or wrong, were done out of care and love for me. That's why. . ."

Cal felt an avalanche of dread fall away from him, and he pulled Dev back into his arms. He whispered thickly, "I love you so much, Dev. I'll support you a hundred percent in your job. I was wrong to ask you to choose between me and your career."

She nuzzled contentedly into him. "Although your job scares the hell out of me, Cal, I'll support you, too."

"So we'll worry about each other." He laughed softly.

"At least we'll be together. The past four weeks have been awful without you, Cal."

"I've never been more miserable."

Dev looked up, her eyes vibrant with love. "And we have ten wonderful days here to enjoy each other. I'm so glad you did this. We needed the time, Cal."

"We needed each other, honey."

DEV RACED out of the breakers, squealing as Cal lunged after her. She dodged his flying tackle and made it to the dry sand before he caught up with her again. Laughing, Dev sank into his arms as they rolled on the beach. Her hair hung in wet sheets around her face that glistened with water. Her eyes sparkled as Cal pinned her gently beneath his body.

"Okay! Okay!" She giggled. "I give! You win!"

Cal gave her a predatorlike smile and then leaned over her, slanting his mouth across her lips. She tasted of ocean salt. As his tongue probed between her teeth, he tasted the utter sweetness of her. Her breasts rose and fell rapidly beneath his chest, and Cal broke the kiss, gasping for a breath. He laid his head on her breast, content to hear the wild beat of her heart. The past nine days had been a miracle. For both of them. Neither had realized just how much pressure they had been under until it had been removed. Cal traced her collarbone with his tongue, feeling Dev respond instantly.

"Mmm, you taste good," he growled, watching her nipples harden instantly beneath her pale-pink bathing suit.

Dev relaxed under him, trying to catch her breath. "If you like salt," she agreed with a laugh, running her fingers across his magnificent shoulders.

Cal propped himself up on one elbow, tracing a path of liquid fire in the shadowed valley of her breasts, feeling Dev press her body suggestively to him. Her firm flesh had taken on a golden glow from hours spent in the sun fishing, swimming and hiking. Cal slipped the strap off her right shoulder, pulling the material away and exposing the curve of her breast. He brought the dusky-pink bud into the moist depths of his mouth, gently sucking on it. Dev stiffened, a tremor rippling through her deliciously loving body, her fingers digging frantically into his shoulders. Cal smiled to himself, lost in the textured sensation of her; she was so spontaneous and giving. Which made him want to give back tenfold. The crash of the surf enveloped them as did the haunting cry of the seabirds who patrolled the cloudless azure sky above them. He felt the noontime sun beating down on them while he pulled off Dev's swimsuit and cast it aside.

As Cal rose on his knees to get rid of his suit, he hungrily absorbed Dev's nakedness. She stretched languidly, her body as sleek and trim as a thoroughbred's. Her hair was damp and tangled with bits of sand, which didn't matter at all because laughter and love were dancing in her blue eyes as they held his. Cal lay down beside her, skimming his hand across her sensitized body, feeling her respond as he caressed her breasts. When his hand followed the curve of her belly, Cal saw Dev's face soften, her movements grow languid, her lips part as he eased his hand between her thighs. He felt the throbbing ache building within him as he grazed her swollen womanhood.

A cry tore from Dev's throat; he continued to touch and please her. She lifted her arms, begging Cal to complete their union. A keening ache sang through her and Cal settled between her legs, his tanned fingers spanning her hips, bringing her to him. Bringing her in union with him. She arched, receiving him into her moist depths, feeling Cal shudder as her body wrapped lovingly around him. He filled her with his power, and the liquid friction of his arousal heightened the screaming need that begged to be satiated. Each thrust, each stroke told Dev of his love for her. Her eyes shuttered closed as a white-hot explosion shook both of them simultaneously, and Dev cried out.

Cal cushioned his fall into Dev's waiting arms, not wanting to hurt her. He gasped for breath, nuzzling her cheek, nose and finally her warm, willing mouth. "God," he rasped, "every time with you is better."

Dev purred, running her fingers across his back, feeling the tense play of muscle. "Every time with you is like the first time," she countered throatily.

He opened his eyes. "The first time was pretty good, wasn't it?"

"The best," she agreed faintly, her body glowing and throbbing in the wake of climax. Neither spoke for almost five minutes, lost in the ebbing euphoria that held them captive to each other. "I'm so glad you brought me here, Cal. I feel like living again." Dev reached out, her hand covering his. "Thank you."

He studied her in the lulling silence, caressing her golden arm. "You know, we've been through a hell of a lot with each other," Cal began quietly, watching her eyes barely open to study him. "And we didn't meet under very ideal circumstances, either."

Laughter gurgled in her throat. "They were the worst!"

"Did I ever tell you that when I walked into the lobby of the Shangri-La, I spotted you immediately?"

Dev shook her head, tiny shivers of pleasure racing through her arms and shoulders where he continued to caress her. "No. I think when I first saw you guys, I just turned and went to the rear of the crowd, hoping not to be seen or even noticed."

A smile tugged at his mouth. "Honey, you'd never get away with that. You looked so fresh compared to the rest of those women who had on layers of makeup and hair spray. When I saw your unruly red topknot, those compassionate blue eyes and—" he leaned down, worshiping her mouth "—those lips, I knew I had lost the battle and won the war." His breath was moist against her flesh as he nibbled on her lower lip. "I liked your style. The way you handled yourself with Mrs. Weintraub."

Dev giggled. "You were awful to her! The poor woman was going to have a stroke, Cal, and you just stood there glaring at everybody in general."

"I suppose you're right," he said a little remorsefully. "Actually, I should write to the American embassy over there and thank her—for you. . . ."

Dev felt bereft when he moved off her, but he drew her beside him, his arm across her waist. She saw the sudden seriousness in his face. Lifting her hand, she removed a few bits of sand from his cheek. "What is it?" she whispered.

"I was thinking . . . about us."

Her heart began a slow pound. The way he looked at her in those crystalline moments made her anxious. Dev's mouth went dry. "Go on."

He picked sand from the strands of her hair, which fanned out around her head. There was a wry quality to his voice when he finally spoke. "My brother Matt's wife once cornered me and asked me why I'd never gotten married. I told Kai that my flying always came first. If a woman couldn't accept that or understand that, then she was out of my life. The ones who accepted were women who liked to be seen on the arm of a fighter pilot. It gave them prestige and importance in the eyes of their friends. Kai laughed at me. She wagged her finger at me on the day of their wedding and told me that someday some woman was going to come along and pull the rug right out from under my arrogant feet."

Cal's gaze moved to Dev. "Kai was right. I had closed myself up a long time ago when I saw how badly Storm was getting hurt for remaining vulnerable. And the military doesn't exactly foster sensitivity and expressive feeling. I ended up cheating myself out of any genuine relationship with a woman. I lived half a life, Dev, up until I met you." His voice grew thick. "You showed me how to give. And how to take. Before, all I did was steal like an emotional thief. With you, I found myself trying to think of ways to please you, to make you happy or bring that melting smile back to your lips. I'm still struggling, Dev. I'm finding myself handicapped because this is the first real relationship I've ever had in my life. I didn't handle you well. I wanted to, but I lacked the sensitivity to put myself in your place. I can't read you as well as I want to, witch. There were many days this past month when we were apart that I felt like a first-class bumbler." Cal forced a smile he didn't feel. "You have an awesome range of emotion, Dev. I'm fascinated by your complexity yet by your simplicity, too. And you allow me to experiment with and express my newfound emotions. In fact, you've always encouraged me to feel and not think. I like that. For twelve or fourteen hours a day, I'm using my logic at test pilot school. My brain's burned out; I'm ready to switch to the emotional side. I like what you've brought out in me, Dev. I'm beginning to be happy with myself for the first time, and it's because of you."

A tremulous smile came to her parted lips. "I think we're two human beings who have found the courage to reach out and trust each other, darling. I know there have been times when we've both been scared to death, for different reasons, to put our life in the other's hands. But we did it, Cal. And look at us. Look how far we've come. Together."

Cal gently moved several drying tendrils behind her delicate ear. "Marry me, Dev," he said in a low voice.

Dev stared uncomprehendingly up at him. He was serious.

"Yes, I'm serious, witch." He ran several strands of her silken hair through his fingers. "I'm damn lonely without you. The weekends don't come soon enough. I find myself cursing because I'm at that school now, and I'd rather be with you. I want what we have on a daily basis. In and out of bed."

She swallowed. "Are you sure, Cal?"

He laughed softly, cupping her chin. "How long have we been going together? Exactly seven months, one week and two days."

"Typical test pilot: you've got all the details."

Grinning, he kissed her, taking sips from each corner of her mouth and then running his tongue along her lower lip. "Quit sidestepping the issue. Marry me, Dev."

"Sure you want to? When I met you, you were the playboy pilot who was making a lifetime commitment to bachelorhood. Are you sure you want to be tied down to one woman for the rest of your life?"

Cal gave her an exasperated look, patiently enduring her pointed questions. "Not only that, but I want to be tied down with a bunch of rug rats, too. Now does that answer all your questions?"

Dev gave him a horrified look. "Rug rats. What are rug rats?"

Cal chuckled and gently shifted beside her. He placed his long, tapered fingers against her belly. "Navy slang for kids. Children. You know."

Dev gave a strangled laugh and sat up, throwing her arms around him. "I love you," she said, her voice quavering.

"Does that mean you want to become Devorah Travis?" He held her tightly, feeling the faster beat of her heart against him.

"Yes," she sobbed. "Oh, yes, Cal."

Dev was crying, and Cal made her sit in front of him while he wiped her cheeks dry. At least these were tears of joy, he thought as he drew her to him once more, pressing a longer kiss on her lips, sealing their love.

"It's going to be rough for a while, Dev," he warned. "I've got another twenty weeks of school left before I graduate."

"I know. Maybe we should wait until you've graduated."

"God, no! I'm like a caged animal at Edwards as it is." His words were fervent. "Why not now?"

Dev blinked and then smiled, sliding her hands up his arms, fingers curling around his wrists. "Knowing you, you've got this whole plan mapped out. Why don't you let me in on the rest of it, Cal?"

He tried to look contrite and didn't quite succeed, grinning disarmingly. He could barely think straight. Dev was going to be his wife! She was going to marry him! How many times he had wanted to ask her. And how many times he had gotten sweaty feet. But it wasn't settling down with her that had frightened him. No, he had been afraid Dev would turn him down. Cal felt the hot tears stinging his eyes. "There's no way to preprogram you. Or me, Dev. How can you pin down a sunbeam? No, the only plan I had was for you to be my wife. My lover. My best friend."

Dev sat there, staring up at Cal, loving him so much that she ached. "Do you know what I want?" she asked softly.

"No. Tell me."

She took his hand from her cheek and placed it once more against her belly, pressing it to her. "Life in me, Cal. Our children. At this stage in my life, I'm ready to settle down and be a mother, your lover and your best friend. Do you know how many times I've dreamed of having a precocious little boy just like you? He'd drive us crazy, but we'd love him."

Tears brimmed in his eyes, and he brought Dev into his arms, holding her in a crushing embrace. He buried his face in her hair, a shudder running through him. "Or a little girl with big blue eyes that would steal her daddy's heart away like her mother's did," he rasped.

Dev sniffed. "Don't forget the freckles, Cal. Every one of our kids will end up with freckles. I promise you."

He stroked her hair and shoulders, unable to hold her close enough. "I love freckles. You could teach them how to fence. We'd have the youngest épée champions in the world."

Dev shook with laughter. "I thought they were all going to end up as test pilots like their father."

"They can be whatever they want," he countered huskily, kissing her cheek, brow and finally her smiling lips.

"Yes, yes. They'll have parents who love them so much."

He met her sapphire eyes filled with the gold of love. "If we can be half as good as your dad and mom were with you, I'll feel we've really accomplished something."

Tears streamed down her cheeks, and Dev sobbed, gripping his shoulders. "I love you so much, Cal Travis, that I hurt. Do you know that?"

"Yes, I know that, my redheaded witch. And so do I. And we'll do nothing more but grow more deeply in love with every passing day, month and year until it's our time to go.

How I'm looking forward to a lifetime of love, exploration and happiness with you, Dev. You've opened my heart, and all I want to do is share it with you. Forever."

Harlequin Temptation

COMING NEXT MONTH